AUTUMN'S BREAK

AUTUMN TRENT SERIES: BOOK TWO

MARY STONE

To my husband.
Thank you for taking care of our home and its many inhabitants
while I follow this silly dream of mine.

DESCRIPTION

Welcome to my bedroom, said the spider to her prey.

Forensic and criminal psychologist Dr. Autumn Trent hasn't had time to unpack her bag before she's asked to join the FBI's Behavioral Analysis Team on another case. This time, she and the team head north, where a web of deceit and murder is being spun.

Up the east coast, wealthy widowers make easy targets for a team of black widows wishing to feast on juicy bank accounts. But in Passavant Hills, Pennsylvania, money isn't the only thing one of their spiders desires. Humiliation, revenge, and human blood is on her menu.

Armed with fleeting clues as the number of victims pile up, Autumn is sure of only one thing...unless she and the team can stop her, their spider will suck her sweethearts fatally dry.

And this time, as the team goes undercover, it could be one of their own.

Autumn's Break, the second book in Mary Stone's Autumn Trent Series, is a riveting psychological murder mystery that will leave you second-guessing every single person you meet.

1

E dwin Gallagher wasn't sure whether to laugh or cry.

Holding a small, silver-framed photograph, Edwin leaned back in his chair and sipped at the twenty-year-old whiskey in his tumbler, using his desk like an ottoman to rest his tired legs. His late wife would've smiled to see his feet up on the old farmhouse table she'd bought him for his home office a lifetime ago.

Doreen would have tickled the soles mercilessly and laughed as he jerked them back. "If you're going to live like you were raised in a barn, you deserve whatever punishment you get."

He gazed at her photograph, the one they'd taken together at their last anniversary. They'd been married thirty-five years. It was supposed to have been their "coral" anniversary, in between the twenty-fifth for silver and the fiftieth for gold. Instead, it turned into their "cancer" anniversary. Their last anniversary. Eight months after she'd smiled into the camera, she was gone.

The signs of it already showed in his wife's face in the photograph, although they hadn't known anything was wrong at the time. She'd said she was tired, but in true Doreen fashion, she hadn't uttered a single complaint or even slowed down. Even as ravished by the hateful disease as she was, she smiled like an angel, her dimples adorable under her thick black curls.

Pancreatic cancer worked quickly. She'd been gone less than a year now, and the shock still washed over him from time to time.

Before cancer had taken her—fifty-eight was too damn young—she had been a force to reckon with. Organized, orderly, and solid. A loud, infectious laugh. Generous to a fault. And so very understanding. Would she understand him now?

Edwin thought about what he intended to do in just a few minutes, if all went well, and tried to imagine her reaction. Doreen would snort, roll her eyes, and poke him in the side. "I told you to take care of yourself, Schmoopsie Poo. If this makes you happy, then I'm happy for you."

He remembered his final moments with her. The curls had fallen out from the chemo treatments, and the dimples had melted away with the rest of her body fat as the demon cancer spread throughout her every cell. Her deep belly laughs had become faint whispers.

He shuddered to remember her final moments. He dropped his feet to the floor and lifted the photograph up to the light.

Doreen smiled tenderly at him, still looking as though she were just about to break out into laughter, or to tell him that she loved him. He looked deep into her eyes and saw only approval for what he was about to do.

"Goodbye, darling…I promised you that I would live the rest of my life to the fullest. I just never thought I'd have to do it without you." He kissed the glass in the frame gently, his lips lingering as he whispered, "Good night."

With a heart that felt pulled in too many directions, he put the photograph away in the filing cabinet under the table, wincing at the sound of the drawer sliding home. It sounded like the closing of a tomb.

His heart gave a jerk behind his ribs, and he put his hand over his chest, his eyes filling with tears. Doreen would have been happy for him, but that didn't mean that it didn't feel like he was losing her all over again. This time on purpose. But did he have a choice?

He took a deep breath, wiped his eyes, and straightened in his chair. He couldn't quite talk himself into putting his feet back up on the desk, and instead slipped them into the comfortable loafers he preferred when he was home.

It was still early evening, although it being mid-January meant that the sun had already fallen behind the horizon. He checked the time on the old-fashioned wood clock on the wall. Five minutes of six.

Five minutes to prepare for a "yes."

Five minutes to prepare for a "no."

In other words, not enough time—or far too much time, depending on how he looked at it.

Edwin stood up and walked to the window, feeling nervous as a boy. His reflection stared back at him, and he frowned at what he saw. His hair was thinning and more gray than blond, face covered with the lines of a life lived well. He hadn't lived as fully as Doreen had, every moment of every day, but he hadn't done too badly. Turning to the side, he patted his flat stomach before flexing an arm, the muscle of his bicep popping up in response. He might be decades older than the woman he wanted to marry, but he didn't look too bad.

He poured another whiskey and stood at one of the windows that looked out onto the driveway. He brushed aside the lace curtains Doreen had picked out and watched for the glow of headlights.

Was he really ready to do this? Tonight?

He patted his pocket for what felt like the ten thousandth time. The little lump was still there. He took it out, a small black velvet box with rounded corners and a gold hinge in the back. He opened it once more and was delighted as the two-carat radiant-cut diamond nearly blinded him with twinkling light.

This was a ring worthy of a woman, and a twinge of guilt nipped at him...not for the first time.

Doreen's ring had been much smaller. Purchased when they were both young and too broke for extravagance, it had been the best he could afford at the time. He'd offered to replace it with something more elaborate, but she'd refused. "You can buy me a necklace or some fancy earrings if you have such a bug up your butt about it, but this is the ring you thee-wedded-me with, and I'm not taking it off."

And she never did. In fact, she had made him promise to let her wear it to the grave. He tried not to imagine what her hand looked like now, as decomposition wore at the skin. The flesh drying and shrinking as...

A pair of headlights turned into his driveway, and Edwin was relieved to have his mind pulled away from the treacherous thoughts. With one last look at the filing cabinet and its lone picture, Edwin took in a deep breath, firmly replacing the past with the present...and he hoped, the future.

The car parked to the far right of the house, and the headlights winked out. He didn't know why she refused to park at the garage, but that was a conversation for another day. Right now, he just wanted to savor the anticipation of what was to come. In just a few moments, his happiness would once again be complete.

The front door opened, and he finished the whiskey and put the ring back in his pocket.

He didn't want to spoil the surprise.

He walked out of the study and into the foyer just as Kim was standing on the patterned entryway rug, taking off her boots. Her coat was on the brass coat hanger stand by the door, her big black leather purse on a nearby barnwood bench like it belonged there.

Which was exactly what he wanted.

He waited until she straightened, his throat almost too tight to welcome her. "Hello, sweetheart," he finally managed to say. "Did you have a good day?"

She brushed long auburn hair out of her face, the old, faded scar at her temple catching the light. Her fingers brushed the puckered flesh, and her face changed to a mix of shame and self-loathing, but only for a second before her hair dropped back down to cover the flaw.

Edwin didn't know why she was so very self-conscious of the scar. He'd asked her about it several times, but she'd always brushed his questions away. The jagged line didn't draw attention from the fit body that was currently hidden under a blue sweater that fell over black tights. In fact, it didn't come close to drawing attention away from Kim's numerous positive qualities, both inside and out.

She squinted at him, waving her arms in front of her as she attempted to peer through glasses that were steamed from the sudden warmth of the home compared to the cold of outside. "Is that you, Edwin, or is it foggy in here?" She laughed playfully, the sound making his heart leap in his chest. "Brr! It's cold out there."

He chuckled and opened his arms. "I'll warm you up."

She stepped into them, standing on tiptoe on the rug in order to snuggle into his arms more completely. She was chilly, as if she'd been driving with the heat off and the window down. He held her tight. She shivered at first, but soon settled into his embrace. He kissed the top of her head, breathing in the scent of her lilac shampoo.

Pulling away from him a few inches, she peered up at him through glasses that were still a little bit fogged. She looked worried. "Are you all right? You seem…" She shook her head and placed her cold hand on his cheek. "Did something happen today?"

The ring seemed to grow heavier in his pocket. In his imagination, what he was about to do had seemed so simple. In reality, he was sweating. He needed to do this here… now…before his nerves got the best of him again.

Here we go.

Taking a single step back, he wiped his palms down his pants and took one of her small, gentle hands in his own. He scratched the side of his nose, which seemed to always want to itch when he was nervous.

Taking a deep breath, he forced the words out of his mouth. "Kim, you know that I love you."

Her face brightened, a shy smile creeping out. "I know." Her expression slowly shifted into a frown. "This isn't some kind of setup for you explaining why you have to leave me, is it? Please don't tell me that you're too old for me or anything like that."

He had to blink to keep his eyes from overspilling with tears. "No, no, that's not it. Not at all. I've been doing a lot of thinking lately. I've decided the age thing doesn't matter to me as much as I thought it did. It was just my way of trying to hold myself back. No, what I really want is to make you happy."

As his leg muscles tensed in order to do what he ordered of them, his heart raced with excitement and hope.

Could he do this?

Could he get down on one knee without falling over?

Could he reach into his heart and find the perfect words to say?

Could he...stand again afterward without asking for a hand up or having his knee pop or give out on the way back up?

Yes, he decided. He could.

And he would.

As his knee sank into the thick material of the rug, he took the small box from his pocket. "Kim...not so many months ago, I thought my world had ended, then you swept in and breathed new life into me. I love you more than I ever thought I could love anything or anyone, and I want to spend the rest of my life at your side." He swallowed hard, emotion burning his eyes as he opened the box. "Kimberly Elizabeth Benson, will you marry me?"

Her hands flew to her mouth the moment she saw the ring, and her beautiful green eyes shifted from one emotion to the next as he watched, his entire being trembling with anticipation. Shock transitioned into delight, then gradually softened into sympathy before her eyebrows pinched into worry. "Oh, Edwin. Are you sure?"

He held the box higher. "I'm sure."

She licked her lips and twisted her fingers together. "What would Doreen think about this?"

It was the last thing he had expected her to say, and the tightness in his throat grew. "Believe it or not, I've been thinking about it all day. I think she would be happy for us."

Her eyes sparkled with tears as she leaned down to his still kneeling form, one arm circling his shoulders, her long hair falling into his face. She leaned against him, resting her head against his shoulder. He soaked in the scent of her soft, floral perfume as he tightened his arms around her.

The soft hiss of a zipper caught his attention, and he nearly fell over as Kim's weight shifted against him. Was she reaching for a tissue? Had she fainted? Why hadn't she said yes?

Worry spiraled through him as she pulled away and stood to her full height. His worry transformed to fear the moment he once again gazed into her eyes. They were no longer filled with love. They were now filled with anger and something else...hate?

Her nostrils flared as her fingernails sank into the back of his neck. "Wrong answer." The words were more like a hiss.

He tried to pull away, but her arm tightened, holding him in place. Fear like he'd never known crawled like spiders across his skin. "Kim? Honey, what's wr—"

White-hot pain made him jerk and twist like a puppet on a string. A horrific crunching sound filled the air, and agony rose straight up his back and into his teeth. His nerves screamed in shock as he struggled, still trapped within Kim's embrace.

She grunted, and the blade in his back turned, sending a new wave of misery following in its wake.

He tried to make his mouth work, wanting to beg her for an answer, but he could barely take in enough air to breathe. "Why?" The sound of his voice was little more than a decaying whisper.

With a final grunt, Kim let him go and stepped away. Her eyes changed as they gazed down at him, still somehow on his knees. They sparkled again, but this time with satisfaction, maybe even...righteousness.

Edwin attempted to stand, but instead, he fell forward, his arms and chest slumping like a heavy winter coat sliding off its hook, carrying him off-balance until he had to use his hands to hold himself up. He raised his head, needing to see her face. She was watching him, a cruel looking knife with a black blade held in one hand.

He blinked, wondering where a sweet woman such as

Kim would have gotten a military knife such as that. As he watched, a drop of blood fell from the tip and landed on the beautiful Persian rug Doreen had purchased so many years ago.

The sight angered him, but before he could utter a reprimand, his hands collapsed underneath him, and he fell, his cheek pressed against the rug before he managed to roll onto his back.

Light from the chandelier hurt his eyes, and he turned his head so that he could get one last look at the woman he loved…the woman who had betrayed him. Killed him.

"Why?" The word was even weaker than before.

The expression of satisfaction on her face widened into a wicked grin. She reached up for her glasses and tossed them to the side. Taking a step forward, she dropped to one knee.

The knife lunged toward him as if it had a mind of its own, as if her hand only obeyed the cold steel's command.

And was hungry for his blood.

"You're just like the rest of them."

She clearly hated him so much. How had he not seen the cruel emotion hiding beneath her beauty? "Kim, I—"

The knife drove into his throat, filling his mouth with the taste of metal.

As his beloved sweetheart pulled the knife away, the space it left behind was filled with an ocean of warm, wet fluid that ran down into his lungs.

His hand clasped his throat, the movement coming without any conscious will of his own. He could no longer control his movements as his body struggled to save itself. But even his deepest instincts could not save him now. Not when he had trusted this woman so deeply and understood her so little.

His heart pounded in his chest, a prisoner beating against the bars of its cage, a quick barrage of beats driven by terror.

Through the pain, he listened to the whirl of his pulse as it grew weaker…slower.

As darkness began to claim his vision, he kept his gaze fixed on her face. She had killed him. With death in front of him, a cave waiting to swallow him whole, he still didn't understand what had gone so wrong.

Why would she do such a thing?

Was she crazy?

Had he failed her?

Laughter echoed through the room, but because he was watching her face, he knew the sound wasn't coming from Kim's lips.

Doreen appeared beside the younger woman, her approving smile turning darker with anger, hatred, jealousy as the giggles turned into howls.

He'd been so wrong. So very, very wrong. About everything.

Doreen hadn't approved, and now she was laughing at him, making fun of him for wanting too much, too soon. Much too soon.

He had failed her.

Failed Kim.

Failed himself.

As his vision dimmed completely, he was certain of only one thing. He would wander the land of the afterworld completely alone.

2

What had I done?

Again.

Killing Edwin Gallagher hadn't been part of my plan. Not really, and especially not tonight.

I'd actually been rooting for the little fellow, hoping against hope that he was a better man than he turned out to be. I'd prayed that he'd come to his senses and realize just how selfish he had been by turning his back on his late wife, especially so soon after her brutal death.

But...

He'd failed Doreen.

He'd failed me.

And ultimately, he'd failed himself.

This was all his fault.

His fault...his fault...his fault!

Taking in a deep breath, I forced the air coming in and out of my lungs to slow down. I was going to hyperventilate or have an anxiety attack if I wasn't careful.

Breathe in.

Out.

Repeat.

Once I was a bit calmer, I took in the scene. Took in myself. What did I feel?

Disappointment was the first word to shoot through my brain.

The disappointment was hard, but I had to admit, the killing had been easy.

Was that good? Or bad?

I couldn't tell.

Of course, I had a little bit of practice by now, and it helped that his end time had come so unexpectedly. I hadn't known that the bastard was planning to go down on one knee. Hadn't known how the fury would rage inside me. Take over me. Lead my every move.

A trill of renewed anger vibrated through me as I recalled Edwin's words and the look in his eyes as he proclaimed that he loved me "more than I ever thought I could love anything or anyone."

It was those words that had condemned him to a death sentence.

Those words had fueled the hate and fury bubbling beneath my skin. Made me reach for my purse. Pull out the knife. Plunge it into his back, which was fitting. After all, with those eleven words, he'd effectively plunged a knife into the back of his late wife.

Tit for tat.

Poetic justice, in my own humble opinion.

But now…I had a problem.

Because I honestly hadn't planned on killing Edwin, especially not so abruptly or with so much blood involved, I had a mess to clean up. I also had a story to weave for the authorities when they came sniffing around to investigate his disappearance, which they would surely be forced to do when one of his kids or friends reported him missing.

What to do?

His body was sprawled on top of the rug, which was so soaked with blood that the pretty Persian was now a solid color. I watched until it stopped pumping out of his body, breathing in and out to further calm myself as the time passed.

It didn't take long for most of the viscous liquid to exhaust itself, but it seemed that hours had passed as I watched. My skin prickled and stung as I waited, like someone had been rubbing pepper into a paper cut.

Despite the gore, Edwin looked almost peaceful. It was a mask, though. Edwin Gallagher had worked hard to maintain the illusion of being a good man, but I knew the truth.

Edwin's wife, Doreen, had died of pancreatic cancer only seven months ago, and the bastard had been quick to get back into the saddle. My saddle, and who knew how many others before me.

The poor little widower had refused to show me photographs of his late wife, saying that he didn't want me to feel like I was living in her shadow. He wouldn't talk about her, and when he spoke of her, it was almost by accident. He would start relating a story about his past but would then cut himself off or change the story so that his wife was no longer present in it. He thought he was being clever, but I knew his actual intentions.

"There was this one time when we went to church…" he'd said just yesterday, then stopped and reconsidered, scratching his nose. He always scratched his nose when he was nervous. "I mean, this one time that *I* went to church…"

He seemed to think that he was sparing me, but I knew the truth.

He was *erasing* her.

Edwin had been systematically removing Doreen from his life for months.

Every trace of her throughout the house was gone. Not a single photograph of her remained on display. Over the short time I'd known Edwin—just under a month—I had looked. I could tell where the pictures had once hung.

As a more or less stereotypical engineer, Edwin didn't have an artistic temperament and hadn't bothered to rearrange the art to conceal the obvious blank places on the walls, the empty spots on the tops of dressers, and the gaping spaces between books where photo albums had once rested on the shelves.

He hadn't noticed.

I had.

It had disgusted me, witnessing yet another man so callously move on with his life, as if the woman who had cared for him had never existed. I'd hoped Edwin would be different. Not just for his sake, but for me too. If just one man would prove to me that not all men were the same, maybe I wouldn't feel so much hate for the entire gender.

But Edwin was exactly the same. He just wanted a younger replacement to fill his bed. To prove to himself that his wrinkled up little dick still held all the power. That he was still a man.

But marriage?

How ridiculous.

I hadn't meant to make him pay with his life…just his life-savings. The savings his sweet wife would never benefit from. But then he sank down on one knee…

Shivering, I recalled that exact moment. Recalled how the light had glittered from the ring. A ring with one intention… to prove Edwin's ownership of me.

I might have gone a little crazy.

There. I admitted it.

Yes. Crazy. But only a little.

Settling a score for his late wife seemed quite sane to me.

I just wish it hadn't been right here. Or right now. And certainly not before I'd drained this pitiful man's lifesavings, taking him for everything he owned.

But by asking for my hand in marriage, he'd forced my hand. The irony wasn't lost on me.

Now, what to do with the body?

I could toss the house and make it look like a burglar had struck, but I'd done that before, and in the end, it hadn't benefited me at all. Because I'd known then what I knew now. The minute I cleaned out Edwin's accounts, the police would know the crime wasn't as simple as a B & E gone wrong.

With my first victim, I'd been forced to toss his place and then walk away, not getting more than a couple thousand dollars that he'd lavished on me during the dating process. Carl Jameson had been so very generous with his gifts, and I hadn't meant to kill him either. He just…he just…

I shook my head, pressing my fists against both temples to keep my brain from exploding. I didn't want to think of Carl right now. Didn't want to remember how he'd sung me that stupid song of love with his stupid guitar. Didn't want to think of his confessions of love. Didn't want to think of my reaction. My lack of control.

So far, the police hadn't suspected that Carl had died at my hands, and I wanted to keep it that way. They just wouldn't understand that his death had been an accident. A happy one, but an accident, nonetheless.

Edwin's death had been an accident too, I told myself. I hadn't intended on killing him. He'd made me. Made me! His fault…his fault…his fault!

Opening my eyes, I realized I was on the floor, though I didn't remember how I'd gotten in that position. Sitting up slowly, I wondered if maybe this entire thing had been a dream.

But no, Edwin was still there. Just as Carl and Brice had been there too. Three deaths by my hand.

Serial killer.

The words whispered around me like a snake.

I'd watched enough crime shows to know that if anyone labeled me as a serial killer, the Feds would be called in. The chances of being caught before I could finish my mission and disappear would increase. And that wouldn't do.

Right now, the authorities hadn't connected me to Carl. Only Brice.

And I couldn't allow them to connect me to Edwin either.

I had to be careful, and make the poor widower simply disappear. I just needed to make sure that I didn't leave anything behind that would give my plan away.

Evidence. It was the word I most feared. That was why I very seldom came to Edwin's or any of my suitors' homes. Most of the time, I invited them back to my place.

Not my real home, of course, but to the cute little apartment I rented for that very purpose. I'd cook for him, and we'd have long conversations by the fire. I'd let him kiss me, even fondle my breast with shaky fingers.

Then I'd send him home, leaving him panting for more.

It always worked.

Sleep with a man, and they thought they owned you. Tease a man, and their ego always had them coming back for more.

And tonight was supposed to have been that night. It had all been so carefully planned. He would have bowed down to me, taken his punishment. Then, he would have eaten out of my hand, if I'd allowed it.

I glanced at the engagement ring again.

A marriage proposal after only a month of dating was a record, and I shouldn't have killed him for it. Not yet, anyway. He was supposed to have been punished first. Plus, emptying a person of their savings took time if one wanted to do it in a way that didn't raise their target's attention.

Of course, my target's attention would never again be raised, so it wasn't too late to help myself to what I could get my hands on. But the authorities...I had to be careful because of them.

I looked at his body, at how quickly it was already changing as death took over.

If I didn't hurry...I'd lose my chance.

First thing first was getting access to Edwin's phone. Being careful not to step in the blood with these particular shoes, I patted his pocket, and sure enough, the device was there. Once it was removed, I looked at his hands. They were covered with blood. I had some cleanup to do first.

Running outside and into the cold, I grabbed my Mary Poppins bag from the trunk of my car. I'd learned at a young age to be prepared for anything, and this bag was filled with items I thought I might one day need.

And tonight, I'd planned to need everything inside, but not for this.

Tonight was the night I had planned to have Edwin submit to me. They always did, even the manliest of them. On their knees, bound, begging for more.

That was how I liked them.

But Edwin had been down on his knee for a completely different reason, so it was his fault...his fault...his fault that he had to die.

"Stop it," I told myself sternly. What was done was done, and I had to stay focused on what needed to be done next.

I'd learned that secret from my dearest daddy. "The past is the past and no longer matters," he liked to say. But all his sage advice really did was give him an excuse to feel no guilt for everything he did...to Mama...to others...to me.

"Stop it!"

The command came out much louder than I'd intended, the words echoing through the stillness of the cold night.

Back inside, I considered taking off my wig but decided to keep it in place. If a hair slipped out and escaped my attention, I didn't want any lethal DNA strands to belong to me. Still, I pulled the long tresses back from my face and wrapped it in a tight coil. No need to leave any evidence at all, especially since I'd paid a king's ransom for the custom-fitted mane of gloriously real hair.

If the authorities were to believe that Edwin simply disappeared, I didn't want to give them any proof that foul play might be involved. A long red hair could muddy the waters unnecessarily.

Next, I pulled out the skintight latex suit I'd brought with an entirely different reason in mind. Shedding my clothes, I pulled it on, the rubbery material clinging to each inch of my skin as I zipped it up.

Tonight should have been so much different.

"But it isn't," I hissed to myself before exchanging my shoes for a pair of comfortable rubber-soled ones, then slipped on a pair of Tyvek booties. One could never be too careful.

Safe sex.

Safe death.

For me, they were one and the same.

After pulling on some latex gloves, I picked up the small velvet box with its betrayal ring inside. The diamond was spotted with Edwin's blood. Fire and ice. The combination was intriguing.

So intriguing.

The flavor of blood was on my tongue before I even realized I needed a taste. This blood was cold…unsatisfying… and before I could stop myself, I was bending and pressing my lips to Edwin's neck, and sucked.

Warmth.

Better.

So much better.

Someone moaned...me, I realized, and the sound pulled me from my trance. Disgusted with myself, I pushed away so hard that I fell onto my ass. What was wrong with me?

"What's wrong with me?" I screamed the question this time, needing it out of my head.

"Nothing." The word was like a whisper in my ear. *"You're just combining his DNA with yours so this moment can be with you forever."*

Yes. That was it. I remembered now.

I was simply carrying Edwin Gallagher with me forever. I was absorbing him into my system so that his essence would fuel my hate.

I licked my lips and looked at the oozing wound again. I turned away. No. Just no. Licking my lips, I knew that one taste was impulse. Two tastes labeled me as crazy.

Forcing myself to focus, I wiped Edwin's thumb with an alcohol prep wipe and hurried to press the digit to the sensor of his phone. This part couldn't wait. In my vast research, I'd learned that dead people's fingerprints changed rather quickly once their heart stopped beating. Decomposition took place immediately, dehydration a part of the process. I could have sucked on Edwin's thumb to rehydrate it, but the blood there would be cold.

Cold couldn't satisfy. Couldn't comfort.

With the phone now unlocked, I went into his settings and turned off all the password protections. Now...I could take my time. I had hours and hours to roam the beautiful house and dispose of the widower. And possibly take pictures that would be profitable on the dark web.

People were so perverted. But money was money. If I was going to reach my goal to have enough to disappear forever, I couldn't turn any of the green stuff or bitcoin away.

And because I'd been impulsive, I might have to stay away from Edwin's other accounts.

Dammit.

Turning slowly, I took in Edwin's vast home. I'd been inside only a few times. Part of my strategy in hooking a catch was to make it well known that I wasn't after his money or any of his possessions, which was why I usually invited him back to my place. My first visit here, Edwin gave me the grand tour, except for his study. On my second visit, he'd carefully slid the reclaimed barnwood door shut then as well.

What he was hiding in there, I didn't know and hadn't asked. Another strategy of catching a man was to never question his intentions. Only question the man...be enormously curious about each and every detail of him. Listen in rapt fascination as he droned on and on about his work, his accomplishments, his interests. Smile and laugh, soften the eyes, gaze at him as if he was the most fascinating human you'd ever encountered.

And just like that...hook, line, sinker.

Edwin's sinker had been the dazzling diamond he'd wanted to brand me with. I didn't want it. I wanted more. Much, much more.

The barnwood door squeaked as I slid it open, and it only took a few minutes to go through his desk. As a retiree, he did very little work anymore. Bills. Bank statements. 401k plans. Keys to safety deposit boxes.

Bingo...a little black book with all his passwords.

Another way I'd reeled Edwin in was by asking him to "teach" me how to solidify my portfolio, and the man had happily whipped out his smartphone to show me the apps he used. Men just loved to educate and instruct. They loved to fix problems by mansplaining ad nauseam.

With the account information now in my possession on the device, I could have hacked them all, but having the passwords saved a great deal of time. I just needed to be careful in how I funneled them to my accounts, if I ever decided it was safe enough to do so. For now, I could start by misdirecting the authorities into believing it had been one of his bratty kids who didn't want to wait for an inheritance.

I'd never met Edwin and Doreen's children, of course. The three were scattered across North America, but Edwin had told me how he regretted spoiling them so much. Regretted how they only called when they needed something from him.

Especially the youngest. Danielle. Hooked on drugs and bouncing from man to man, she would be the perfect fall guy for my plan. Flipping through the little black book, I found exactly what I needed. Danielle's bank account information. A little transfer from one of the accounts of Edwin's vast portfolio should lead authorities on a merry little chase.

Smiling now that I'd created a plan, I continued to search his office. I found the jewelry store receipt for the engagement ring Edwin had purchased just a few days ago. The amount would have been impressive, if it hadn't been an attempt to buy freedom from guilt in betraying his wife. The receipt was in a folder called "taxable items," and my heart hardened even more. This folder was for his accountant.

For men like Edwin, romance was just a business expense.

Pocketing the receipt, I yanked open the final drawer in the file cabinet and paused as a face stared up at me. Two faces, actually. Edwin and a pretty woman with curly black hair and dimpled cheeks.

Doreen.

I'd found pictures of the woman online. She'd had social media accounts, and volunteered her precious time at a number of charities. But this was the first picture of her I'd seen in Edwin's house.

One picture, tossed into the very bottom of a drawer.

So pathetic.

If I'd had even the slightest tinge of guilt for sinking that knife into Edwin's flesh, I didn't anymore.

The two of them sat together at a small table with a bottle of Chianti and a red rose between them. Edwin's arm was around Doreen. She was very thin, her skin sagging at her jawline, making me wonder if the photograph had been taken shortly before her diagnosis.

As tired as her eyes looked, though, she wore a genuine smile.

Edwin? Not so much. His expression was flat and emotionless. Even cold.

I ran my finger over the woman's smiling face. "Well, Doreen? What do you think? How does it feel, knowing that your 'one true love' couldn't wait barely six months before he went looking for a younger model?"

Doreen didn't answer, partly because she was dead, and partly because she had no doubt been the kind of woman— good-hearted, open, generous—who hadn't been able to see the bad in anyone.

Ever.

My throat tightened. The woman in the photograph seemed to smile ruefully at me, as if to say, *Love is blind, kiddo. It's hindsight that's twenty-twenty.*

"Isn't it, though?" I asked the photo wryly.

The snapshot was in a silver frame engraved with *Happy 35th Anniversary Edwin & Doreen.* It had a stand-up back, so I carried it out to the foyer and put it on a side table so it could face Edwin's dead body as I worked.

And I had much work to do.

Disposing of the body was the most urgent...and most dangerous. But I had no other choice. I couldn't just leave it here where Edwin's weekly housekeeper would find it in a couple days.

Delaying discovery *always* meant that less evidence could be collected. But I also liked the idea of it, of cleaning up after the guy so that he was being erased too, the way he had tried to erase his wife.

I found cleaning supplies in a closet that I was sure nobody but a weekly maid had touched since Doreen's death, and used them to mop up the worst of the blood that had oozed out from the sides of the rug. I did *not* want to be tracking my way through that.

"Even from the grave, it must sting," I told the photo. "To spend your entire life loving a man, and then to have *'til death do us part* taken so literally...that's just unforgiveable, right?"

Doreen didn't answer. The smile plastered on her dying face looked a little fake and strained, to be honest. Just because women had to learn to smile through their disappointments didn't mean it was easy.

Pausing in my work, I realized that I was treating the situation a little more flippantly than it deserved. I faced the photo again.

"I'm sorry. This is a serious moment, and I don't mean to sound sarcastic." I placed my gloved hand over my heart, hoping to demonstrate my sincerity to the dead woman. "I have nothing but sympathy for you. I swear, I never intended to try to take your place. As a matter of fact, I took a vow to put things right. And I promise I'll get you out of here soon. I just have a few more things to take care of."

A glance at the clock gave me a jolt of surprise. I'd spent hours going through Edwin's office. Needing the cover of darkness to do what I must now do meant I couldn't dally any longer. It wasn't even midnight yet, but I wanted to give myself plenty of time.

Rushing to the kitchen, I snatched up the keys of Edwin's flashy Mercedes-Benz GLC-Class and went into the garage. Opening the tailgate, I folded the back seats down before covering the now extended cargo area with several layers of heavy plastic I found on the garage's well-stocked shelves. After that, I hurried to the merry widower's weight room and snagged forty pounds of free weights. He wouldn't need them again. The idea made me even madder, thinking of the older man trying to get in shape for a younger woman when he probably didn't give a shit how he looked when he was married to Doreen.

Taking a deep breath, I refused to think about that anymore. I needed to clear my mind for the task ahead. Being upset over things I couldn't control would only distract me and lead to mistakes.

I couldn't make any of those. Too much was at stake.

With those tasks complete, I went back to the foyer and put on a disposable raincoat I kept in my bag in case of unanticipated splatter. As tightly as I could, I made an Edwin burrito by rolling the rug around him, then rolled the entire thing in a tarp I'd also found. He was heavier than I'd imagined he would be as I dragged him through the house, grateful that the floor was tile, making the task much easier. Still, I was sweating by the time I reached the garage.

Grunting and cursing, I hefted the entire burrito into the cargo area, making sure the plastic stayed firmly in place. With a sigh of relief, I slammed the tailgate shut before continuing with my work.

I cleaned up the mess as best as I could, using a custom mix of hydrogen peroxide and other household cleaners that should help break down the hemoglobin in the blood and make it harder for any probing crime scene investigator to track. Well, from luminol, at least. I had no doubt that there were more high-tech ways to spot blood, but if I was very clever, law enforcement would never have a reason to use them. Only time would tell.

When that was done, I wandered around the house, tempted to take small items that I knew were incredibly valuable. I didn't, of course. Physical items could be traced, and to sell them I would need a buyer. When more than one person knew your secrets, it increased your risk of exposure.

And too many people already knew.

Something else I didn't want to think about too closely.

In the basement, I spotted a rug that looked very similar to the one that was currently serving as Edwin's casket. My high esteem for Doreen went out the window as I unrolled yet another expensive Persian. How could anyone just toss such a beautiful object into a storage space like this? So very wasteful. Maybe she did deserve to waste away from the cancer after all.

With the abandoned rug firmly in place in the foyer, I took a tub of disinfectant wipes from my bag and set to work wiping down everything I'd touched. On my hands and knees, I made sure that not a single hair could be used as evidence against me. A final sweep and mop of the area, and I was certain that I was safe.

Soon, the kitchen, foyer, and garage, and everywhere I'd snooped, were as spotless as I could make them, and the rags, mophead, and leftover cleaning supplies were either packed up in my purse or in garbage bags in the trunk of my car.

Pulling on Edwin's coat, I secured his hat down over most of my forehead. Changing into a fresh pair of gloves, I was ready to leave. I locked the front door, went into the garage, and started Edwin's Mercedes. My own car was on the oppo-site side of the driveway, as far away from any nosy neighbors as could be, and its current location meant I wouldn't have any trouble backing out.

It didn't take long to make it to a bridge three counties over. In the movies, the killer was always putting a dead body into the driver's seat, starting the car, and jamming a rock on the gas pedal. They set the car in drive, and it would then shoot over a cliff to a crescendo of dramatic music.

And then the cops recovered the car and found some damned piece of evidence in it.

Me, I just parked the car as far out along the embankment as I dared, checked for oncoming traffic, and dragged the Edwin burrito out of the back and over to the embankment on the upstream side of the bridge.

Just as I was about to heave him over, I realized that I'd forgotten the weights. I didn't want him floating up too soon. Or ever, hopefully. I ran back to the SUV and grabbed the weights and a roll of tape from my bag, then carefully stuffed the heavy cast iron into the rug, using the duct tape to secure everything nice and tight.

As I worked, I flinched every time I thought I heard a car approach.

None did. I was lucky.

When everything was ready, I looked up at the dark sky. "You're free now, Doreen. Vengeance is yours, and you may now truly rest in peace."

With the very last of my strength, I hefted him over the side of the near-vertical embankment and watched him tumble downward, crossing my fingers that he wouldn't get stuck on a rock or a branch. The last thing I wanted to do was try to climb down there in the dark.

But he landed in the water with a slushy splash. Seconds later, he was consumed by his watery grave.

Walking a half mile or so down the river, I found a particularly wide area and threw the knife with all my might. It disappeared just as easily as Edwin had.

Well, that was that.

The cold air felt wonderful on my heated skin as I walked back to Edwin's SUV. I drove back to the house and reentered the garage. Once the door had closed, I wiped down every surface with cleaning wipes and then used the shop vac in the corner to make sure I didn't leave any random strands of the red hair.

Removing the collection container, I stuffed it along with Edwin's hat and coat into a large black bag. I walked carefully back through the house, searching for anything I might have missed. Back in the foyer, it was just me and Doreen again.

I picked up her photograph. "Time to go, sweetie. Soon, we'll have a ladies' night. I promise."

I also picked up the engagement ring, scowling at the ten-thousand-dollar diamond. I would worry about disposing of it later.

Considering my night's activities hadn't been planned, I thought it had all gone smoothly. And yet...I was left feeling unsatisfied. I'd been initially fulfilled, knowing I had rid the earth of a man who didn't deserve to breathe the air that Mother Nature produced, but now, after handling all the details, I felt tired, achy, and hollow. Although I was still glad that I'd killed him for Doreen's sake, the magic of the night had rubbed off already.

What was missing?

Was it just too much time spent cleaning up afterward? Should I have been more cruel? Made sure that he fully understood why I'd turned on him?

Probably.

As I backed out of the driveway and headed out onto the road, I brainstormed ideas for making my future Romeos suffer more. Pain only lasted so long. Unless it was my pain, and then, it was never-ending.

It was the anticipation of pain that built the suspense, I realized as I pondered the thought. Now, all I needed was more anticipation.

And when I selected my next victim, he would suffer more. I would see to that.

3

The Mosby Detention Center was a fortress of solid slabs of cement and endless miles of coiled razor wire, a place where dangerous men were held pending their trials. The atmosphere couldn't have been more discouraging if they'd put up a sign over the door reading *Abandon all hope, ye who enter here.* If there was any difference between the detention center and an actual supermax prison, Dr. Autumn Trent couldn't tell.

"May I see your driver's license and the secondary ID you submitted with your request?" The guard at the front desk in the reception area held his hand out, only glancing in her direction, still staring at a computer screen that was large enough to take up most of the small space.

Even though this wasn't her first visit here, she handed over her driver's license and her ID from Shadley and Latham, a full-service psychology consultancy that focused on threat assessment, insider threats, counterterrorism, investigative consultations, and operational training.

Her company covered everything from stalkings to school shootings to workplace violence while also creating criminal profiles to assist in a variety of investigations, including building profiles for cold-case homicides. They identified employees who were at risk for committing things like fraud and corporate espionage. When requested, they even researched radicalization techniques for the FBI.

She loved her job.

At least she had until a couple weeks ago when one of the smarmy owners decided that she was the perfect candidate for his unwanted advances. She wasn't, and she'd let him know that in no uncertain terms. The solid kick in the balls she'd delivered when he'd pushed her too far in his hotel room communicated more than words ever could.

Adam Latham was now currently on a leave of absence while the original owner of the firm, Mike Shadley, figured out how to dissolve the partnership without ruining the company's reputation.

Which was what Autumn wanted too. She adored Mike, and she believed deeply in the mission of the firm. One snake shouldn't undermine it all, though Autumn was still contemplating the idea of pressing charges. It wasn't a decision she was taking lightly.

Nor was she taking the possibility of joining the FBI lightly either.

Autumn had been recruited heavily by Special Supervisory Agent Aiden Parrish since she entered the FBI's orbit as the victim of a crazy neurosurgeon who'd been intent on studying her unique brain. Autumn had managed to escape Dr. Catherine Schmidt's clutches with the help of Aiden and her new best friends, Winter Black and Noah Dalton, who had both been rookie agents in the Violent Crimes Unit at the time.

Since that day, Autumn had been called on to assist the FBI on a few cases, and although she'd found herself in a few tight places, she loved being out in the field. Loved hunting the criminals down and saving victims, much as she'd been saved herself.

Aiden Parrish, smart man that he was, had pounced on her love of the job, going so far as to create a new position within the FBI Behavioral Analysis Unit. Because of her unique qualifications as both a forensic and criminal psychologist, not to mention her Juris Doctorate, the highest law degree in the country, Aiden felt that the new position was justified.

Autumn hoped so. She'd worked her ass off to become competent in both specialties.

Criminal psychologists spent most of their time focusing on determining a motive and creating a profile of the perpetrator of a crime, while forensic psychologists most often specialized in the aftermath. Once the dust had settled, forensic psychologists then were often called on to evaluate a suspect's mental state in order to assess things like their competency to stand trial, which was what she was at the prison to do today.

Most psychologists chose to focus on either forensic or criminal, but Autumn hadn't wanted to choose. She'd wanted to know it all, knowing that both methodologies gave her an edge that was highly sought after in her field.

And now...she knew where she wanted to be. She knew which ID she wanted to carry in her pocket. At least she thought she did.

By joining the FBI, she would be putting herself in danger on the regular, and she'd be giving up her cushy desk job with its enormous paycheck too.

The good news was that, for now, she would continue to work as a consultant as the specifics of the new position was nailed down and she went through proper training, which she desperately needed. During that time, both she and

Aiden would determine if she was as perfect for the job as he thought she was.

She just had to be patient as the hoop jumping concluded and the red tape rolled.

The guard took a plastic tray out from under the desk and laid it in front of her. "Thank you, everything checks out. Please place your personal items here."

He went through the litany of rules and regulations, along with the list of what she could take inside with her and what she couldn't. She removed her jewelry and tucked everything but a short pencil and non-spiral bound notepad inside a locker.

"Follow me." The guard led the way down a narrow observation corridor, passing through a multitude of gates before reaching what would have looked like a classroom…if the students all sat in cages with chairs and tables bolted inside.

A whiteboard at the front had English and Spanish words written in neat cursive. *Hermano*—brother. *Tío*—uncle. At least something constructive was taking place in this hell-hole. At least Autumn hoped that was the case, and this room hadn't been created to only make it look like it was.

In the far corner of this "classroom" was a closet-sized space that was vastly different. Made of a heavy steel frame with thick plexiglass panels, it reminded her somewhat of a fishbowl. Aside from two places to sit, the place was sterile. One was like a school desk, the kind with the seat and desk attached to each other. It was bolted to the floor and had all kinds of bars and hinges attached.

The other was just a stacking chair with molded plastic that was shaped to better fit a person's ass, though Autumn knew from personal experience that the curve didn't provide much added comfort.

The first chair already held a young man. He was wearing

orange scrubs, shower flip-flops, and handcuffs with an extra-long chain between them, one that was also fastened to the chain running between his ankle restraints.

Justin Black. Nineteen years old. Serial killer.

Her best friend's baby brother.

Autumn first met Special Agent Winter Black during an investigation into yet another serial killer, a pediatric neuro-surgeon who targeted children with traumatic brain injuries, hoping to study those children when they turned into adults to better understand how the mind worked.

Autumn had been one of those children.

Her father, a piece of shit with a bad temper and even worse drug habit, had knocked her headfirst into a heavy coffee table, forcing Autumn to have surgery to relieve the pressure on her brain.

Unbeknownst to anyone at the time, the neurosurgeon had noticed something unusual about Autumn and had "marked" her for future research...by implanting a tracking device along the side of her stomach. With that tiny GPS signal, the doctor could find her when she was ready to prepare Autumn for "study."

The doctor was crazy, but she had also been right. There was indeed something unusual about Autumn. She had gained an ability to somehow feel people's thoughts and feel-ings with no more than a brief touch.

The neurosurgeon had wanted to know why. What made Autumn's brain fire differently than others? And she'd wanted to learn how Autumn's brain worked by examining it...one slice at a time.

The mad scientist had come very close to doing just that. Winter, Noah, and Aiden, as well as many others on the FBI team helped save Autumn's life, and Autumn had gotten to know the team very well during that scary time.

She liked them. They liked her in return.

Friendships grew, as did professional respect.

Soon after her close escape, Autumn had been asked to consult on a case the Violent Crimes Division was working. Then she was asked to consult again…and again. During one case, Autumn helped Winter catch her baby brother, a madman and serial killer in his own right.

Now, Autumn helped Winter in a very different way.

She was also helping herself, if she was being brutally honest.

Having the chance to study a young serial killer's behavior was practically a dream come true. Especially this serial killer, who had been raised on another serial killer's knee.

Justin Black had been abducted and raised by The Preacher when he was only six years old. The Preacher had killed Justin's parents and had left his sister, Winter, for dead.

His case was fascinating to Autumn. Had Justin possessed homicidal tendencies upon birth? Or had sitting on the knee of a madman been the sole reason Justin had gone on his own rampage of destruction?

More importantly, could he be helped?

For his and his sister's sake, Autumn hoped so…but she had her doubts.

And now, as she lowered herself into the seat across from Justin, those doubts rose by several degrees.

Because of his level of violent tendencies, she wasn't allowed to move her chair within six feet of the prisoner. She wasn't allowed to touch him, nor were they allowed to exchange any item, no matter how innocent. If either of them even raised their voices, the guard, who was standing outside with his back to the door, clearly within view, would end the interview.

And she was only allowed to take a notepad and a short, non-mechanical pencil with her into the room, in order to take notes. It didn't bother her to have to use such simple tools. She had long since embraced the fact that writing down notes in longhand enhanced her understanding of the subject. In this situation, she would need every advantage she could get.

"Hello, Dr. Trent." Justin tried to smile but couldn't quite conceal the strain in his eyes. He had been locked into the desk by means of a heavy steel staple that secured the stretch of chain between his wrists, and a bar that swung over the chain between his feet. He sniffed the air deeply and leaned forward in his chair. "You look nice."

"Thank you." Autumn was wearing her olive blazer again. This was only her second visit, and she had chosen nearly the exact same clothes as she'd worn on her first meeting with him. Déjà vu maybe, but she felt it was important to stay neutral in her appearance. "How are you today, Mr. Black?"

Justin was a slim young man with dark hair, pale skin, and vivid blue eyes. He resembled his older sister, except for the fact that Winter radiated strength and confidence while the person in front of her was hunched over on himself, making him look closer to ninety than nineteen.

"I asked you last time to call me Justin." His lower lip jutted out, and Autumn fought not to roll her eyes.

"Yes, you did. I just wanted to make sure you feel the same way today."

"I do." He straightened a little, those piercing blue eyes coming up to meet hers for a moment. "They told me you were away on a case. I was a little mad about it, actually. I think I said some mean things to my sister. Wrong things." He inspected his fingernails, which had been chewed down to the quick. "I told her that I didn't want to see her again until you came back. I got it in my head that she was trying to keep you away from me."

Autumn kept the pencil and paper in her pocket for now,

loathe to bring them out until she needed them. The last thing she wanted to do was give Justin the impression he was being studied like a dead bug pinned to a piece of foam backing.

"What makes you believe that to be true?"

A flash of rage crossed his pale features before he ducked his head again. "Because I don't trust her. She makes me nervous, and when I get nervous," he yanked against the chains, his hands moving up but not quite touching his face, "it's like a switch flips in my head, and I just want people to get away from me."

"You don't feel that way now?"

More docile now, Justin pulled at a ragged cuticle on his thumb. "No. I started to realize it was all in my head."

"What was your head saying?"

His thumb began to bleed, and he watched the red spot with what appeared to be genuine fascination. "She was telling you to stay away from me. She was saying that I didn't deserve to get help. That you should abandon me too."

Autumn's gut twisted in sympathy, and she forced the emotion away. Justin Black was very clever, and he knew how to get people on his side. Knew how to play them, and Autumn refused to be played.

"How does that make you feel?"

It was a fallback question every psychologist used, but it was a fallback for a reason. It worked to help get the client talking.

Justin's gaze finally came up to meet hers, his expression pleading. "Just tell me that you're not going to abandon me, okay? I'll try to hang on to that, instead of the crazy stuff I normally think."

Autumn forced herself to hold perfectly still and meet his gaze with a calmness she didn't exactly feel. Making promises wasn't in her best interest...or his. "I'm here, and I will do my best to stay on board with you. I'm committed to helping you get the help you need."

His expression changed, but only for a second. In a blink, he transformed from a handsome young man and into...The Preacher. With another blink, his gaze was back on his bleeding thumb.

"That isn't a promise." His voice was deeper too, more Southern. Crazier. More...Preacher.

What did anyone expect, really? After his parents' murder, Winter went to live with her loving grandparents while Justin lived by the law of Douglas Kilroy.

Autumn shivered, though she didn't allow her body to move.

Justin glanced back up again, his eyes seeming to bore through her skull. His voice rasped in the back of his throat, strained and painful sounding. It had lost the hard edge of The Preacher, and now sounded more like a little boy. "Will you? Will you, Dr. Trent? I have been let down by so many people. It's hard to trust anyone. Even you."

Many troubled people seemed to change their attitude when they were most vulnerable, becoming defensive, angry, accusatory, and in some cases, even abusive. It really was like flipping an emotional and mental switch, and Justin's was flipping back and forth so quickly, it was proving to be difficult to keep up.

The question was...was this real or an act?

She maintained eye contact. "I understand."

"Do you?" His tone turned accusatory, the switch flipping to anger now. His lip curled, his fists clenching and unclenching in his lap. "I don't think you do. You said something last time about having been in the foster care system as a kid, after your dad knocked you into a table." He tried to point toward his forehead, but the chain at his wrists stopped him. "You had brain surgery. I remember. I'm not saying you never had it bad, but I don't think you had it as bad as I did. You said you were finally accepted by the people who adopted you. I think that after you got adopted, it was nothing but smooth sailing."

He clearly had more to say, so Autumn sat calmly, meeting his gaze. She let silence draw him out even further.

"You finished school. You went to college to get your fancy degree. I didn't even get to graduate. Kilroy made me drop out. He said that the government was brainwashing me. I had to study under him, but it was crazy stuff about women and Jews and…and all sorts of things. And church. Literally every person in my life who stuck around was crazy."

He raised his fists. For a moment, Autumn thought he would pound the table with them. But instead, he glanced toward the guard standing outside the door and lowered them slowly to the scarred wood.

"So, which one are you?" His eyes glittered with tears. "Are you the crazy person who sticks around, or are you the normal person who lies about being there for me but only shows up when they want something?"

Images flashed through Autumn's head…being yelled at, being slapped, being locked in a closet for wetting the bed, locked in so long that she had wet herself again and was further punished for it, going without food until she could barely remember what it was like to be hungry.

And worse, she found herself remembering her younger sister, Sarah. For years, Autumn had been so hurt and jealous and happy that her little sissy had gotten away. Her bio dad had gotten cleaned up, then came swooping in to claim her right as Autumn was recovering from her brain surgery.

Ryan Petzke had fought for custody of Sarah, and when he'd brought Sarah to the hospital to say goodbye, Ryan had held Autumn while she cried, promising that he would come back for her too.

He never did.

Which was probably for the best. He hadn't stayed clean for very long. Then he and Sarah had seemed to disappear from the planet. Autumn didn't even know if her baby sister was alive or dead.

Did Justin think he was the only one who had suffered?

Did he really believe that his suffering compensated for his evil acts?

"Well?" Justin demanded when she continued to do nothing but study him. His impatience seemed to come off him in waves that bounced off the see-through walls. "Talk to me!"

He needed to see that he could push her, and she wouldn't react the way everyone else in his life had reacted. She wouldn't walk away, nor would she fight back. She would be a steady presence, observing and offering help where she could.

"Are you finished?"

The question seemed to surprise him. "Finished what?"

"Making our time together about me instead of about you?"

Long seconds passed as he just glared at her. Then he regrouped, his face transforming into a sneer. "Afraid to tell me?"

"Not at all, and if I ever write my biography, I'll personally autograph you a copy, but right now, my life, past and present, isn't our focus. Our focus over my next few visits is to determine if you are competent to stand trial."

The sneer turned into a scowl filled with so much anger that a cold slice of fear ran through her system. "Fuck a trial. I refuse to be judged."

Autumn lifted a shoulder, keeping her face carefully neutral. "I'm afraid you don't have a choice in the matter. Do you understand what competency means in this situation?"

The muscles in his jaw popped. "I'm not stupid."

"I agree. You're actually very bright, and I still need to know if you understand what competency to stand trial means."

For a moment, she thought he would transition back to anger again. She watched his eyes play through several emotions before his shoulders collapsed, and he began to rock in his chair. "I'm not sure."

He was lying to her, but she didn't push it. Not yet. "A competency assessment establishes whether a defendant, meaning you, is able to understand and rationally participate in the court process. You and I will be—"

Justin slammed his fists on the desk, making Autumn jump. "Order in the court!" He yelled the words so loudly that the guard turned to look through the glass wall.

Striving to calm the adrenaline rush his unexpected actions caused, she took a deep breath and gave the guard a thumbs-up, letting him know that she had everything under control. Her sweaty palms told another story, and she wiped them slowly down her legs.

Justin was grinning big enough to show nearly every tooth. A drop of saliva dripped from his lower lip, drawing a wet line down his chin.

"As I was saying, you and I will be going through the competency assessment on our next visit, although the completed assessment could take more than one visit."

He straightened. "When?"

"As soon as I schedule the time."

He pounded his hands on the desk again. "When?! Give me a date. A time. Is that so hard, you stupid bitch?!" Spittle flew from his mouth by the time he was finished with his tirade.

He was testing her, she knew.

Just as she was testing him.

When she didn't stand and leave, Justin Black, brutal serial killer that he was, burst into tears. She didn't believe them. Not completely.

Autumn couldn't help but think that every move and emotion Justin produced was perfectly calculated to get the result he desired. She felt quite sure that he had total command of his feelings. Most children of abuse did.

Autumn included.

Children of abuse knew when to stay silent. They knew how to keep their face calm.

She waited until his tears had run their course, which didn't take too long. Ten seconds, maybe fifteen, and he was wiping his nose on his sleeve and making a show of bending over until he could brush his cheeks with his hands.

"I-I-I'm sorry." He sounded like a little boy again.

It was interesting, and although she was formally here to discuss the upcoming competency assessment with him, she couldn't stop herself from asking, "When did you learn to turn your emotions on and off like this?"

He blinked, but the movement of his eyelids was so slow that the reaction didn't come from surprise. The second the blue irises appeared again, the switch had flipped. They were back to anger.

Before he could lash out, she held up a hand. "This is getting boring, Justin. Surely it must bore you as well."

His pupils dilated. Finally, an unrehearsed emotional response.

Better.

But not good enough.

Autumn wondered if his shifting mood swings were on purpose. Did he intend to simply exhaust the person he was speaking with to the point in which they basically surrendered and gave him whatever he wanted? Or were they a distraction? Or a tool he used when he wanted to be left alone?

It wasn't a bad plan.

"Did you just tell me I was boring?" The hard edge, the Preacher edge, was back.

"Not at all. I said that your *actions* were getting boring." She leaned forward, genuinely curious. "Is that your goal?"

As a psychologist, she rarely used open-ended questions, but there were times when a quick yes or no gave away more than a carefully scripted answer.

He opened his mouth, then closed it so hard his teeth ground together. Seconds passed before his jaw loosened and his lips curved into what some might call a smile.

"I don't have a goal, Dr. Trent."

She nearly laughed at the response but managed to keep the sound behind tightly clamped lips, her face the neutral mask necessary for her profession.

"Then what do you want?"

He studied her for a very long time, his face softening until he finally lifted his blue eyes to meet hers. "I want to make amends to the people I've hurt."

"Since most of those people are dead, how do you plan to make those amends?"

His jaw tightened again, but he covered quickly, his face falling into an even deeper well of sadness.

Was this how The Preacher had seduced his victims into letting him into their homes? Did Douglas Kilroy teach Justin how to control each muscle of his face so that he could do the same? And more importantly, what else did The Preacher teach the boy?

Autumn was torn.

She knew that delving deeply into Justin's psyche would take many more sessions than the competency assessment allowed. And even though she suspected that Justin was faking his level of competency, she questioned whether she should report his actions as malingering.

On one hand, her gut told her that he was grossly exaggerating his psychological symptoms, but on the other hand...how in the world could the young man not be psychologically unstable to a very large degree?

She weighed her options. If she reported him as faking his illness, he very well might not receive a fair trial because of an inability to best assist his attorney in his defense. If she assessed him as incompetent to stand trial, that didn't mean that he'd get away with his crimes. It just meant that he would get the mental health treatment he so desperately needed before taking the stand sometime in the future.

But she hated to be played. And worse than that, she hated for Justin to think that he was getting away with his role playing.

But that was her ego talking, and she needed to set it aside and focus on what was best for the young man across from her.

Autumn let the silence continue, waiting patiently for Justin to address her point. His chin was on his chest, his fingers linked tightly together. His breathing was ragged, and his face was even paler than normal.

Just when Autumn thought she'd be forced to lose this battle of wills, Justin lifted his head, tears streaking down his face. "I can't remember their names."

Autumn had no similar lack of memory. "Kelsey and Adrian Esperson. Sandy and Oliver Ulbrich. Willa Brown. Dana and Timoth—"

"Stop it!" Justin's chains rattled on the desk as he slammed his hands onto the surface. Spittle flew from his mouth, tears and snot mixing in a noxious looking mess on his face. "Stop it! Stop it! Stop it!"

Justin Black could certainly not go to trial like this, and

she certainly couldn't continue to treat him or even research him under the current conditions. She stood up from her seat.

The guard, who seemed to have eyes in the back of his head, turned and faced her on the other side of the glass, his eyes narrowed on Justin. The young man was now attempting to slam his fists into his face, though the chains around his wrist kept him from doing any damage.

"I'm sorry. I'm sorry." His voice was back to that of a little boy's. "I didn't mean to get angry. Please don't be mad. Don't be mad."

The door opened and the guard stepped inside.

Autumn nodded at the man. "I'm finished here for today."

Justin moaned and began rocking back and forth while he yanked on the chains. His fingernails dug into his hands, leaving long deep red scratch marks in their wake.

"Are you going away again? Don't go away again. Don't go. Don't go. Please don't go."

She held her ground. "I'll visit again another day when we can communicate more easily. We still have the competency assessment to complete."

He blinked rapidly, the tears still flowing. "When? When will you be back? Please come back."

"I may be going out of town again, and I'm not sure how long that will take. If you like, I can have another therapist assigned to complete the—"

"No!"

The guard pulled his baton from his belt, and Autumn nearly gasped at its presence. Moving quickly, she stepped between the guard and Justin.

"That's not necessary," she pleaded with the burly man.

Justin made a giggling sound that seemed on the edge of hysteria before parroting her words, "That's not necessary."

She turned to him, giving him her sternest look. "Don't do that."

Justin's lip turned up in a sneer. "Don't do that."

Autumn exhaled a long breath, better understanding the presence of the baton. She just might bring one with her next time.

Mentally shaking the thoughts of violence away, she bent to pick up the pad and pencil from the floor. "I'll see you next week, Justin."

His lower lip jutted out, and his thumb tried to make its way to his mouth. "Do you promise?"

Behind her, the guard growled before muttering, "For fuck's sake."

She didn't blame him. Autumn had been in this room for less than a half hour, and her nerves were hanging on by a thread. Riding Justin's emotional rollercoaster was one thing. Keeping her composure during the ride was another. Every muscle in her body felt like it was pulled tight.

"I'll visit again after my trip."

His blue eyes seemed like needles under her skin. "Are you going with my big sister?"

Autumn watched him closely. "Actually, I am."

He began rocking again, the blue eyes seeming to grow hotter even as his mouth sagged and drool slipped from his lips. "She's pretty, you know."

Autumn watched his eyes, continuously looking for his triggers. "Yes, she is. You both have similar coloring."

His reaction was as expected as it was explosive. He jumped to his feet, at least as far as the chains would allow. He screamed his sister's name, followed by a string of words so nasty that Autumn nearly covered her ears.

The guard was on him before Autumn could react. His hand on Justin's shoulder shoved the young man into the seat so hard that the clank of his teeth jolting together was unmistakable. A second later, blood mixed with the saliva on Justin's chin.

"Tell her that her baby brother can't wait to see her again!"

The words followed Autumn out of the room. She didn't run, though she badly wanted to be rid of this place.

"Tell her that it's not over yet!"

Flesh connected with flesh, and she didn't turn, not even when Justin howled in obvious pain. She didn't want to witness what was happening in the fishbowl of a room.

In the hallway, she moved to the side as two other guards rushed down the hall and into the room. One pointed in her direction. "Stay there."

She nodded her consent. Now that she was away from Justin, her eyes prickled with tears. It was like stepping out of a room filled with toxic fumes.

Breathing in…she mentally calmed herself.

To her way of thinking, the competency assessment wasn't even necessary. Faking or not, Justin Black needed more help than the penal system could give him.

The door beside where she stood opened again. Autumn forced her face back to its previous blankness.

His voice much weaker now, she heard cries from inside the room, followed by, "I'm sorry. Tell her I'm sorry."

The door shut with a firm click. "Ms. Trent, this way please."

It was one of the new guards, and she followed behind him without saying a word. It wasn't until she was retrieving her belongings from the little locker that she managed a smile. "Thank you." She took a step closer and asked the question she should have asked minutes ago. "Will he need medical attention?"

The guard's face didn't even flinch. "No, ma'am. He'll be just fine when we get him settled."

Fine?

As she thanked the guard again and turned away, she didn't think any part of this scenario was fine. And she didn't think anything would ever be fine again.

AFTER JUSTIN HAD BEEN ESCORTED BACK to his cell, he spent twenty minutes banging on things, alternating between rocking back and forth, sucking his thumb, and keening to himself—too softly to summon a guard, but too loudly for his next-door prisoners to ignore.

When the man in the cell next to him finally muttered, "Jesus fuckin' Christ, somebody just tranquilize that nutcase or hit him with a stun gun already," Justin smiled and lay back on his bunk and thought about Dr. Autumn Trent.

Her pretty face, green eyes sparkling. Eyes that were easy to transform into distress and even tears. Her beautiful curves, clear to see, even under that ugly green blazer.

What would it be like to slowly remove all her clothes, to cut them away, her arms tied behind her, a gag in her mouth, watching her eyes fill with panic and dread as she became more and more vulnerable?

Better yet, what would she say?

Mentally, he started his fantasy over.

He was chasing her through woods at twilight, the leaves wet from a recent thunderstorm. The air smelled like musty leaves and ozone. He had a hunting knife at his side, and a slim piece of wire looped loosely around his wrist.

Fleeing from him, she'd gotten lost in the dark, but she didn't know how to be silent. As she ran, twigs cracked underfoot. She searched for a path, but it was too dim for her eyes to see the difference between a path to safety or an animal trail.

Silent as a panther, Justin followed in her wake, making just enough noise now and then to ratchet up her terror. To let her understand that he was still behind her. That she wasn't safe. Would never be safe while he lived.

If she called for help, he came closer. If she tried to run silently, he fell back and gave her a few moments of hope.

The animal trail disappeared beneath her, and she turned back and forth, trying to find another direction to go. He watched her in the deepening shadows and dragged the tip of the knife across the bark of a tree trunk just to watch her startle in fear.

"Justin?" He could almost hear the tremble in her voice. "Justin? Is that you? It's just me, Autumn. Don't you remember me?"

From behind, he approached her in perfect silence while she stared blindly into the shadows. Mouth near her ear, he whispered, "I remember you, Autumn," and looped the wire around her neck.

A snare for his little rabbit.

"Yes, I remember you, and I remember how you abandoned me."

At the most perfectly timed moment, he giggled.

People didn't like when he giggled. The sound was eerie. Yet another talent he'd learned while sitting on Grandpa's knee.

Would she *cry*?

He hoped so.

He hoped she would weep and gibber hopelessly, telling him all the secrets in her heart, anything—*anything*—to keep him from killing her. He hoped she would beg.

It was a nice fantasy. Not reasonable, but why have reasonable fantasies?

Justin frowned as the small door in his cage slid open, and

a metal tray screeched across concrete as it slid inside his cell.

Breakfast.

He wasn't very hungry, but he rolled from his cot and retrieved the tray, his mind still on Dr. Autumn Trent. He might not get Autumn out into the woods alone with a hunting knife at his side, but at least he could wriggle a few of her secrets out of her heart.

And find a way to turn them to his advantage.

Because Justin always found the advantage.

Too many people were relying on him to fail.

Lifting the lid on the tray, he winced at the smell of runny eggs and a biscuit so hard that it could be considered a lethal weapon in nearly all fifty states. But it was the pile of gravy he was most interested in.

Dipping his fingers into the gelatinous pile of white goo, he smiled as he touched the plastic baggy. Pulling it out, he licked his fingers before wiping the opening of the ziplocked sandwich bag clean with his tongue.

It was a letter.

Typed in neat print were six little words that made him smile even bigger.

Plan A in progress. Stay alert.

4

Traffic wasn't bad. It was seldom bad at six in the morning, especially in the suburbs of Richmond, Virginia, which was why Aiden Parrish liked to get to work extra early. After a greasy breakfast, of course.

He pulled into his favorite restaurant, a small Southern-style diner just off the interstate and ordered his usual. His stomach rumbled at the upcoming feast, knowing the rest of the day would only bring healthy selections that would make any cardiologist proud.

The breakfast "garbage plate" included generous helpings of hash browns, spicy sausage, pimento cheese spread, and hot pickled peppers. The next layer consisted of a generous helping of grated cheddar cheese with two eggs cracked over top. It was the kind of place where the waitresses all liked it when you called them "hon."

His waitress gave him her usual level of sass, and he left her his usual five-dollar bill tucked under an empty plate. With an overly full belly, he got back into his two-year-old Lexus and followed the curving road through a neighborhood full of identical houses, a community college, a middle school, and several softball parks. It was the kind of area that rang with baseball bats, children's bicycle bells, and ice cream trucks all summer long. In January, it was a little quieter, with only a few yellow school buses trundling through the streets.

He put on his blinker and turned into the drive leading to the main Richmond FBI Office. After parking in his usual spot, he checked his tie, making sure there were no breakfast leftovers on the patterned silk before he got out. The guard at the door, a sixty-year-old man named Jim Wheeler, was, as always, scrupulously polite, even though they'd been greeting each other for at least a decade. "Good morning, Special Supervisory Agent Parrish."

"Morning, Jim." Aiden nodded at the guard and lugged his briefcase up the steps in lieu of an elevator. He had some calories to work off, but each bite had been worth it.

Stopping at the break room, he cursed whoever hadn't made coffee and started a pot. As he waited for it to sputter out the first cup, Max Osbourne, Special Agent in Charge of the Richmond Violent Crimes Unit, stepped into the room, his stocky form taking up a good portion of the doorway.

"Good morning." Max's rumbling voice was even more threatening than his appearance, but he took the cup Aiden handed him with a more or less friendly smile. "Did you get my message?"

"Sure did, and I'll be running it by the team this morning." Aiden scrutinized the SAC's face. "You sure you don't want to take point on this one, being friends with the chief and all?"

Max pulled at his tie. "Would love to, but we've got serious movement going on with that school bombing, and I don't want to lose momentum."

Aiden didn't blame him. Every politician in the country was on Max's ass to solve that case.

"I want to take Black, Stafford, and Dalton, at the very least. I'll be bringing in Dr. Trent to assist since my team is spread thin right now."

"Take Sun Ming too. With the staffing issues we're having in cyber, she'll help with tech."

Shit.

It wasn't that Aiden didn't appreciate Sun's intelligence, but he was still kicking himself for letting their relationship move beyond professional years ago. Their breakup hadn't been easy, and he didn't need to be a profiler to know that Sun still harbored more than a little animosity that she enjoyed flinging in his direction.

Keeping his face neutral, Aiden nodded. "Will do. A six-man team should be plenty."

Max nodded. "Keep me apprised."

"Will—"

"Parrish!" This new voice might have been feminine, but it shot through the room like a bullet. Turning slowly, Aiden found Cassidy Ramirez, the Associate Deputy Director of the Richmond FBI office glaring at him. "Meeting. My office. Now." Without another word, his boss turned and strode away.

Aiden didn't move, and it pissed him off that Max Osbourne had witnessed the dressing down. Eager to show just how unconcerned he was, he waited until a single cup of coffee had landed in the coffee pot and poured himself a cup, adding sugar just so he would have a reason to linger in the break room as he stirred.

At the door to the ADD's office, he knocked. Cassidy looked up from her desk and waved Aiden in. "Took you long enough."

Aiden lifted his cup, as if needing caffeine this early was explanation enough. "What's the emergency?"

Cassidy's nostrils twitched. "Autumn Trent."

"*Doctor* Autumn Trent," Aiden reminded her, enjoying the moment when Cassidy's nostrils flared again.

"Doctor or not, what the hell are you trying to do? It takes a minimum of three years of law enforcement expertise to get hired on at the FBI...which she doesn't have. And then you have to spend ten years as a special agent before you break into the BAU...which she hasn't done. It smells like special treatment."

Aiden settled back in a chair, squaring his feet and getting ready for a fight. Trying to convince Cassidy of *anything* was like trying to lead a bear to water on a leash.

"I understand that it looks that way." Aiden had wondered when this confrontation would occur. "But Dr. Trent brings with her a wealth of knowledge that far surpasses anything I can provide."

Cassidy rocked back in her seat a little. "More experience than *you* can provide? How long have you been the head of the Richmond BAU?"

Aiden blew on his steaming cup. "Long enough to know when I've run into a unique skillset that could be vital to my team's success. Dr. Trent is both a criminal and forensic psychologist and has intuitive skills about how serial killers tick that are almost preternatural. Capturing her early in her career instead of waiting until she is tenured somewhere else just makes sense. We train her while picking her brain."

Cassidy's eyes narrowed. "It's a total reversal from our standard operating procedures."

"Maybe our SOPs need to be reversed at times." Aiden forced out a weary sigh. His breakfast was sitting like a lump in his stomach now. "She's new...but she pulled more out of the suspect of our last case than one of our more seasoned agents ever could and did it while being sexually harassed and manipulated by her boss, Adam Latham."

Cassidy tucked a strand of black hair behind her ear with

an angry flip of her wrist. "Get to the point, Parrish. I'm not arguing about Dr. Trent's credentials. I'm arguing about her hiring process. It's disruptive to the team."

"The members of our teams who know Dr. Trent know that she's an ideal candidate for a position within the BAU."

Cassidy didn't even blink. "Again, I'm not arguing that point with you, Parrish."

Aiden held up both hands. "What point *are* you arguing? Because I'm not seeing it."

"I'm arguing that her hiring process is unfair, biased, and completely cuts out any chance of an internal candidate taking a coveted BAU position."

"Which is exactly why we're creating a *new* position. The remainder of my team stands exactly the same. She hasn't forced anyone out nor is she taking a spot that one of our more tenured agents would benefit from." Aiden waited a beat, letting that sink in before driving in the last nail. "And… I've already spent as much on consulting fees as her salary would be with us. That young woman is willing to slash her income in half to come work with us."

Money. The bottom line in any conversation.

Cassidy slowly blew air out of her cheeks as she stared up at the ceiling, clearly wanting to shoot Aiden's idea down but struggling to find a solid argument for doing so. Cassidy's eyes fixed back on Aiden. "You'll have to post the job and have her go through the normal application process. And she *cannot* have the title of Special Agent…unless and until she meets the regular requirements."

Aiden pushed to his feet. "You know, that's a great idea. I hadn't thought of that. I'll get the job description and requirements written up right away."

Cassidy's eyes narrowed. She was smart and knew when she'd fallen into a trap. "What if another internal candidate outshines her?"

Aiden suppressed a smile. "Then I'll hire that candidate, no question. Do you know another agent with Dr. Trent's set of credentials?"

Her lips flattened into a straight line. "You maneuvered me into this, didn't you?"

Aiden tried to look offended. "I'm not sure what you're talking about, Cassidy, but I really don't have time to discuss it. I have a job description to write. It'll be on your desk this afternoon."

He left Cassidy's office, whistling as he returned to the break room to refill his coffee. A few members of his team were coming in, and he greeted them as they passed.

They hadn't generally started out as early risers but there wasn't a single one of them who wasn't hungry for their next case, and Aiden always gave out the best assignments first thing in the morning.

"Conference room in twenty," he told the group before heading back to his office.

With great satisfaction, he pulled up the files he had already written for Autumn's job description and sent the job rec to human resources. He then checked the rest of his files to make sure they were in order. The rest of the week, at a minimum, was going to be busy.

He was on his third cup of coffee that morning when Autumn Trent appeared at his door at precisely eight a.m. She was slim, pretty, had bright red hair and was tallish for a woman. She wore a tailored black suit over a silky silver and black houndstooth shirt. A slim red belt cinched tight at the waist was the same color as the twin Bing cherry earrings that were the only hint that this professional looking woman had a playful side.

He found himself staring and quickly looked away. He'd promised that their relationship would be purely professional. Dammit. It wasn't often that he met a woman with a mind as fantastic as her body.

She'd been to the office before, so she was familiar with the building and office layout. Nevertheless, she seemed to be studying the place as if she'd never seen it before.

She leaned against the doorjamb. "So, where's my new desk?" From the twinkle in her green eyes, he knew she was joking. Or maybe testing him. With her, it was sometimes hard to tell the difference.

"It's on order." He waved to the stack of papers that he'd only recently completed. "In case you didn't realize it, government agencies sometimes work at a snail's pace."

She smiled and pushed away from the door. "I've heard such rumors but thought the great Aiden Parrish would be in possession of some magical mollusk that was turbocharged."

He barked out a laugh. "I am, but the damn thing keeps ramming into the red tape strewn everywhere."

The smile slid from her lips as she closed the door behind her and took a seat across from him, placing her enormous tote bag in her lap. "Are you trying to tell me something, Aiden? Has there been a change in plans?"

The woman was astute.

"Not at all. I actually spoke to ADD Ramirez just this morning, and we have a plan to quick start your employment while staying within the lines human resources requires."

An eyebrow shot up. "Can you please speak plainly?"

Aiden cleared his throat. "We are creating a new position within the BAU that will be open to all internal candidates per agency policy." He pushed the job description across the desk to her, watching her while she read.

Her green eyes met his. "Will this cause a problem?" She pushed the job description back. "Anyone with two brain cells to rub together will understand that the job is tailor-made for me."

He lifted a shoulder. "And they will also come to the conclusion that only one person in this agency has the specific skillsets we need. If they want to go back to school and broaden their scope of education, they are welcome to do that."

"I don't want to cause conflicts or take away a position from someone more deserving."

He held up a hand. "You aren't taking anything away from anyone, and I'm of an opinion that conflict can be good for an organization at times. For those who wish they had the qualifications for this position, I'll welcome them to return to school and gain those credentials. I believe in hiring people smarter than me, and if I'm not intimidated by you joining our team, I don't see why any of them would be intimidated either."

Autumn didn't seem convinced and actually looked more than a little embarrassed. She wasn't used to accepting compliments, especially to that degree, which made Aiden even more certain that now was the optimal time to bring her on his team. She had no idea how bright she was...how unique...how gifted. How much money she could make in the private industry. Her salary at Shadley and Latham was huge, but in a few years, she would be able to command much more.

He needed to snap her up now, make her addicted to chasing a crime. No desk job with a big paycheck could beat the adrenaline rush of taking down the bad guy.

Now, he just hoped that nothing would screw it up.

She fingered the straps of the tote bag as she watched him closely. "You seem certain."

He didn't hesitate. "I am."

"And you don't waste time."

"Wasted time is wasted lives." He pushed to his feet. "And

right now, it's time for our briefing session." His hand was on the doorknob when he turned to her. "Ready?"

She was the picture of poised professionalism as she adjusted the strap of her bag higher on her shoulder. "Ready."

They stopped in the break room for more coffee while Aiden mentally went over the details of the case he was about to toss out to his team. Thoughts of murder didn't stop him from noting that Autumn liked an enormous amount of cream and sugar, making her coffee more of a latte than the black acid threatening to burn through his cup.

Winter Black was the first to notice him enter the conference room. Her piercing blue-eyed gaze was eager and held more than a little suspicion. She seemed to always be hungry for a new case, but her caution was well-placed. New cases were exciting, but they also ate at an agent, especially one who wore her heart on her sleeve like Winter did. Her heart competed with the chip she carried on her shoulder and the two always seemed to be at war.

Winter did a double take when Autumn followed him into the room and was on her feet in an instant. The two friends hugged, making Aiden wonder when they'd last seen each other. Women were complicated beings. These two would probably react the same whether they hadn't seen each other in hours or weeks.

"Please tell me that you're joining us for this case."

Autumn gave her friend a final squeeze before stepping back, a big smile on her face. "I'm joining you for this case."

Noah Dalton, a fellow special agent and Winter's boyfriend, cracked his knuckles. Tall and athletic, Dalton was far too laid back for Aiden's tastes. The man was a professional, but he didn't always act like one. And he had a tendency to go for jokes at Aiden's expense.

"I heard we were borrowing you from Shadley and

Latham again." Dalton's lazy Texas drawl scratched across Aiden's nerves. "Any idea what we're hunting today?"

Autumn placed her heavy looking bag down on the table. "Nope. As long as it's not spiders or snakes, I'm ready for about anything."

Next to Noah, Bree Stafford snorted, her perfect set of white teeth a stark contrast to her dark skin. The oldest of this crew, Bree had worked for the agency for more than twenty years. At nearly six feet tall, she was a commanding presence, and Aiden had little doubt that she was the person most likely to give Noah Dalton trouble on a basketball court. She was athletic and friendly and was often paired up with the big Texan.

Since Noah and Winter had confessed to having a personal relationship, the two of them were now on separate teams for professional reasons. The two worked well together, but Noah and Bree worked equally well. The Texan and the seasoned agent were like a pair of retrievers: friendly, open, and absolutely impossible to distract from a suspect they were supposed to bring in. Bree held out a hand for a high five, and Autumn slapped it.

Aiden was pleased. Having Autumn accepted by the Violent Crime Unit was important, and it appeared as if everyone was glad to have her here. Except Sun Ming. Well, it wasn't as if the reticent agent was displeased, exactly. It was a rare thing for Sun to do more than scowl, so the nod she gave Autumn was the only confirmation Aiden needed that Sun didn't oppose the addition.

The members of the BAU would be a harder team to crack, but that was another matter for another day. For now, each of the members were busy on other cases, which was becoming more and more commonplace within his department. While there were thousands of agents within the FBI, there was only a handful assigned to each agency's Behavioral Analysis Unit.

Sometimes, his agents simply provided profiles and never left their offices, but heading out into the field was becoming more and more a commonplace occurrence. The BAU had originally been formed to help the agents connect the dots between an unsub and a crime, analyzing behavior, motivation, and language as well as demographics based on similar crimes and criminal actions in the past. The role was quickly evolving. It was one thing to analyze behavior from a spreadsheet of descriptors, and quite another to see it come alive more fully at a crime scene.

Aiden called the meeting to order the moment he set his coffee cup down. The room quieted and every person's attention turned to him. He knew they could feel a big case coming, and he rearranged his folders a couple times to draw out the suspense.

"As I mentioned in my message, we have a predator in our midst…" he paused for added suspense and to also tap the laptop connected to the smart screens awake, "but it's possible that our unsub has recently crossed the line from theft to murder."

"Possible? We're going to take a case on a possible?" Sun looked pissed. She didn't like games and her sense of humor could use a little humor.

Aiden continued to tap, pulling up the case file he'd assembled the night before. "That's why we've gathered here instead of three hundred miles away. Before deciding to take on this case, I wanted us to puzzle together the pieces to see if they make a complete picture or if they belong in another box."

No one groused because, as much as they loved being in the field, they loved puzzles almost equally as well. And what was law enforcement if not taking pieces of evidence and assembling them in an organized way?

"Here is what we know so far." He tapped the first file that showed a map of similar crimes dotting various communities up the northeast coast. "Starting about twenty-seven months ago, there has been a slew of crimes against recently widowed men that resulted in those men losing a large majority of their lifesavings."

Sun tossed down her ink pen. "You want us hunting down a con artist?" Disgust mixed with disbelief practically dripped off the question.

Autumn crossed her legs. "Do you mean sweetheart scammers?"

Aiden ignored Sun's question and the way in which it was delivered as well as the smoothly delivered correction from Autumn.

"These dots most likely represent a small percentage of the crimes that were actually committed to similar victims within that same time period. As you can imagine, being taken in and systematically ripped off by a beautiful young thing would hit most men in the pride. We don't know and probably will never know the extent of money taken or the number of victims."

He then clicked a button that categorized the crime spree by dates. From the corner of his eye, he glimpsed Autumn lean forward. "The spree moves up the coast in a sequential fashion."

Winter nodded, also leaning forward. "It's the same unsub."

"Or unsub*s*," Autumn added.

That was what Aiden thought too. "Several days ago, SAC Osbourne got a call from Keith Mazur, the Chief of Police of Passavant Hills Township Police Department in Pennsylvania. Chief Mazur and Max go way back, so our look-see is also being based on a lifelong friendship."

Sun Ming rolled her eyes so hard he was surprised when they didn't get stuck in her brain. "Seriously? We are—"

Aiden held up a hand, letting his annoyance show. He and Max Osbourne didn't always get along, but Aiden understood friendships and the ties that bound people together over time. The young agent could learn a thing or two about building bridges instead of burning them to the ground.

"As you've already seen, the dates of the crime spree offer a pattern that can't be ignored. Chief Mazur, though, didn't call SAC Osbourne about anything as simple as a bunch of widowers losing their pensions. The chief feels that our unsub has escalated, and he is afraid that this escalation is only the beginning."

He had them all now. Their eagerness to learn more was radiating off them in waves.

"What's happened in Passavant Hills?" Autumn asked.

"In Passavant Hills, widowers are not only losing their pensions…they're losing their lives."

5

Autumn had heard her military and agency friends speak of having a "go bag" filled with necessities ranging from toiletries to shoes and clothes in order to travel at a moment's notice. She desperately needed one of those, she realized as she waited with Aiden Parrish for their rental car.

Had she remembered to pack her deodorant and an extra pair of shoes? Had she left her beloved pets, Toad and Peach, with enough food for Leslie Zane, her very lovely and accommodating neighbor turned pet sitter, to feed them on their schedule?

If she was truly going to join the FBI, she needed to get her shit together.

She'd been given exactly half an hour after the meeting to pack and contact Leslie to make sure she was available to pet sit. If Leslie had been out of town or otherwise indisposed, Autumn would have been forced to turn to her Aunt Leigh, who wasn't really an aunt but her adoptive mother's best friend. Aunt Leigh would have dropped everything to help in a crisis, but as owner of a busy bar, The Lift, she didn't have much time for dog watching or litter box scooping.

Autumn desperately needed more friends. Friends with jobs that didn't take them away at a moment's notice would be most helpful.

The distance from Richmond to Philadelphia wasn't that far, but the time between departure and arrival had been short, and as usual, the admins of the Violent Crimes Unit and the BAU had overdone themselves in getting the earliest possible flights for the team.

Which meant that Autumn was riding along with Aiden in a giant rented Tahoe that looked, sounded, and even *smelled* just like the one she had been stuck in with her former boss, the manipulative and highly inappropriate and unethical Adam Latham.

Her mind continued to wander, fastening finally on the memory of her kneeing Adam in the balls when he'd attacked her at the hotel. She sniggered, the sound bursting out before she could stop it.

Aiden gave her a quick glance as he drove. "What's up?"

She adjusted the seat belt that was cutting into the skin of her neck. "My mind was wandering into unpleasant places, so I steered it to a more pleasant memory."

"It must have been a good one, whatever it was."

"It was." She shot him a sideways glance, her smile growing wider. "I was remembering kneeing Latham in the balls that night at the hotel."

"I hope you knocked them loose for him." It was his turn to glance her way. "What have you decided about pressing charges?"

The smile slid from her face. "I'm going to file when we get back from this case."

He was nodding before she'd finished speaking. "I'm glad."

She was actually more than a little ashamed of herself for not having already gone through the procedures. "I'm…worried."

There.

She'd admitted one of her concerns, but if she were being fully honest, a better description would have been that she was scared. She didn't like being scared.

To Aiden's credit, he didn't provide any comforting platitudes. He actually looked grim. "That's understandable. Court cases can get ugly, and as I'm sure you well know, Latham's defense attorney will attempt to drag you through the mud." He reached over and squeezed her arm, but only for a moment before his fingers were back around the steering wheel.

"'He said, she said' is an ugly game, but I don't think I can look at myself in the mirror if I let him just get away with his harassment and assault. How could I ever attempt to convince one of our victims to press charges if I'm not willing to do it myself?"

He was nodding again. "He's losing his partnership with Shadley, right? At least Mike is taking this seriously."

Poor Mike Shadley, the boss she respected and adored. The last time Autumn had spoken to him, he sounded as if he'd aged twenty years.

"Mike is actually looking to rebrand the entire company, taking both Shadley and Latham off the logo and replacing it with a name that more fully reflects what the company offers."

"Good thinking. That strategy will require less explanation regarding Latham's disappearance, and the name and logo won't need to be changed if Mike decides to retire or brings on a new partner."

Autumn refused to remember how she'd had big dreams of her own name being part of that logo not too long ago.

Not that Mike wouldn't welcome her as a partner after she'd spent a few years earning the title. That type of work just didn't satisfy her any longer. Sitting at a desk didn't suit her anymore.

Right here, in the field, was exactly where she belonged.

"I'm stopping for gas before we brief with the police chief. Want anything?" Aiden pulled into an enormous station with twenty pumps.

Autumn went inside and bought a vanilla latte out of a machine as well as a couple of candy bars and packages of almonds. She didn't think she was hungry but found herself tearing savagely into the first PayDay. She tucked the rest of her treats into her trusty tote bag before she was tempted to scarf them down too, then headed back to the Tahoe.

She found Aiden with a finger in one ear and his phone tightly pressed to the other. Seat belt in place, she powered her iPad back on and scrolled over to a victim's folder. Brice Sutter, the widower killed just three days ago in Passavant Hills and the reason SAC Osbourne had assigned them to this case.

Poor man.

Tapping on the crime scene photos, Autumn mentally apologized to the naked man taking up her screen. Brice Sutter hadn't gone quietly into that good night. The expression on his face had been marbleized by death into a mask of fear and pain. And that wasn't all. His death was clearly meant to be a form of humiliation. Control. Was it also a message?

She made herself a note to follow that thread of thought later.

The man was on his knees, held in place in that kneeling position only by the belt around his neck. His hands were bound behind his back while a ball gag was visible between his teeth. Stripes marred his pale skin. Well, the skin that wasn't covered in blood.

Two wounds were obvious in the photographs. The smiley face looking cut gapped open just under the belt, running nearly ear to ear. From the amount of blood that had poured from the gash, Brice Sutter had clearly been alive when his throat was cut. A second wound on his back still held the knife that had been slammed into him to the hilt.

Another message?

She typed *Stabbed in the Back* into her notes. A betrayal of trust, an act of treachery.

Who had Brice Sutter betrayed?

What was the spider trying to tell them?

Autumn zoomed in on the wound on the victim's back, then zoomed in closer. The stab wound offered a surprising lack of blood, but she suspected that was due to the massive blood loss from the neck wound, it actually made sense.

"What is that?" she murmured to herself before scrolling through the photo gallery for another image, one that focused more closely on the area surrounding the knife.

When she found one, she zoomed in again. Yes, this image showed the same anomaly. A streak, for lack of a better name, started several inches below the blade. The streak stopped at what appeared to be an odd-shaped circle.

Autumn looked closer, then shivered. Was that a mouth mark? Lips pressed against flesh? Was the streak created by a tongue licking the blood away?

Surely not. But still, she wrote the questions down in her notes. *Did the suspect lick and then kiss the victim's flesh below the knife wound?*

"Time of death?"

Autumn looked up from her iPad, observing Aiden's set jaw as he pressed his phone hard to his ear. He glanced her way, his expression grim.

"We'll meet you there, then reconvene the briefing for afterward." A long pause was followed by, "Very well. We'll meet you back at the station in two hours."

She waited until he'd tossed the device into a cup holder before turning in her seat. "Did our sweetheart scamming spider strike again?"

"Yeah." He rubbed his face with both hands before pushing the button to start the engine. "Chief Mazur is just leaving the crime scene and will be busy with his team for a couple hours. We'll head to the victim's home now, then meet up with the chief later."

Another murder. So close on the heels of the last. "Widower?"

Aiden nodded. "Yes. Less than a year."

"Bondage?"

Aiden exhaled a long breath through his nose. "From what the chief shared, the scene is a near duplicate of Sutter's."

She gazed back down at her iPad. The gruesomeness was hard to look at, but the calculated humiliation made it so much worse.

What had happened to the woman—because Autumn felt sure this was the work of at least one woman—who had done this? What had triggered her to transition from robbery to murder?

What message was she trying to send?

As she pondered these and other questions, Autumn listened as Aiden conference called the other teams. He rerouted Winter and Sun to the crime scene while Noah and Bree were directed to report to the police station and start going through files.

Autumn mentally armored herself, preparing to face the new aftermath this heartless spider had inflicted.

6

As the team closest to the scene, Winter Black discovered firsthand that their heartless spider did more than spin a web of treachery and deceit. Their spider was evil. Or nuts. Or both.

In the bedroom of sixty-three-year-old Allen Newhouse, Winter took in several deep breaths, hoping that by forcing the stench into her entire nasal cavity, her body would soon realize that it had no choice but to get used to the scent of death.

Newhouse was completely naked, but that wasn't the part that was shocking. That came when the mind penetrated through all the blood and realized just how vulnerable the poor man had been. Vulnerable to the rope that was cinched tightly around his neck. Vulnerable to the gaping wound just below the rope. Vulnerable to the knife that was still wedged firmly in his back.

The man was handcuffed in a kneeling position on the floor with what appeared to be leather covered cuffs. A black leather BDSM mask covered his features, providing only a glimpse of the red ball gag that was wedged between his teeth.

As Winter walked around the body, she felt tremendous pity for the man. The humiliation of being found and photographed in such a vulnerable position would have been mortifying, she felt quite sure. And his poor son...

"Looks like this guy was screwed."

Winter closed her eyes against the gallows humor as well as the round of laughter the cop who'd made the joke received. From a psychological standpoint, she understood the comedy was a much needed coping mechanism and would never chastise a person doing their best to cope with a stressful situation.

But she didn't have to like it.

Just like she didn't have to like the blood that was splattered across the floor and walls. It reminded her too much of another bedroom years ago, though, thankfully, no crosses or Bible verses had been written here.

She forced her mind away from that terrible night. She had been focusing on it too much lately. Probably because of Justin and the emotional trauma finding him had caused.

Wasn't it always that way? The thing that you wished for the most didn't always turn out the way you hoped it would.

She'd imagined tearful reunions. Crying and holding hands. She'd imagined evenings spent telling stories and catching up on the time they'd missed.

Instead, she was scared for her brother. Scared *of* her brother. Scared for herself.

Scared because, deep in her heart, she simply wanted to run away from him. Let him live out his days in prison or a mental institution. Focus on building a life for herself, a life she hadn't let herself live because she'd been so intent on the past. On bringing her parents' killer to justice. On finding her brother.

Life was ironic that way.

Shaking off those thoughts, she took another turn around the room. She needed to focus on this man before her, give him all her attention so she could stop the person who did this from doing it to another.

Shifting her attention from the body, she squatted to study the drops of blood as well as the footprints the crime scene techs had already photographed. She wasn't a blood spatter expert, but even she could see the void pattern. The spider had stood in front of this man, facing him while she slit his throat. Blood had sputtered out in a great gush, except for where she was standing, hence the "void."

The spider must have been covered in his blood.

"Has the shower been checked?" Winter asked one of the techs standing closest to her.

"Sure was. No blood detected. We checked each drain in the house."

That was a surprise. "Our offender wouldn't have walked out of this house with so much blood on her."

"Latex body suit." That came from Sun Ming, who was standing by the door, her face pale.

Winter studied the scene again and nodded. It made sense. With the BDSM scene that had apparently played out, this man had clearly been the submissive while the spider had played the Dominant. A full body latex suit would have been easy to clean of any bodily fluid. Or to simply strip out of and change into something else.

"I believe she knelt here after most of his blood was drained," the lead crime scene investigator, Laurie Kirk, said from where she stood at the rear of the body.

Winter studied the area were Laurie pointed. "How can you tell?"

Instead of answering that question, Laurie walked in front of the victim, being careful to stand only on the areas carefully marked. "My initial impression is that our victim was involved in erotic asphyxiation, hence the rope. I haven't touched the body, but I noticed some light razor marks here and here." The CSI appeared to be in her late forties, but only a few lines creased deeper as she frowned at the cuts on the insides of Newhouse's thighs.

"So, they were acting out a scene?"

Laurie nodded and shrugged at the same time. "At first, at least. She gets him bound and gagged, then plays with him a little. At some point, though, she cuts his throat, then walks around him to plunge what is probably the same knife into his back." She pointed at the two darker areas on the floor near the man's feet. "I believe those are knee marks from where she knelt."

In sorrow?

No. That didn't feel right.

This spider knelt for a darker reason.

Suddenly cold, Winter thanked Laurie for her input, then took one more turn around the room. This time, she was searching for a different type of evidence. She wanted… urged…pleaded for her intuition to pick up an important impression from the room. An impression that might even glow a hopeful red so that she could Scooby Dooby Doo this case and get the hell out of Pennsylvania.

She also wished that Autumn would hurry and get here. Between the two of them, maybe the special abilities their individual head traumas had left them with would help pinpoint the person who had humiliated this poor man so terribly.

Early in their friendship, Autumn had confessed to Winter that she was able to pick up the mental states of the people she touched, a form of empathy so accurate that it bordered on the parapsychological.

Winter's talents were similar but triggered by the visual

rather than physical contact. Most frequently, a red haze appeared when she was around hidden signs of violence. But she could also be taken down by strong hallucinations that both exhausted her and dragged her out of the real world.

If she pushed too hard, stayed too driven and stressed out, the visions could be dangerous. She'd learned that the hard way.

Lately, she'd been trying to learn how to hold some of herself in reserve and not operate at a hundred percent every waking moment of her life.

Perspective was what a former therapist called it. *Balance. Creating healthy boundaries.* Winter hadn't told the therapist about her visions, though. It was a bit difficult to have perspective or balance or boundaries when things around you glowed for your attention.

Not that she was ashamed of her unusual abilities. Well... not really. But she'd felt like a freak for the majority of her life. She didn't go out of her way to share information that others would use as ammunition against her, making her feel even more isolated and different.

She'd take isolated and different right now, though, if only she could intuit a clue that would help them find this man's killer.

Standing in the corner now, she focused on each aspect of the room. The walls and carpeting were a light seafoam green while the furniture was dark wood with brass hardware. Porcelain plates of famous sailing ships perched on shelves of different sizes. Prints of seacoasts were hung randomly about. Miniscule dots of blood seemed to coat everything, a relatively sure sign that, after the victim's throat had been cut, he'd exhaled a good amount of his aspirated blood.

Interestingly enough, the large four-poster with its pale green coverlet and abundance of pillows was nearly the only thing in the room that had escaped the spray. Had the spider spun her web in such a way that her prey was strategically positioned to avoid the marital bed from being dirtied?

As she took in the room, her wish was granted, and a red haze crossed her vision. She blinked several times, wondering if the haze was just a reflection from the large amount of blood in the room.

It wasn't.

Moving close to the spot she was being drawn to, she squatted and tried to read what the haze was trying to tell her. Three small circular imprints on the plush carpet formed a type of triangle. Leading both to and away from the circles were blood scuff marks that Winter thought might be footprints.

"What do you see?" It was Laurie, the crime scene tech, just behind her.

Winter first pointed at the scuff type marks. "Are those footprints where maybe the suspect scooted her feet?"

Laurie squatted. "Yes. We actually found a full footprint on the tile in the bathroom. Size seven, so I'm thinking a woman. She was smart, though. Except for that one print, she must have dragged her feet to avoid leaving a full one."

Winter had been thinking the exact same thing. She now pointed out the three circular imprints. "There, there, and there."

Laurie waved the photographer over. "Get closeups, please." Then she set a ruler down to give the marks perspective.

Once that was done, Laurie marked each one with tape. "A tripod?"

Winter nodded, and a small wave of dizziness blurred her vision. She steadied herself. "That's my guess too."

Another figure appeared at her side. It was Sun Ming. Her face was getting close to the same shade of seafoam green as the room as she visibly swallowed chunks of nausea. For all her tough, dispassionate exterior, the agent was horrified at the sight of blood.

Winter kept her face carefully neutral. Sun would hate to learn that her discomfort was so obvious. "Why don't you go downstairs and check on the security system."

Sun's jaw clenched, and she swallowed once again. "No, I'm fine. That does look like it could be tripod marks. Do you think our unsub videoed the show?"

That was exactly what Winter had wondered. "It's a good possibility. The marks are still relatively deep in this carpet." She would have to have someone study how long a tripod would need to sit there to make those particular marks before she would vote her theory as being true.

"Did you see the mess in the bathroom?" Sun asked. "There's more bondage stuff in there."

Winter looked around the bedroom. Her gaze rested on crops and whips and other implements she didn't recognize. Heck, she wouldn't have been able to name them if she'd been threatened with a butt plug. "There's more?"

She followed Sun down a narrow hallway with his and hers walk-in closets on either side, to what had to be the biggest bathroom outside of a sports arena that Winter had personally ever seen. The bathroom was bigger than some of the apartments Winter had lived in before and seemed even bigger than the bedroom itself.

It sported the same color as the bedroom, though the countertops were a much darker green marble. The gold-plated fixtures dated the style as did the Audubon bird prints decorating the walls. There were two toilets on the far side of the room along with separate showers. An enormous tub big enough to swim in sprawled in the middle.

A crime-scene tech was still logging evidence and looked up as she and Sun approached. Sun led Winter to one of the showers, where a black mass lay on the tiled floor. The door of the shower was marked off with *DO NOT CROSS* tape but she could easily see through the clear glass.

Strange. "And we're sure there is no blood in the drains?" Winter asked the tech.

He didn't even look up from his work. "Nope."

Sun pointed toward a ring surrounded by studded leather straps. One of the straps led to a pair of buckles. "I'm not entirely sure what that is, but it's too complicated to be a dog collar."

A sense of heaviness pressed down on Winter's face, as ominous as the first signs of a migraine. She closed her eyes and rubbed the sides of her nose.

Sun shot her a look. "You okay?"

Winter blinked, trying to force her vision to clear. "Headache."

Sun grabbed her arm when she swayed. "You look like you just saw a ghost."

It wouldn't be a ghost, but Winter knew she was about to see something just as mysterious.

At the first warmth of blood trickling from her nose, she grabbed a tissue from her pocket and turned on her heel. Walking quickly through the series of rooms, she didn't stop until she was out the front door. She was about to have a vision—something she'd wished for earlier—and she didn't want to pass out anywhere that might contain evidence.

Be careful what you wish for!

Outside, she sank onto the expansive brick patio in front of the house. It was chilly out and the cold seeped in through her pants, but it felt good on her heated skin.

Sun was beside her, watching her intently, a phone clutched in her hand. "What just happened?"

Winter forced a smile. "Migraine. I'm fine."

"If you pass out, I'm dialing 911."

There had been an ambulance on the scene when Winter and Sun first arrived. Winter glanced up and realized that the EMS bus had been replaced with a line of reporters. Shit.

Winter wanted to get out of sight of the cameras, but a wave of pain and dizziness hit her before she could. The warm drip of blood that normally accompanied her visions flowed from her nose. She pressed her ever present tissue just above her lip.

"I'm—"

The seafoam paint was back, and Allen Newhouse stood as still as a statue as a young woman clamped a pair of cuffs around his wrists.

"Have you been a bad boy?"

Allen made a sound that was half laugh and half strangled lust as the woman used a tiny razor blade to cut through his skin. He moaned as she lapped at the blood with a long stroke of her tongue. "Yes, Mistress Kitty."

The vision was gone as quickly as it had come, and Winter groaned when she realized that she didn't get a glimpse of the woman's face. Just long dark hair tied back in a high ponytail. A black catsuit covered the rest of her slim body.

"Winter?" Sun's tone had transformed from worry to irritation.

"I'm fine. Like I said, just a migraine. It'll be over soon."

Sun didn't look convinced but didn't appear to be interested enough to ask additional questions either. Which was a good thing because Winter had zero answers to give.

With the fading of the vision came the aftereffects. Winter flexed her fingers. After visions, she was almost always drained and disoriented, but lately, she'd noticed that her fingers were swollen too. Her doctor said that was a common symptom.

For migraines, at least.

Winter swallowed, her mouth suddenly dry. She licked her lips and tucked the bloody tissue into her pocket. "Was this a crime of passion that got out of hand?"

Sun frowned, and Winter wasn't sure if it was a reaction to the change of subject or to the question itself. "With *that* much blood?"

"Should I emphasize 'out of hand?'" Winter tried to think of a way to bring up the subject of drinking blood without giving away her vision. "I'm not an expert on bondage, but isn't blood play or needle play part of the BDSM lifestyle for some people? Vampirism isn't unheard of either."

Sun was growing pale again. "You think our Black Widow could be a vampire?"

Feeling stronger now, Winter attempted to think back to one of her psychology courses that delved into various fetishes, and even as she desperately wished that Autumn was here, she spotted a black Tahoe pulling through the reporters. A flash of bright red hair confirmed that her friend had arrived.

She held up a finger to Sun. "Ask me that again in about sixty seconds."

Sun followed her sight line, her mouth turning into a thin line as Aiden Parrish opened his door. Winter couldn't help but think that Sun and Aiden's past relationship still carried some painful weight on her fellow agent.

Autumn's smile was broad as she approached the pair first. Then, she looked more closely at Winter and frowned. A quick rummage in the enormous tote bag slung over her shoulder produced a small container of wet wipes. She pulled one out and gestured to Winter's nose.

Even as she thanked her friend, she gave Sun the stink eye. Was one woman seriously going to let another woman walk around with blood on her face? Next time Sun had spinach in her teeth, there would be payback.

"Could our unsub be a vampire?" Sun blurted.

Autumn's double take was almost as funny as watching Aiden's eyes open so wide that the whites showed all around his cool blue irises. The SSA was rarely ruffled and normally had control of his facial expressions. It took a full five seconds for him to get control of it again.

"Excuse me? Did you say vampire?"

Sun colored a shade of pink that was rarely witnessed on her pale skin. That didn't stop her from baring her teeth and offering a, "Yes...an 'I vant to suck your blood' kind of person." She even made a couple slurping noises, which made Winter smile. It was the most relatable Sun had ever been in her presence.

Autumn was still frowning, looking back and forth between them all. Aiden just shrugged while Winter tapped underneath her nose. With the gesture, she was silently explaining to Autumn that she'd seen blood drinking in her vision. Well, blood licking, at least.

Autumn's eyes widened as the dots connected quickly and hard. She cleared her throat, and Winter knew she was stalling to let her thoughts re-collect. "Well, perhaps I should examine the crime scene so that I can better understand what type of vampire you're speaking of."

Sun's hand went to her throat. "There's more than one kind?"

Autumn didn't answer. She just squared her shoulders and took a step toward the door. She stopped when an engine roared down the street and reporters scattered as a big truck pulled into the driveway.

A middle-aged man stalked in their direction. He wore a nice wool suit that was a surprising contrast to the mud-covered truck he drove. He went to duck under the crime scene tape, but a local officer backed him up quickly enough.

Winter headed his way. "May I see some identification?"

Although his nostrils flared, the man pulled out his wallet and handed her his driver's license. "My name is Louis Newhouse. I'm Allen's son. I found," he swallowed a few times before finishing, "him."

Compassion slammed into Winter, trying to imagine a son finding his father in such a position. "I'm so sorry for your loss, Mr. Newhouse. I'm Special Agent Winter Black with the FBI." She extended a hand. "If you will wait one moment, we'll get you logged in."

A few minutes later, the crime scene book had been signed, and the team led the younger Newhouse into the kitchen. Winter offered the man some water, and when it was refused, she sat down across from him. "Can you please share what happened?"

He made a face and stared down at his clasped hands. "I paid Father an unexpected visit last night, but I've told the police all about that already. We had an argument about finances on the phone earlier yesterday, and I decided to come to the house and finish it in person. Sounds bad, doesn't it? He was dead when I got here." He cleared his throat a few times. "I was angry at him, but he didn't deserve anything like *that*. Nobody deserves that."

Winter nodded solemnly. "What time was the argument, and what time did you arrive here?"

"The argument was at…" Louis looked at his watch, as if the device held all the answers. "Three oh three. I was at work and then I had a late meeting that ran until after nine-thirty. I drove straight here, and remember it was around ten-fifteen or so. Which would have been about right since my office is a good forty-five minutes away."

"You were so angry that you drove that far after a long day of work?" Winter kept her voice soft, knowing the question could seem more like an accusation.

Louis didn't seem offended. "Yeah, I guess so. It just bothered me, you know. He'd started dating again and was, I don't know, changing. Spending a lot of money on things that he wouldn't talk to me about. I thought if he had to look me in the eye, I might get him to explain."

"Did you hear anyone else in the background when you spoke to your father?"

He frowned at her. "No. Why?"

Winter smiled. "Standard question. Your mother passed in April. This has been a very hard year for you."

The man blinked several times but held his composure. "Yeah. Mom's death was from a heart attack. Real sudden, but heart attacks are, you know, normal." Louis looked up at the ceiling. "What happened to Dad wasn't normal."

"Do you know the name of the person or persons he was dating?"

Louis's head jerked up. "Person? Don't you mean woman?"

Winter just gazed at him. At this point, besides intuition, they only had a single footprint as evidence that the person who had murdered Allen Newhouse was female. Well, except for her vision, which she very well couldn't count as evidence. "Mr. Newhouse, at this point, we can't rule anything out."

"Well, you can rule out my dad being a fag, for one." Winter mentally flinched but kept her face carefully blank. It was sad that people were still judged so harshly in today's society, but she needed to do nothing that would make this witness walk away. "He'd met some woman online named Kitty."

Winter jotted down the name. "Kitty as in Catherine."

Louis made a sound that dripped of bitterness and something else…disgust? "I asked him the same thing. You know what his answer was?" When Winter shook her head, he made the bitter scoffing sound again. "He said, 'Kitty as in *meowwww.'"* He made a flirtatious clawing gesture with one hand, a clear imitation of what his father had done.

Winter couldn't stop the wince this time. "Ouch."

Louis laughed, the bitterness still clinging to every sound he made. "Ouch is right, and another ouch came when I tried to warn him about young hot women who took advantage of older men. He just laughed me off and said that he wasn't going to give some damned tramp his bank account number, no matter how many times she spanked him."

Behind Winter, someone snorted, then coughed to cover the sound. It sounded like Sun, but she didn't turn to look.

Louis pointed toward the ceiling. "That wasn't just spanking or any of that shit up there. That was..." His face fell, his shoulders dropping with it.

Autumn pulled out a chair, and Winter was relieved, feeling like a basketball player being tapped out of a shitty game.

"Louis, as hard as it is to think about our parents having personal lives, no child should have to witness what you did. And please know that, many men, especially after being married to the same woman for so long, cross barriers with their sexuality in ways they never did before."

Louis looked miserable as he pointed to the ceiling again. "But isn't that a little extreme?"

Autumn gave him a gentle smile. Damn, the woman was good at her job.

"Not for someone who enjoys that type of lifestyle. For them, it's natural and normal, and it isn't anything we can judge. What we need to focus on right now is the person who killed your father. That is the only official bad thing that happened in that room."

Louis straightened a bit, seemingly comforted, at least a little. "I told him that, no matter how smart he thought he was, con artists always have more practice conning their victims than he had with not getting conned. He just waggled his eyebrows at me and said that I'd see just who was getting screwed. He was always kind of, uh, dirty-minded. Except around Mom. He loved and respected my mother."

The first tear fell, and Winter knew this interview was mostly over. The team would rake Allen Newhouse's financials with a fine-tooth comb. They'd dive into his technology life, ripping into his privacy one gigabyte at a time.

Winter took over again. "Did your father show you a picture of Kitty?"

Another snort. "Yeah, but only on his phone. He didn't send it to me, if that's what you're asking."

"Do you know the name of the dating website or other forum he might have been using?"

Louis scrubbed his face with his hands. They were losing him. "Pervs-R-Us?" Yet another snort, but this one came with a glint of tears. "Damn…I still can't believe this."

"Do you know how long your father and Kitty were seeing each other? And do you know if he was dating anyone else?"

Louis shook his head. "She was the only one I knew of, and it was maybe three or so weeks ago when he first mentioned her name. From what I gathered, they'd seen each other a few times before he shared anything with me."

"You mentioned that your argument was about his finances." Winter hated to bring the sore subject back up, but they needed more details. "Can you share what you were most worried about?"

Air streamed from between Louis's lips as he let out a breath for nearly ten seconds. "Dad called me, wanting to know the best way for him to go about refinancing this house. When I asked him why he'd want to do such a thing, he finally admitted that he'd blown through his entire checking and savings accounts." He met Winter's gaze. "Over three hundred thousand dollars...gone." He snapped his fingers.

"Do you know what he spent it on?"

The bitterness was back. "Her."

Winter's pen was poised. "Jewelry? A car?"

"Student loan."

Winter blinked. "Your father paid off Kitty's college student loans? Did he say where she allegedly went to school? What her degree was? Her age?"

Louis's face turned hard as stone. "He never said her age exactly, but he finally confessed that she was in her mid-twenties. She apparently received her Ph.D. in psychiatry, and she told him that she was desperate to start a practice, but no bank would loan her money with such a high student loan bill."

"So, your father paid off the loan."

Louis nodded, looking even more miserable than before. "Two hundred was for the loan and the other hundred was to purchase a building for her to set up practice."

Winter's heart cracked a little. She could almost imagine the hope and excitement the dead man upstairs felt as he financed the dreams of a beautiful young woman who, from all appearances, fulfilled a part of him that had probably never been fulfilled.

And to be taken for a fool would have been bad enough.

But to be killed?

Why?

The image of the young woman licking Allen's blood resurfaced in her mind, making her shiver.

With nothing more to ask, Winter jotted down Louis's contact information and handed him her card, asking him to contact her if he thought of anything else that might be helpful. She took him through the steps and probable timeframe they were looking at before he would receive his father's body so he could plan the funeral.

Louis pushed to his feet. "Just burn him."

Autumn got to her feet as well, giving Winter an *I'll take this over* glance. Winter was happy to let her and closed her ears against Autumn's impromptu counseling session with the man as she led him outside.

Minutes later, Autumn was back, her arms crossed over her chest as she leaned on the doorframe leading into the kitchen.

"So…" Autumn's voice sounded wary, "let's talk about this vampire stuff."

7

"According to research, vampires are ordinary people with no special powers who claim that they require additional human energy in order to sustain such things as their physical, emotional, or even spiritual health."

Autumn pressed her lips together, hoping to suppress a smile as each person in the police station conference room stared at her in a mixture of horror and disgust. They'd left the Newhouse crime scene less than a half hour ago, rendezvousing at the station for the briefing that had been diverted earlier.

"You're serious?" The question came from Police Chief Keith Mazur, whose stocky body looked like it could very possibly be knocked over with a feather.

"Very serious. These vampires can take this energy in a number of ways. For some, their feeding—"

A loud groan cut her off, and Autumn looked around to find a hand clamped over Bree's mouth. The normally composed woman just looked shocked, not on the verge of losing her lunch, so Autumn went on.

"For some, their feedings can be satisfied by ingesting

small amounts of human or animal blood. These types of vampires often call themselves sanguinarians and use willing donors for their source. Others report that they require sexual stimuli to be satisfied. Those vampires, who are sometimes called Eros or tantric vampires, feed off the sexual energy of a willing donor, and often engage in bondage and discipline, dominance and submission, and sadomasochistic practices."

Noah leaned over and whispered something in Winter's ear. A millisecond later, a loud thump was followed by an even louder grunt as Noah reached under the table to rub his shin.

Everyone laughed but Winter, who looked like she might grow fangs herself at any second. Noah, red-faced from pain and poorly suppressed laughter, held up both hands in a gesture of innocence.

"Pay attention, children." Aiden's voice attempted to be stern, but his twitching lips gave him away.

With that small display of humor, the entire room seemed to exhale a long breath.

Noah's little act did exactly what Autumn knew he had intended—broken the tension within the room. Noah was like a mix between a highly trained guard dog and Labrador puppy. The lazy smile creeping back on his face showed a hint of satisfaction as he nodded for Autumn to continue.

"Is our unsub a vampire?" Autumn asked and answered the question she knew was coming next. A shrug was followed by a helpless spreading of her hands. "I don't know."

Chief Mazur cleared his throat by coughing loudly into his fist. "Why exactly are we talking about vampires in the first place?"

Autumn glanced at Winter. To be perfectly honest, she really wasn't sure why the subject had been brought up at the Newhouse scene. She hadn't been given even a second alone to ask Winter in confidence. She hated to put her friend on the spot, but there was no choice at the moment.

Winter linked her fingers together. "I could be very far off base, I admit, but when I was examining the crime scene, I had the thought that the murder hadn't been intentional. Well, not at first. Then I remembered reading a case involving blood play in BDSM, and how that got out of control for the participants and led to a woman's death."

Noah's face had lost all sense of humor as he turned to Winter. "I remember reading something about that. The dominant of the couple considered himself a vampire, right?"

Winter nodded, a little snarl curling her upper lip. "There was just something about the blood spatter that made me feel like there was some sort of connection. Maybe from the way she knelt beside the body in the pool of blood. But again, I could be way off."

Mazur made a face that looked like he'd eaten something immensely sour. "Let's hope you are."

No one at the table disagreed.

Autumn remembered the smear in the blood when she was reviewing the Brice Sutter crime scene photos. She picked up her iPad and scrolled through to the correct image. "When I was going through these images, I noticed this smear." She turned to Mazur. "Do you know if any saliva was found on Sutter's body, particularly here around the knife wound?"

Mazur moved closer to her and took the iPad from her hands. She could tell from the way he was staring at the image what his answer would be even before he picked up his copy of the medical examiner report on that particular crime. He read for a moment before shaking his head. "No." He looked supremely embarrassed for having not caught it before. "It doesn't appear it was found or tested."

Autumn tried to not look disappointed. "Can you ask the

ME to swab any area that might appear to be the least bit suspicious?"

He nodded and jotted down a note.

Aiden stood and moved to the whiteboard centered on the longest wall of the small room. "How about we talk about the things we currently know about this case?"

Mazur, who still looked grim, took the lead. "Newhouse is the second widower to lose his life in Passavant Hills within the last week. This follows numerous previously reported financial thefts from other recent widowers who lost a large chunk of their wealth. A few days ago, I did some PSAs on social media and the local TV channels warning the public about these scams. Since then, I've had six more men call in to report similar crimes."

Sun began tapping on her computer. "Both Sutter and Newhouse were online dating?"

Mazur nodded. "We found both profiles on several dating apps, and Newhouse's neighbors claim to have seen him in the presence of a young woman. They never got close enough to tell anything about eye color or any other distinguishing feature, though. Both men's accounts have been drained as well."

Autumn had been scrolling through the list of financial scam victims that had been reported since the PSA. At the very bottom of the list was a name marked with several question marks. The name was also marked with MP—missing person. She looked up. "Who's Edwin Gallagher?"

Mazur scratched the tip of his nose. "Sixty-one-year-old widower whose wife died about seven months ago. Got a call from one of his kids saying she hadn't been able to get in touch with her father in the past few days. Sent a patrol out to do a well-visit check yesterday morning. Car in the garage. House in good shape except the garbage that had started to rot. No Edwin. No evidence of foul play."

"Did crime scene techs sweep the house?" Noah asked, paging through his iPad for the case.

"Sure did. Spic and span, except for the stink of the garbage, as I mentioned. Grout around and under the rug in the foyer looked several shades lighter than the rest, so we tested that since it was in plain sight. An oxy type cleaner had been used in that specific area and came back negative for blood."

Autumn knew that oxy cleaners disrupted the hemoglobin in blood, making it much more difficult to detect. But oxy cleaners were also a popular choice for many households because they cleaned so well. Many houses would have a bottle or two on their shelves.

Taking a look at various pictures of the foyer the chief was describing, Autumn noticed that a rug normally sat on top of the space that, did indeed, have lighter grout lines than the rest. Could someone, very innocently, have cleaned the rug with an oxygen infused solution? It was likely, she had to admit.

Winter reached for a file containing physical photographs of the Gallagher home. She frowned as she flipped through, then started over again. "Did the crime scene techs sweep the car?"

Mazur shook his head. "It was only a wellness check, so while I felt comfortable testing the grout lines that had been in plain sight, I didn't push the scope of our rights by opening a locked car."

Searches were a tricky subject, Autumn knew from her years attaining her Juris Doctorate. If one little mistake was made, a defense attorney would pounce, and all the hard work put into an investigation could easily slide down the drain.

Noah grabbed another folder. "Was Gallagher dating anyone?"

Mazur glanced at his notes. "Yep. Young redhead for about a month, and yes, his profile was also on a number of dating sites. That's why I've added him to our list of possibles. Neither the neighbors or his three children seem to know the young woman's name and hadn't yet met her. From what we were told, she'd only been to his house a time or two, that anyone knew of, at least."

Noah glanced up. "No security cameras on a house that big?"

"Negative."

Autumn kept scrolling through the crime scene file. "What about the financials?"

"Working on getting a warrant for those. None of the Gallagher children are on the accounts, so..." He shrugged, lifting both hands to duplicate the helpless gesture. "The first judge we went to wasn't convinced that Mr. Gallagher hadn't just run off for a little fun with his new sweetheart, so refused to sign the warrant. Adults are allowed to run off if they want, and until we have any evidence to prove otherwise, it will be hard to get any judge to sign off on one."

Autumn chewed on a nail, trying to get her legal mind to come up with a work-around. "With the new victim, you'll most likely have a better chance proving a pattern."

The police chief nodded. "That's what I'm hoping. Not many judges will stick out their necks and approve a search through such personal information with 'lighter grout lines' as the only evidence, but a pattern of theft and now murder might loosen those rules a bit."

Sun, as tactful as ever, rapped her knuckles on the table. "We should bring in our own crime techs to go back over the scene. Your boys might have missed something important." For emphasis, she tapped on the picture with the smear.

Mazur's face turned red, but before he could respond, Aiden picked up a marker and headed to the whiteboard.

"Who are the six men who came forward after your public service announcement?"

Still more than a little red in the face, the chief flipped through his notebook, slamming one page down before turning yet another. "We've got Marcus Freemont, Peter Kelley, Thomas Hill, James Roberts, David Myers, and Dennis Hughes. All in their sixties and seventies. All recent widowers. All wealthy. Five of the men came forward on their own while the other one had family members call in the complaint."

"Which one had the family member call, and who was the family member?"

"Peter Kelley, and his daughter called it in."

"Ouch," Noah said.

Autumn couldn't disagree. She could only imagine how difficult it was when the tables turned and children had to start parenting their parents.

Aiden glanced around the room, and although she hadn't been working with the team for long, she knew that look. He was about to start assigning tasks.

"Sun, I'd like you to stay here and do a deep technology dive, but since Vasquez hasn't arrived yet—"

As if he'd been waiting outside with his ear pressed to the wood, the conference room door opened and the man in question appeared. "Miguel present and accounted for," Miguel said with a bright smile. "What do you need me to do?"

Aiden didn't miss a beat. "You'll team up with Dalton, and as masochistic as this is about to sound, I'm thinking these older gentlemen will be more comfortable sharing their stories with other men."

Sun snorted. "That doesn't sound masochistic at all." Sarcasm dripped from the words.

Aiden ignored her. "You two will meet with the five men

who self-reported the crimes. Get those names and contact numbers from Chief Mazur. Autumn and I will visit with the other one and his daughter. Sun, I want you deep diving into the dating websites our victims used. Connect with Chief Mazur's tech team and assist however you can. The second we get a warrant on Gallagher's financials, work with cyber to follow any trails."

Sun's snort was closer to a grunt, and it was during times like this that Autumn missed Ryan O'Connelly, a former con artist tech genius turned good guy who'd helped the team on a couple cases then had moved away to be closer to his sister and her kids. Autumn hoped they were happy, and that Ryan was staying on the right side of the law.

Ava, one of the FBI's cyber space specialists, was pregnant with twins, but due to a series of complications, her doctor had ordered bed rest just a month or so ago. Ava was as bright and as sunny as Sun was dark and grumpy, and Autumn missed Ava's positive attitude and deep sense of team spirit.

"Winter and Bree, we need a deeper dive into the other sweetheart scam cases leading up to this spree of murders. We need each victim contacted again and all their information categorized so that we can find any additional similarities. We need to create not only a profile for the unsub but of her victims as well."

Mazur raised his pen. "How sure are we that our suspect is a woman?"

Aiden glanced at Autumn. She met the chief's gaze. "Ninety-nine percent. There is a very small chance that our spider is only the bait who lures our victims in, and then their partner, a man, finishes the job."

"But you don't think that's probable?" Mazur asked.

Autumn didn't hesitate. "I don't. I believe our suspect is a woman who is sending a message with these killings." When

Mazur frowned, she went on. "Stabbing someone in the back is known as a betrayal of trust or an act of treachery. Our suspect could be telling us that she punishes those who display those traits." She stepped out farther on the limb of her theory. "And since each of our murder victims have been widowed for a short time, she could be telling us that she doesn't approve of them jumping back on the horse, so to say, so quickly."

Winter was frowning. "She's trying to teach other men a lesson about betraying their late spouse?"

"I think that's a distinct possibility. After all, she could target any number of rich men, but she's purposefully targeting those who have been widowed less than a year."

Mazur didn't look convinced. "Why would she do that?"

"I'll need more time to come up with a specific profile, but it could be that someone in her life has betrayed a person she was very close to. Perhaps, her father might have dated or remarried quickly following her mother's death."

"Then why didn't she kill all the men?" Mazur lifted his list containing the names of the victims of the sweetheart scams.

Autumn raised a shoulder. "That's a question we need to answer, but there are a couple possibilities. One is that our suspect simply snapped for some reason when she was with Brice Sutter, then upon that first kill, got a taste of blood…" She paused, realizing that her choice of words was an idiom but also disgustingly true. "Sorry, but I guess I could be correct in saying that she might have gotten a taste of blood, both literally and figuratively."

Mazur's nose wrinkled. "You said there could be a couple possibilities. What's the other?"

Autumn allowed herself a moment to think. "Some of the men could have passed some type of test." She tapped a crime scene photo. "And some didn't pass that test."

"What test?"

She'd been expecting Mazur's question and was already pulling up the picture showing the knife in Newhouse's back. "Betrayal. Treachery."

Mazur's face changed. He was beginning to understand. "I see."

Winter leaned forward, her blue eyes bright. "Newhouse didn't have pictures of his late wife anywhere that I noticed."

Autumn took a mental walk back through Newhouse's home. All she could remember was seafoam green and bird pictures everywhere. "I don't remember seeing any either." She met the chief's gaze. "Do you know if Sutter and Gallagher had visual displays of their late wives? Pictures? Marriage certificates on display? Anything like that?"

Mazur studied the wall before he shook his head. "I don't remember, but it would be easy enough to take another look."

Aiden stepped back to the board. "Chief, can you or some of your men do that?"

Mazur nodded. "Absolutely."

Autumn felt a hum of excitement. She felt in her bones that her preliminary profile might be correct. Another thought occurred to her. A thought that had been tickling the back of her mind.

"I don't think that Brice Sutter was her first victim," Autumn said.

Every head in the room whirled to face her. Mazur looked particularly doubtful. "By now, I think we'd know if another murder with these specific characterizations had occurred."

Autumn gave herself a second to think it all through before meeting his eyes directly. "Serial killers normally have a gestation phase to their fantasies, with those fantasies staying in their mind until something stressful happens. This is called a stressor. Some call it a trigger."

Aiden nodded and stepped in when she paused. "A stressor could be anything that weighs heavily on the person's mind. Things like getting fired from a job or having a relationship end are examples of stressors."

Autumn nodded her thanks and took back control. "The stress gets to be too much, and the person snaps and fulfills their original fantasy…killing. The thing is, once they cross that barrier and kill that first time, the next murder comes easier. The person plans more thoroughly, determines ways to improve their technique."

Mazur scratched his head. "That's interesting, but I don't see how that information leads you to believe that Newhouse wasn't the first."

All eyes were on Autumn, intent on her explanation. That was okay. The more this conversation flowed, the more certain she was that she was right. "The first murder is almost always an impulsive act," she told Mazur, focusing only on him. "Brice Sutter's murder was elaborately planned. So was Allen Newhouse's. Our spider learned from previous mistakes."

The color drained from Mazur's face. "How many?"

Autumn lifted a shoulder. "I don't know. Can you think of a murder in your area or nearby that involved either a slit throat, or most importantly, a knife in the back of a widower? Most likely a widower who fits our particular victim profile?"

She held her breath while Mazur thought. When his eyes widened, she could have shouted in celebration. She knew it. There was another case.

Mazur frowned. "We had a burglary a couple months back. It was clearly a B & E."

Autumn leaned forward, pinning him to the spot with her

gaze. "Was the victim a widower who had begun online dating? Did his wife pass less than a year before? How, exactly, was he killed?"

The chief just stared at her, and she almost read his mind. She wasn't at all surprised when he lifted a finger and left the room. Less than a minute passed before he was back, a file folder in his hand.

Carl Jameson, age sixty-four. Wife, Dorthea, passed eight months prior to his death. Knife in the back. House was tossed, jewelry was taken. No prints. No suspects."

Winter lifted her chin. "I'd bet my career that our spider sank that knife into his back."

Mazur looked angry now. "But his bank accounts were intact. There was no bondage implements in the house of any kind. He was fully clothed."

"Were there pictures of his wife in the house?"

Mazur just stared at her for a moment before shaking his head. "I don't know."

"Do you have copies of his dating profile? Did you question the woman or women he was dating?"

The tips of his ears grew red. "Carl had only been seen with a young woman one time, which was a couple weeks before his death."

"Do you have a description, by chance?" Autumn softened her expression and voice. She was pushing too hard, making the chief feel inadequate. "There was no way you could have known about our unsub preying on local men at that point, Chief Mazur, and knowing now that Jameson might be her first or one of the first victims helps me with our killer's profile. Thank you."

When Mazur gave her a reluctant nod, the room seemed to let out a collective breath.

Winter raised her pen, grabbing Aiden's attention. "What about contacting the law enforcement agencies of those towns hit by the sweetheart scammers to have another look at any deaths that fit our victim parameters?"

Aiden was nodding before the question was finished. "Good thinking. Chief Mazur, if you could check back through your files, we'll work on the other towns. Winter, you and Sun split those tasks and have cyber help. With Ava and O'Connelly gone, they're stretched a bit thin but I'm sure they'll do whatever they can. Autumn and I will dig into the case of Carl Jameson. Any questions?"

Sun had a question for Mazur, and Autumn tuned them out.

Aiden checked his watch. "We're going to work this case, and that means put every single detail in Rapid Start." He gave them all a stern look. "Every detail."

Rapid Start was an information system where every team member could add their notes to a case.

With each assignment given, the team dispersed, and Autumn ate her second candy bar while Aiden made the call to schedule their meeting with the scamming victim. Feeling guilty, she shoved the half-eaten PayDay in her bag when he finished the call.

"Hungry?"

Her stomach immediately growled, and she sighed. She wouldn't be able to think clearly with her blood sugar in her toenails. "Very much. Can we grab something in the next hour or so? I'd hate to interrupt our victim's tale of woe with this." She pressed her hand over her belly button as her insides churned again.

"Peter Kelley can see us in an hour, or so his daughter says." He tapped an address into his maps app. "It'll take us fifteen minutes to get there, so we have plenty of time."

She followed Aiden to the Tahoe, and as he drove, Autumn looked through Mr. Kelley's file. There wasn't much. "So, his daughter called in the theft of her father's life-savings? This is just so sad."

"Which part? The whips and chains?" A smile played on the corners of Aiden's mouth as he pulled into a deli that appeared to have a steady stream of customers.

"To each his or her own, I always say, but what I find so sad is that these men were all married for a number of years. It might seem cold for them to start dating so soon after their wives' deaths, but what most people don't understand is that many men need the comfort of a partner, especially as they age."

Aiden made a scoffing sound. "Many, but not all."

She grinned as she pushed open her door. "True. Some men need to stay at least ten feet away from women their entire lives."

He didn't rise to the bait. They joined the order line, dropping the subject for the time being. After ordering—a three cheese panini for Autumn and a roast beef on rye for Aiden—they grabbed a corner table and discussed their plan of attack for the interview with Peter Kelley.

"Are we blindsiding him with our visit or did his daughter let him know we are coming?"

Aiden wiped his mouth and took a large drink of his tea. "She said that she would warn him."

Autumn was relieved. She hated the idea of just showing up on this man's doorstep and asking him such personal questions. She raised her panini halfway to her mouth. "I'm trying to think how to ask him if he enjoyed a little S&M." She chomped into her sandwich, taking in a little too much and was forced to hold a napkin over her mouth so she didn't spit crumbs everywhere.

Aiden bit into his pickle. "I just wish I was a fly on the wall when Dalton and Vasquez ask the same types of questions to their victims."

When she was finally able to swallow, she blew out a breath. "It's terrible that we're laughing about this. These poor men. They—"

In an instant, she was staring at the palm of Aiden's hand. When he dropped it back to the table, he was giving her a hard look. "You've got to stop thinking of them that way, Autumn. They aren't your patients. You have a case to solve, and as much as I know you'll care for their mental health, you have to put your focus on asking questions that will make them uncomfortable or even angry or sad. You can't let their feelings get in your way of gaining the information we need to create a viable profile of this woman." His gaze grew even more intense. "Unlike how you went at Mazur."

She lifted her sandwich, stinging a little from his rebuke. Not about Mazur, exactly. She wouldn't apologize for asking hard questions, but these widowers. Couldn't she do both? Care about people and work a case? And if she wasn't allowed that bit of humanity, was the FBI the best career choice for her?

Pushing the unwanted thoughts away, she focused on the case. "We've talked about there being more than one woman involved, and I still think that's a probability."

Aiden raised an eyebrow. "But?"

"But...I don't think there are two women doing the killing. What if these two women are a team, but one has fallen off the edge?"

Aiden wiped his mouth and took another drink, clearly thinking it through. "One killer feels right to me."

She relaxed a little. "Me too. Of course, the entire string of cases could be coincidental, and these crooks are just increasing their scams now in order to pay off their Christmas credit card bills from last month."

Aiden's mouth twitched in amusement as he glanced at his watch. "We better get going."

Autumn practically hoovered the rest of her meal, unsure when she might get another. If she were drawing a line on a piece of paper, with "pros" and "cons" of joining the FBI on either side, one "con" would be the lack of scheduled meal times. Or having a life.

But on the "pros" side, she'd never felt more alive. Wasn't that what life was, anyway? Not just breathing in and out, but enjoying each and every breath?

After gulping the rest of her tea, she wiped her mouth. "I'm ready."

Peter Kelley lived in what appeared to be an affluent suburban neighborhood. His two-story brick home looked well cared for and boasted an American flag fluttering out front.

A slim older man with white hair sticking out over his ears, furry eyebrows, and not much hair anywhere else on his head answered the door with a friendly grin. "Hello, are you here to sell me something? I already have a vacuum, but I might be in the market for a set of encyclopedias."

Aiden held out his badge. "Special Supervisory Agent Aiden Parrish of the FBI. My colleague and I would like to ask you some questions."

The man's face fell, the very tips of his ears turning pink. "My daughter told me she'd ratted me out." He looked from Aiden to Autumn, his ears turning even pinker when he met her gaze. "Well, come on inside and have a seat."

Autumn gave him a warm smile and held out her hand. "I'm Autumn Trent. Thank you for being so gracious."

Peter smiled in return before holding the door wider. He led them into the house, which was decorated in a combination of white, black, and light blue. "Let's sit at the table in the kitchen. You can't get enough sunlight in the winter, I always say."

Autumn noticed several photos of Peter and a pretty

woman she believed to be his wife. There were even more photos of the couple with their growing family...first a boy, then later, two girls.

So...Peter Kelley hadn't created a shrine to his dead wife, but he hadn't forgotten about her either. Was that what had saved him?

The small breakfast nook table was indeed surrounded by windows that let in bright winter sun. The space was cozy and still carried a feminine touch in the well-worn tablecloth covering the surface. "I'll make tea."

Autumn had just sat down but pushed to her feet. "Let me. If you'll just point me in the right direction, you can talk with SSA Parrish, and we'll be out of your hair that much sooner."

Peter's eyes trailed from her bright red hair down to her shiny black shoes. "Do you like to cook?" He bobbed his eyebrows at her. "I'm a sucker for hair color like yours."

Autumn gave him a warm smile. The older man was a true flirt...and so adorable that she didn't feel threatened or offended in the least. "Trust me, I can boil water but that's about it." She waved to the table. "Go. Sit." She watched him closely to see how he'd react to the dominant orders.

His eyes practically sparkled as he bowed his head slightly. "Yes, mistress."

Well, that answered that question.

She watched him walk to the table. The man could have been joking, or the orders could have spun him toward a subspace response. She couldn't be sure which was true for him. Not with such a brief exchange.

And did it matter?

It certainly could. If their victims all enjoyed BDSM, that could be an important aspect of their victim profile. If nothing else, it narrowed their profiles down significantly.

As she ran water into the kettle and set it on the burner to heat, she mentally added sex clubs and sex sites to the places they needed to investigate. Terrific. She just hoped she didn't end up having to go undercover. Or maybe it wouldn't be—

"I take mine with cream."

The request brought Autumn back to the kitchen and away from the direction her mind had wandered. Which was a good thing. She didn't even want to count the number of months since she'd last been with a man.

Geez...now she was thinking about sex.

She gave herself a mental shake. "Cream it is."

Prowling through Peter Kelley's nicely stocked refrigerator, she forced herself to listen to the small talk occurring at the table.

"Karrie Nicks was really something." Autumn's heartstrings tugged in response to the wistfulness in Peter's voice. "It was a May-December romance." He put one hand on his chin and batted his eyelashes at them. "She seduced me."

Aiden shifted in his seat. He was obviously trying to ignore Peter's goofy sense of humor. That made Autumn like Peter even more. Seeing the great Aiden Parrish uncomfortable was a treat. "Please tell us everything you can about her. We're trying to determine whether your case is connected to any others."

"Oh, I don't think so." He patted his heart with his hand, the wistful expression still on his face. "She was one of a kind."

"What can you tell me about her?"

"Not much." As Autumn poured water over the tea bags in three oversized blue and white mugs, Peter stood and opened what turned out to be a junk drawer. He dug around for a second before pulling out a little photo album. He flipped through several pages before stopping and running a finger down the slick plastic of the photo cover. His expression was a mix of longing and affection, not the anger she would have expected.

Autumn stopped her tea preparations and moved closer. She frowned. She'd been expecting...what? Beauty, sure. Sexual rawness, perhaps. What she hadn't expected was a young woman with frizzy red hair and a nose that was much too large for her slim face. Her eyes were a pretty blue, but almost too blue...contacts? Dressed all in black, the woman known as Karrie Nicks had a friendly, although pleasantly witchy look, but she certainly didn't have the beautiful seductress mistress vibe that Autumn had expected.

Peter slipped the photo from its cover. "You can have this one. It's just a printout from the local one-hour photo place." His gaze shifted past Autumn and Aiden, staring into the far distance. "Lovely, isn't she? I knew something wasn't quite right, of course. But I chose to do the gallant thing anyway. *Several* times."

He winked at Aiden. If older men were supposed to be shy about their sexual conquests in front of women, you couldn't have proven it by Peter Kelley.

Aiden studied the photograph too, looking as puzzled as Autumn felt. "Can you think of anything else to add?"

"Not really." Peter tossed the photo album back in the junk drawer. "It was all such a whirlwind."

"When and where did the two of you meet?"

Peter looked down at the floor, his toe rubbing at a tiny stain on the grout. "Why is that important?"

For all that Peter Kelley seemed open and friendly, he was definitely steering the conversation away from having to give details about his former love.

Before Autumn or Aiden could ask another question, a car door slammed outside.

Peter's shoulders sank. "Who could *that* be?" His tone

carried so much sarcasm that Autumn might have smiled if he hadn't seemed so distressed.

Without a knock or even a pause, the kitchen door slammed open. The new arrival was a woman in her thirties, bottle-blonde, wearing a thick layer of mascara, a white blazer, and gold jewelry. She walked into the kitchen, dropped a large designer purse on the counter, and stared daggers at the three of them.

"I would have expected you to wait for my arrival." Peter Kelley's daughter planted her fists on her hips. "After all, I'm the one who reported this terrible situation."

Peter seemed to have shrunken into himself with the arrival of his daughter. He scratched at his chin and seemed to have aged a decade in a span of a few minutes. "I was just making tea."

The blonde shook her head, giving her father a pitying look. "Oh, Papa. Tea at a time like this? What are you thinking?" She scoffed, the sound filled with bitterness. "You're clearly not thinking...again."

Autumn's hackles rose, and she took a step forward, feeling very protective of this older man. True, Peter Kelley had placed his trust in someone who shouldn't have been trusted. Yes, he'd clearly been out to sow some oats, but that wasn't a crime. He wasn't a criminal.

He was the victim, and Autumn refused to let him be victimized again.

"I'm Dr. Autumn Trent, working with the FBI."

Peter gestured toward his daughter. "Sorry. Where are my manners? This is my daughter, Tina Kelley. Tina, in addition to the lovely Dr. Trent, we have..." He squinted, clearly trying to remember Aiden's name.

Aiden stepped forward, his hand out, and did the introductions himself. Tina seemed hesitant at first, but finally relented and shook the SSA's hand.

After clearing his throat, Peter moved toward the table. "They're here to ask questions—"

"I know, I know, Papa." Tina rolled her eyes. She apparently thought that letting her father finish his sentence was a waste of time. "You're here to ask questions about that bitch, Karrie Nicks. You can ask me anything. Papa doesn't like to talk about her." She sent her father a scathing look. "Do you, Papa? But the *rest* of us would like to see her arrested and get Papa's money back for him."

Aiden glanced at Autumn. She had already been thinking the very same thing. Divide and conquer.

Autumn took a step toward the door leading to the living area. "Ms. Kelly, please come with me into the other room."

"Why?"

"Procedure." Autumn didn't feel gracious enough toward the woman to give more information than that. She headed out of the room, glad when the other woman's heels click-clacked after her.

Tina followed her into a comfortable looking living room with oversized blue corduroy couches. "How long will this take?"

Autumn sat at the corner of one couch. "Not long. What can you tell us about Karrie Nicks? What was she like? Please share everything you remember about this woman."

Tina's nostrils flared as she sat across from Autumn. "How to sum up the whole Karrie experience...let me think. Oh, yes. I have the perfect term for it. The woman was a gold digger. She didn't give a damn about my father. She just wanted his money." Real emotion flashed across the woman's face. "And she got it."

Autumn felt a little stab of sympathy. "Start from the beginning, please."

Tina took in a deep breath. "It all started when Mama died. She'd been sick for years with one respiratory infection after the next. COPD and then lung cancer. My mom smoked like a freight train since she was a teenager, and I'll be shocked if I don't have lung cancer too before I hit forty. Secondary smoke should be considered child abuse, I think. I…"

When it was clear that the woman had just started her rant on the evil of cigarettes, Autumn cleared her throat. "I'm so sorry for your loss, Ms. Kelley. For now, can you tell me about Karrie Nicks and how she came into your father's life?"

Lines wrinkled the woman's forehead as she frowned at the interruption, but she waved a hand in her face like a fan. "Sorry. I just get so emotional about it all."

Autumn gave the woman her best sympathetic expression. "I'm sure, and again, I'm so sorry for all your family has been through. When did your mother pass?"

"Nine months ago tomorrow."

Tina sniffed, and wiped an invisible tear away from her cheek without touching her mascara. Autumn's moment of sympathy vanished. "What happened after that?"

"Papa went a little crazy in the aftermath. And by 'crazy,' I mean sex crazed." She hissed out the last two words. "You won't share any unnecessary details with the press, will you?"

Autumn shook her head. "Of course not."

Tina flashed her a perfectly fake little smile. "Good. A few months after Mama was gone, Papa was attending one of those new 'speed-dating' events at the community center. It was a cover for some kind of illegal setup, in my opinion. The women were all much younger than many of the men. What younger woman in her right mind wants to date someone like Papa? The kind who can't legally advertise her services elsewhere, that's who."

Autumn privately thought that if the men involved all had

to deal with daughters like Tina, then perhaps they deserved a little relief. "That is a possibility."

Tina rolled her eyes theatrically. "It's nothing more than the truth. This Karrie woman suddenly found my seventy-four-year-old father 'very attractive' and they started 'dating.' Within a couple weeks, it came to light that Karrie had... surprise, surprise...some crushing student loan debt to pay off. Papa soaked up the debt for her. Papa melted like butter in the microwave and gave her a huge loan to help her 'get ahead of her payments.' He told her there were no strings attached, but we all know what that means. S.E.X."

Peter's voice came from the kitchen. "She was grateful."

Tina snorted but lowered her voice. "Not *that* grateful. She wasn't satisfied with her loan. She needed more. She couldn't pay rent. She wanted to buy her mother a nice birthday present. It went on and on. Of course, I didn't learn any of this until it was too late. Not until the day *I* needed to borrow money from him to refinance my house. Just a small place, nothing like *this* mansion." With flying hands and arms, she gestured at the large home.

"You only learned about Karrie Nicks when you asked for money?"

Tina's chin came up defensively. "Exactly. I just needed twenty-thousand dollars to refi at the new lower rates. It would have saved me hundreds of dollars each month and thousands over the course of the loan. Plus, that money was supposed to come to me one day anyway, so I didn't think it was overreaching to ask for a little of it early."

Autumn held up a hand. "I'm not judging. Just trying to keep the timeline straight."

Tina didn't look convinced, but her shoulders relaxed a little. "Yes, that's when the whole sordid story came out. His bank account was nearly empty. He's lucky that most of his money is locked down in certificates and he couldn't get to it fast enough to suit that bitch."

Peter appeared in the doorway, his face flushed. "I heard that, Tina. I told you I'll come up with the money soon."

She turned on him. "You're a fool, Papa. You're worse than a man who sits down at a slot machine until he's completely broke."

His face grew even more red, and Autumn worried about his blood pressure. "I may have made a few mistakes, but you have to understand. Karrie made me feel alive for the first time in years. I—"

"Don't you *dare* imply that Mama didn't make you feel alive!" Tina stood up and tossed her hair. "You were just a horny old man who tossed money to that ugly twat like she was some kind of prostitute."

Autumn was on her feet just as Aiden appeared at the door. He shook his head just a bit. He wanted to let the scene play out.

"Did you tell them, dear Papa, about the handcuffs and the whips...and...and...nipple clamps?" The last two words shot out of her mouth like bullets. She pointed a finger at him. "It wasn't even just sex. It was kinky sex. Disgusting sex." She whirled on Autumn. "And Papa wasn't even the Christian to Karrie's Ana."

Autumn was a bit embarrassed that she knew the characters of which Tina was speaking. Of course, what thirty-something female hadn't read or seen *Fifty Shades of Grey*? Across the room, Aiden looked confused at the reference, and she deeply hoped he didn't ask about it later.

"Oh no," the daughter continued her rant. "My father, it seems, likes to be...spanked!"

How in the world did a daughter know such intimate things about her parent?

"My sex life is my business," Peter argued, stomping his foot hard enough that a vase on a shelf rattled a bit.

Tina stomped her foot right back. "Then maybe you shouldn't have left those pictures out on the kitchen table for me and the entire world to witness your…your…depravity!"

Enough was enough.

Autumn held up her hands in a universal sign for time-out. "This isn't helping either your relationship or the case we need to investigate."

Tina threw up her hands and tears shone in her eyes, real ones this time. "Do you know how I felt to have the man I always looked up to, the man I respected with all my heart, my daddy, my hero…" Her voice broke on the last word, and she gulped in great mouthfuls of air. "To see him kneeling like that, looking so broken. So used."

Autumn inhaled deeply. She didn't look at Aiden because she knew she was about to step away from being a law enforcement agent. As a psychologist and as a person with a big heart for people who were hurting, she needed to help this pair mend their relationship if it was at all possible.

"Tina…" She waited until the blonde met her gaze. "What you saw in those pictures would have been upsetting for anyone. None of us want to think about our parents' sex life or their sexual preferences."

Tina snorted and said something that sounded very close to, "No shit."

"I want to share some information that you very well might not be aware of. Information that might help you see your father in a different light. May I?"

Peter shifted from foot to foot but didn't walk away from the conversation. Tina's eyes slid to him then back to Autumn before she shoved her hands through her hair. "Some things can't be unseen."

"True, but sometimes, if you shift your interpretation of what you saw, you can think of it differently."

Tina didn't look convinced as she crossed her arms over her chest. "That will take more shifting than I think my mind can manage."

Autumn sat down, inviting Tina to do the same. For a moment, Autumn thought the woman would refuse, but she finally stepped over to a chair and just sank, almost like her legs had given out from under her.

"I could talk for hours about male and female stereotypes in society today," Autumn began, knowing she needed to get the point she wanted to make across quickly. "The thing is, and what I want you to hear me say is this...maybe your father needed a break from the expectations placed on him for most of his life. Providing a good home, being strong when everyone was weak, being the shoulder or the stiff upper lip of the family while your mother was so very, very sick."

Tears glistened in Tina's eyes again, and she quickly whisked them away. Her mouth tightened back into a straight line as she fought back any emotion for her father. "So, he needed someone else to boss him around for a while? Is that what you're saying?"

"Not completely, although there might be some truth in that. I'd imagine being able to turn away from society's expectations for a little bit must have been a relief."

Autumn glanced at Peter, who gave her a small nod. He cleared his throat but didn't say a word, for which Autumn was grateful.

"But what I also want to share is how many people don't understand what it is to be submissive. Many think being submissive simply means you enjoy being ordered around and told what to do or not to do. But in a Dominant/submissive relationship, the truth is that the submissive is the object of desire. The submissive is the center of attention."

Tina glanced at her father again. "I guess all our attention was focused on Mom for a long time."

"Which was exactly what you needed to do at the time," Autumn assured her before she could take a journey down the yellow guilt road. "Your mother was very sick for a long time, and your father's job was to be strong for each of you. When your mother passed, having the opportunity to lay that strength aside and be cared for must have been very appealing."

Tina frowned. "I don't see how spanking someone equals being cared for."

"On the surface, it doesn't, but if you think about how the brain works, being the submissive in a relationship can cause a person, male or female, to enter an altered state called 'transient hypofrontality.' This altered state is associated with a reduction in pain, feelings of peacefulness, and feelings of living in the here and now."

"Are you serious?" Tina asked with another look at her father. Her expression wasn't quite as scathing this time.

"Yes, I'm very serious. There is much more research into this subject that I don't want to bore you with right now. Right now, we need to focus on finding the woman who stole from your father. Your father is the victim here. He was used by a professional manipulator who knew how to prey on what he needed the most. Having you be understanding and have some compassion would benefit him greatly, I'm sure."

A real tear fell, and Tina brushed it away. "I just don't know if I can forget what I saw."

Autumn made a mental note to ask for those photographs. She needed to know who took them, when and where, and if they were part of a blackmail attempt to siphon Peter's bank accounts.

"Unfortunately, our minds don't have a delete button for those things, but if you can work to look past those photographs and see your father...that man right there." She waited until the daughter locked eyes with the father. "See *him* and remember the man who raised you and cared for you for so many years. That hasn't changed. If your father had been robbed at gunpoint in an alley, you would have supported him. Just because he was robbed in a different way doesn't make him less deserving of your support."

"I wish she had just killed me," Peter muttered. The friendly and playful mask that he normally wore was gone now. In its place was raw pain.

"Oh, Papa." Tina shot to her feet and went to him. They both seemed to hesitate, as if touching each other wasn't something they were accustomed to. "I'm glad she didn't." Then, the father and daughter were embracing.

At the man's side, Aiden gave her a little nod. Carefully, Autumn went around the pair and followed Aiden to the kitchen.

"Nice job," Aiden said.

She gave him a small smile and went back to the kettle to reheat the water. "Thanks. They needed to clear the air so they could help with this case."

The kettle clicked as it came to a boil, and Autumn had poured four cups by the time the pair rejoined them in the kitchen. They both looked drained but also more peaceful.

"I'm going to go now." Tina grabbed a paper towel and used it as a tissue. "This is Papa's story, and he'll be more comfortable sharing it with you all if I'm not here."

Peter walked his daughter out, and Autumn had three cups on the table by the time he returned. She placed the cream and sugar in the middle. Peter smiled at her, and she gave his hand a quick squeeze.

With the touch, she caught his feeling of the rich,

complex love he had had for his wife, one that had stretched over the years, had its ups and downs, and left him devastated with its ending. She caught the love he had for his children. More than any of that, she caught his need to feel excitement again.

That was what the spider had preyed on, and Autumn hated her for that.

She squeezed his hand even tighter. "There's nothing wrong with wanting to love again."

"It does look bad, though, doesn't it? Less than a year I waited. It felt like longer. And Karrie made me feel so young again. I never thought I'd turn out to be such a stereotypical old man. Such a...*sucker*!"

"Do you know where Karrie is now?"

Peter gave her a quick glance. "Am I hiding something, do you mean? No, I don't know where she is. But give her my regards if you find her. I must say, I had a lovely time. And it's not as though..."

Through his skin and into hers, Autumn felt a twist of pain run through Peter's emotions, a fear of death, of abandonment—of the lonely years stretching out in front of him.

She patted his hand before letting him go. "I understand."

"Thank you."

They finished the interview over the course of the next half hour. Peter swore that he had destroyed all the images of him and Karrie. He also swore that she hadn't blackmailed him at all; he'd very willingly given her money because it had felt good to do so.

"Mr. Kelley, did you know the pictures were being taken?" Aiden asked.

"Of course." His gaze fell to his mug. "Yes, of course I did."

He was lying, Autumn could tell, but she didn't call him on it. The man needed to conserve what pride he was able. In fact, she could tell that Peter Kelley was growing weary. Aiden seemed to sense the same thing.

After offering him their cards and asking him to connect if he thought of anything that might be helpful, they ended the interview.

Leaving the house was an emotional relief.

Back at the Tahoe, Aiden tossed her the keys. "Let's head to the Passavant Hills Police Department to check in with the others." While Autumn entered the address on her GPS and followed the directions it gave her, he checked his phone, sent a few texts, and made a call back to the Richmond office.

But Autumn could feel that something was on his mind.

Finally, he dropped the phone in his lap and rubbed his eyes with both hands.

"You okay?" she asked.

"The man was played so bad. It's hard to imagine how anyone could let something like that happen to them."

"Really?" Autumn stopped at a stoplight. "Can't you imagine how lonely Peter must have been after the long, drawn-out death of his wife? When you have that kind of love in your life and it's taken away, can't you imagine what it would be like to have someone offer that love to you again? Offer to take all the decision-making pressure away? Promise only an altered state of being where pleasure was the only end result?"

"Maybe you can imagine it, but I can't." Aiden's jaw was set at a stubborn angle. He picked his phone back up, abruptly ending the conversation as his thumbs went flying across the screen.

Autumn suppressed a sigh. What was it with men who thought they were too strong to need anyone?

She could easily understand why Peter had been drawn to someone like Karrie Nicks.

Karrie hadn't *looked* like a heartbreaker. That was the

problem. Just a young, nonthreatening woman with a charming smile.

Not a thief.

Not a murderer.

Which led her to her next question.

What triggered their spider to kill?

8

Black Widow Strikes Again

I glared at the Passavant Hills newspaper's headline. Similar block letters practically sprang from the other newspapers from the surrounding areas, even as far as Philadelphia.

But seriously?

Black widow?

Couldn't the reporters be even a little bit more creative? Or accurate?

I wasn't a widow. In fact, I'd never been married at all, nor would I ever be.

Marriage was a trap. Not a web a clever spider would ever want to weave. A trap with balls and chains and shackles and gags.

No, I would never be a widow.

How little these reporters knew me. How little most people did.

Which, for now, was a blessing I wouldn't argue with. Because as much as I wanted to correct them...make them understand...I still had much to do. I needed to be cautious.

Careful. There were still lessons to teach before I left this horrid town with too many memories.

I skimmed each article, looking to see if I'd made a mistake. Of course, the police wouldn't share every detail or piece of evidence they found. That was just good detective work. For every murder the police offered a reward on, or even asked for leads, there would be a thousand phone calls offering false leads, spurious "tips," and fake confessions. The police needed to hold back information so they could determine whether they had found their killer—or just had a crazy person on their hands.

Was that why they didn't mention how Allen Newhouse was discovered? The bonds? The mask? The degradation? Did they hold those elements away from the press in order to make sure they caught the real bad guy?

Or was it something else? Was the good ole boys club at play again?

If Allen had been a woman, would they have kept the whips and chains part private, or would that have been part of the sensationalism of the case?

I would put my money on the latter.

The good ole boys would protect other good ole boys. They wouldn't want to embarrass one of their own.

It wasn't fair. It wasn't just.

But what could I do?

I could publish the pictures myself, of course. I knew enough about online security to route a few very revealing photographs to the gossip mags, which would eat each image up like candy. I could even sell the video of Allen begging for his life to not only perverts on the dark web. Plenty of "normal" good ole boys would want to jack off to it too.

I had options. Plenty of them, actually. But I couldn't be distracted from my current goal.

And Edwin had been distraction enough.

If I were honest, his death worried me more than a little. Not only for any legal ramifications that could come my way. And not only because it hadn't been part of the plan. More than any of that, I hadn't been able to control myself.

That wasn't good.

Not good at all.

Not because of the increased risk of leaving evidence behind, but because…I'd liked it. And I very much wanted to do it again.

Little girls were taught from a very young age to play nice, to share, smile pretty. They were taught to mind their manners and be seen but not heard.

I wasn't being quiet now.

In fact, I was shouting. Screaming from the highest roof, even though no one could see me. I didn't even have to open my mouth to be heard…my knife blades spoke for me, said everything I'd never been allowed to say.

But even now, I had to be careful.

Hush, my child.

Closing my eyes, I forced my mother's voice out of my head and tossed the newspaper down on the stack. I thought about clipping the articles out and putting them in a scrapbook. But that would be stupid. I was already taking a risk by keeping the wives' photographs. I had hidden them well, but one never knew what a thorough police search might turn up.

Of course, I had no plan to have the police search turn on me.

I was clever. Much more clever than most people believed.

When all of this was over, I still intended to take the photographs with me, so I could show those poor women a good time. A little too late for them to truly enjoy it—but it was at least something for *me* to look forward to.

When I had finished rereading the articles, I turned on my laptop and scanned the online news while waiting for the facial mask to dry. I sat in my bathrobe, the rest of my body covered in a thick layer of moisturizing lotion. It was important to use a healthy skin care routine when one was stressed.

When I was finished scanning the online sites for any additional information, I reached for my tea, only to discover that the cup was empty. Running my thumb over the words written in a pretty script across the pink mug, I said them aloud. "No regrets."

Did I have regrets? Remorse?

As I poured fresh water into the kettle to heat, I searched my heart for any feelings of guilt. It was like feeling around with your tongue after you'd had your wisdom teeth removed, trying to find out whether it was sore or not.

My search was inconclusive.

I was still more than a little disgusted by the way the men had behaved, but that wasn't the same as remorse. I didn't feel as satisfied as I had imagined feeling, but that wasn't remorse, either.

In the future, it would be better to take men to a place where I could control the situation a little better. The events of the night I killed Allen Newhouse had shaken me more than I liked to admit. I hadn't expected his son to intrude so abruptly—I had only just gotten started with Allen and hadn't had time to really satisfy myself. I'd also had to leave a few things behind in my rush to get out of the house without being noticed.

But remorse? No, not much.

Was that bad?

Carrying my fresh mug of tea upstairs, I washed the mask from my face and considered sinking into a hot bath. Quickly rejecting the idea, I took a quick shower instead, knowing I was too restless to spend much time in one confining space.

Besides, I had things to plan. I needed to choose someone to add to my list of losers.

And choose the new me.

I'd already been Kasey, Kate, Kim, Kitty, Karen, Karrie and Kay, and those were only the ones within the past year. Before that, I was Kendra, Kira, Kora, Kara, and Kali. Right now, I was Karen to a man I'd been only talking online to for a few weeks. There were more, but I couldn't remember all of them right off the top of my head.

It got confusing, sometimes, but I'd learned to respond to any name that started with a "K." That made it easier. Just as it got easier to look men in the eye seconds before I robbed them blind.

That was the original goal. Money. Just that and nothing more.

Then something had changed. I'd started spinning my web—maybe I was a spider after all—a few states away, not wanting to shit where I ate, or so some foulmouthed someone once said. But as I made my way up the eastern coast, something had shifted inside me. Something I couldn't explain.

The closer to home I got, the more enraged I'd become.

The more those men reminded me of—

A key rattled in the lock downstairs, and I froze where I stood in only my satin robe, a towel wrapped around my hair.

Plastic bags rustled as they were placed on the kitchen table, on top of the newspapers.

"Are you okay?"

I closed my eyes in response to the question, glad I couldn't yet be seen. I had more acting to do, this time with someone who knew me well.

Forcing strain into my voice, I sniffed loudly before calling out, "Fine."

A huff was followed by a slamming cabinet door. "According to the newspapers, things didn't go fine at all." Another cabinet door slammed, harder this time.

I needed to defuse the situation. Looking up at the ceiling, I allowed my mind to go back to the one place that always made me cry. It worked, and soon, tears were pouring down my face, and I was taking in great gulps of air.

"Oh, honey." A moment later, a comforting arm came around my shoulders. "I'm sorry. Tell me what happened."

I looked up and met blue eyes the same shade of mine. I watched the surprise force them wide, listened to the harsh curse that accompanied the gasp.

The purple bruises under my eyes were from my own fist, as was the split lip. A hammer had left perfect finger-sized bruises on my arms and legs.

Dipping back into the deep well of sadness that lived in my soul, I began to cry harder, so hard that the cold tea splashed over the sides of the mug and onto my bare legs. Hands took the mug away, then I was pulled into a familiar embrace that brought both comfort and additional pain.

"He deserved it then."

It wasn't a question this time. Last time, I'd heard the uncertainty and doubt behind the questions I'd been asked.

Why did you do it?

Why didn't you just leave?

How could you allow that situation to occur?

What are we going to do now?

"He left me no choice."

"Why didn't you call me?" The arms squeezed tighter. "You know I could have come."

And ruined the whole thing.

I sniffed hard. "By the time I realized he was dangerous, it was too late."

Lips pressed into my hair. "Did he find out about the money?"

I nodded. "Yes. I don't know how."

"I *told* you to leave him. Get the money and go. Don't hang around to give them one last goodbye."

I wiped my nose on my sleeve. "It's supposed to defray suspicion, you know that. Take the money, have one last fling with them, and say there's an emergency and disappear. You're *supposed* to leave them wanting more. That way, they don't call the cops."

The arms dropped away, and a long, hissing sigh filled the room. "Maybe it's time to move on."

My heart picked up speed. "No!" The word came too quickly, and I forced myself to calm. "We need to stick to the plan."

Those blue eyes found mine again, searched my face. "Killing these men isn't part of the plan, either. This is too dangerous now. This place is too dangerous. We need to leave and never, ever come back."

There was truth in the words, but I wasn't ready. Not yet.

This place might be dangerous, but it was also feeding something deep inside me that had been neglected and starved for too long.

"Soon. The plan was for two more. We'll have everything we need after that." I turned on the stair and placed my hands on the sides of a face I loved so much. "We can't let a couple assholes throw us off track."

Doubt wrinkled a forehead. Worry creased the corners of eyes. Fear tightened a mouth.

"I don't know. We need to talk to—"

"No!" Again, the word burst from me, and I smiled to soften my tone. "We don't need to talk to anyone about anything. We just need to spend the next couple of weeks wisely, follow through with the plan."

"Then what?"

"Then we finish what we started and move far, far away."

The lips curved a little bit, but the creases around the eyes didn't soften. "Promise?"

It was my turn to comfort this time, and as my arms wrapped around the familiar body, I pressed my lips into soft hair. "I promise. It will be over soon."

"Nothing but lint?"

I smiled and kissed the soft hair again. "Nothing but lint."

That had been the goal from the beginning. Pick these rich, unfaithful men's pockets until there was nothing but lint left to remind them that we had scurried into and out of their lives.

Scurried.

The word reminded me of spiders again. Maybe Black Widow was fitting after all.

Yes, I might want their money, but I wanted something else from them as well.

Step into my parlor, I said to the fly.

Dance into my heart and let me taste your soul.

Show to me that you are devoted to the one you should miss.

Prove to me that you will not betray her for the sake of a single kiss.

Convince me that you are noble.

Confirm that you have nothing to forgive.

And in return, I'll demonstrate my gratitude to you.

In return, I'll let you live.

9

Noah and Miguel got out of their rented Explorer and walked up to the front door of the Passavant Hills Township Police Department, a new, one-story brick building that practically gleamed in the bright January sun. It had been a shitty day filled with shitty conversations from men who felt like shit because they'd fallen for scams that made them feel shitty.

Yeah...that about wrapped up his day.

As he reached the front door of the station, he noticed a poster taped to the inside of the glass.

Be Aware of Scams!

Passavant Hills is proud of our seniors. Unfortunately, seniors are often the target of scammers. Chief Mazur advises you to watch out for the following:

Social Security Scams: Do not give your Social Security Number to anyone who claims that they need it in order to provide your benefits. The Social Security Office already has your Social Security Number and will never contact you by phone.

Utility Scams: No one from the Utility Department will come knocking at your door to demand immediate cash payment for your utility bill! Several scammers are going door to door and saying that the owner of the property owes thousands of dollars in unpaid bills. If you are worried about your bill, call your utility office—don't fall for the scammers!!!

If you're not sure, call the PHTPD!

A third warning had been taped under the first two, in a different computer font:

Online Dating Scams: Beware sending anyone money who you haven't met in person, and never give out your credit card number!! If someone you have recently met needs financial help, ask for the information of the company and pay the bill directly to their customer service department.

Remember, as I always say, A trustworthy person never tries to guilt trip you by saying, "Don't you trust me?"

Noah approved. The world was full of scammers. It didn't do any good to pretend otherwise. Whoever had composed the posters clearly loved their community. Maybe they had a *small* problem with exclamation points, but that was forgivable, particularly in the face of seniors who thought they knew everything. Some older folks just didn't listen to good advice, thinking it wouldn't apply to them.

Miguel had his hand over his brow and was scanning the area. "I see a couple of other sparkling clean SUVs in the parking lot. I think that means the others are here already."

"Good. Maybe that means they're done passing out all the paperwork." Noah opened the door and led the way inside.

"What? I thought paperwork was an FBI agent's best friend."

Noah had a list of what paperwork actually was, but he kept it to himself as they approached the receptionist's desk. A uniformed officer with a balding head and wind-chapped cheeks was jotting something on a sticky note. He was about to ask where the briefing would be taking place when Chief Mazur came striding down the hallway.

He barely rose past Noah's chest, but he was built like a Greco-Roman-style wrestler. He took Noah's hand, and the two of them shook like two men about to step into a ring, definitely sizing up each other's strength.

Noah accepted in a split-second that he wouldn't be able to take the guy down in a fair fight. He was just too tall. Chief Mazur would be able to throw down power and leverage too fast and twist him up like a pretzel. Now, if they were talking about a team sport, Noah would definitely have the advantage. His long legs could carry him halfway across a field or a court before Chief Mazur could blink. But in the wrestling ring...

He'd get eaten alive.

It didn't bother him. Every body had its strengths. Noah had gone with his, and Chief Mazur had probably selected differently, but with the same optimization in mind.

Miguel specialized in efficiency. Kind of like a sloth.

"Did you wrestle in college?"

Chief Mazur laughed. "Yep. Paid my way through school that way. Basketball or football?"

"A little bit of everything...*except* wrestling."

Mazur led them down a hallway. "They haven't been waiting too long. Just got here about fifteen minutes ago. They're in the Forkston Room."

Winter, Aiden, Autumn, Sun, and Bree were already working hard, manila folders spread out across the table. Bree was working on a laptop, entering notes from a legal pad sitting beside her. Sun was buried in writing notes on another legal pad, stopping to cross out several lines.

Aiden sat at the head of the table, studying something on his iPad. "Gentlemen, Chief Mazur. Let's get started."

Noah grabbed a chair, one of the legal pads off the top of a small stack, and a pen, resisting the temptation to put his feet up on the table. Miguel sat and took a piece of candy out of his pocket.

Aiden tapped at his screen. "Autumn and I interviewed Peter Kelley, age seventy-four. Contact information in the file I just sent you."

Noah tapped the message app on his own screen and filed the report before opening it. "Let me guess. Guy was seduced by a homely looking woman who convinced him that his life would be complete if he just let her tie him up and have her way with him."

Aiden nodded. "That sounds very familiar." Aiden shared the meeting with Peter and Tina Kelley and how Autumn had talked the daughter down from a ledge.

Autumn flipped to a page back on her legal pad. "I'd like to add that Mr. Kelley seemed genuinely fond of Ms. Nicks and asked for us to tell her hello if we ever found her. I got the impression that he had been very lonely after the decline of his wife during her long respiratory illness and subsequent death, and I believe he said something about it feeling far longer since her time of death than it had really been."

"Daughter sounds like a real gem," Miguel muttered.

Sun lifted her head. "I'd be a real bitch if my father gave away my inheritance to some money grabbing criminal just to get into her panties."

Miguel lifted both eyebrows to his hairline. "*That's* what would turn you into a bitch?"

Sun's eyes narrowed dangerously, and Noah seriously thought she might go for his partner's balls.

Autumn stepped in. "Talking to him, I felt like I understood his decision to get conned by Karrie, if that makes sense. He was so lonely that he didn't care whether he was getting screwed over. I even wonder if he regrets giving the money to a young woman who was patient with him, rather than his daughter."

Mazur still hadn't seated himself. He stood by the door as if guarding it. Given his physical build, it probably seemed as though he were guarding *everything* he stood next to. "I did a thorough interview with Peter after Tina yelled at him for spending her inheritance. I have a list of all the 'loans' he gave this Karrie woman, including dates that he gave her money and dates that he remembers going out with her, if you need them, but to sum up, she wiped his checking and savings out. Not his total portfolio, but enough to set Tina Kelley's hair on fire, that's for sure."

Aiden nodded. "I'd like a copy of that information whenever you get a moment, Chief Mazur. Noah? Miguel? Were you able to contact Marcus Fremont? What do you have to report?"

Noah leaned back in his chair, flipping a pen between his fingers, and glanced at his partner. Their interviews had gone well enough, no problems. But Miguel was always trying to get out of giving reports. It was *his* turn to talk.

When Noah said nothing, Miguel blew out a breath. "We did get most of the details, but I'll sum up. Marcus Fremont, age seventy, address and phone available in our report. I'm going to say that his story sounds a lot like Peter Kelley's, only it started at a speed-dating event. Her name was given as Kasey Ayers. I've sent the photograph we have of her around to your iPads."

Everyone stopped to look at the photo, which they had received from Marcus Fremont. Fremont hadn't wanted to let them have it, even though he clearly had printed out several copies of the same digital photo and left them sitting around his house in fancy gold frames.

The woman known as Kasey Ayers was pretty but not beautiful, with blue eyes and a golden-brown bob cut. She had dark eyebrows and a wide, wide smile, and was wearing a big, floppy straw hat and standing in front of a grassy field, holding up a painted birdhouse. She had a prominent birth-mark on her right wrist that was visible as she gestured toward the birdhouse.

Studying the image on her iPad, Autumn she reached across the table and snagged another printed photograph of a woman, setting the two side by side.

Noah leaned over her shoulder.

She pointed at the picture that wasn't of Kasey Ayers. "That's Karrie Nicks, the person who targeted the other victim, Peter Kelley."

The photo was of a redheaded woman with an unfortunate nose and a crooked smile nothing like the wide smile that Kasey Ayers beamed toward the camera.

Miguel was still speaking. "Marcus's wife, Jennifer, had passed away in…" He checked through the file again.

"October," Noah prompted.

"October," Miguel confirmed, reading off the report. "He hooked up with…" He cleared his throat, giving Sun a pointed look. "Excuse me, he *dated* Ms. Ayers in April."

Aiden stood and went to the whiteboard, uncapping a black marker along the way. "April? Peter Kelley was seeing Karrie Nicks in April?"

Chief Mazur shrugged. "I had the same thought as you guys. I checked the dates between the two cases. They didn't often coincide, but in a couple of cases, both men were out on dates with their lovers at overlapping times, although not locations. It would take some pretty sophisticated hijinks for one woman to manage both men at the same time in public."

Noah laced his fingers behind his head, leaning back in his chair. "I am a hundred percent on board with the idea that there's a girl gang out there targeting well-off senior men who have just lost their wives. I would go see that movie in a theater, as a matter of fact. Repeatedly. Ladies, no disrespect."

Winter pressed her lips together. Her frown had made some of the most hardened criminals cower, but Noah glowed with happiness at the sight. He knew she was struggling not to laugh—and he loved making her laugh.

Autumn rubbed her wrist, a pained looked crossing her face. "Actually, I'm with Noah on this. Maybe not something quite as Hollywood as he's thinking, but it would explain why the M.O. doesn't quite fit between each of the incidents, yet they still seem to connect. The women would have different styles." She tapped the photos. "And different looks."

Noah pulled out the pictures from the other men he and Miguel had interviewed. The entire team stood to get a better look at the women side by side.

"They all are so different," Bree said, pulling one of a brunette closer to her. "Or..." She pulled one of a blonde closer, squinting hard at each image. "Her nose is different in these two photos, but the facial structure is very much the same."

Sun waved her hand for the photos and Bree slid them across the table. Using a scanner that wasn't bigger than a notebook, the team watched Sun do some computer magic and then the images flashed up on the projector screen.

"Bree is right." Sun shifted the images until they were nearly black and white. "When I make them the same size and overlay them on each other—"

"The bone structure matches," Winter murmured.

"Son of a bitch." The curse came from the police chief, who was picking up another picture. "What about this one?"

Sun scanned it in, tweaked the resizing and contrast settings. When she overlaid the new image over the old, she was already shaking her head as Mazur said, "They're different."

He wasn't wrong. At first glance, they looked very much the same, but... "The last one's eye sockets are bigger." Noah looked even closer. "And maybe her face is a bit, I don't know, wider?"

Everyone nodded.

In a few minutes, Sun had each of the photographs up on the screen. Mazur had run a second set of full color prints, and Aiden had created two columns. Unsub 1 and Unsub 2. Noah kept waiting for a third unsub to appear, but unless their analysis had missed one, so far, they were looking at only two women.

Aiden tapped at the board with the marker. "Unsub 1 appears to be the same woman who ripped off Thomas Hill, James Roberts, David Myers, and Dennis Hughes."

"That we know of." Noah shrugged when everyone looked in his direction. It was true. These poor saps could be the tip of the sweetheart scam iceberg.

"And all four of those men are alive?" The question came from Autumn.

Noah nodded. "Yep."

"Any BDSM play for them?"

Noah flipped through his notes. "Nope. Just Marcus Fremont."

They all studied the picture of the woman Sun pulled up on the screen.

"Unsub 2 appears to be the same woman who dated Marcus Fremont, Brice Sutter, Allen Newhouse, and Peter Kelley." Parrish wrote the names on the chart.

"That we know of," Noah reminded them all.

Parrish nodded, looking grim. "That we know of."

Noah scratched his chin. "Two dead and two alive. Why?"

The room was quiet before Autumn leaned forward. "Marcus and Peter might have followed the spider's instructions while Brice and Allen didn't."

Winter frowned. "What instructions?"

Autumn shrugged. "That's one of the things we need to find out."

A thought popped into Noah's head. "What about the missing guy? Edwin Gallagher. Do we have a picture of the woman..." he flipped until he found the name, "Kim Benson?"

Sun held up a finger before clicking away. "I found a cached paged for a Kim Benson when I was going through one of the dating sites. The page was deactivated yesterday, which is why I remember."

A few moments later, a woman with pale skin, long red hair, green eyes, and glasses appeared. Again, she looked different, at least at first glance, but when Sun tweaked the coloration and size and laid this image over the other image of Unsub 2, they matched.

"Shit," Noah muttered. It was what he had been afraid of.

Autumn looked over at Mazur. "Do you think that's enough to get that search warrant now?"

The police chief wiped a hand down his face. "I'm guessing so." He nodded at Sun. "Can you send that to me?" His phone beeped almost before he had all the words out. He glanced at the screen. "Thanks."

Aiden walked over to a blank board. "So far, we believe we are looking at two women who may or may not be working together, who are targeting widowers who have lost their wives less than a year before they began dating again."

Autumn nodded. "Whether they are working together or not, these women are well-trained and well-coordinated. Internet savvy. Makeup and prosthetic savvy."

Noah pulled one of the images closer. "You think the nose is prosthetic?"

Autumn tapped the forehead of one of the women. "This scar could be too. Or a chin."

Bree's nose was wrinkled. "But wouldn't a facial prosthetic be noticed when it, um, falls off during sex?"

Noah had to agree, it was a good question.

What would he do if he and Winter were getting it on,
and she started doing a little oral exploration...and her
freaking nose fell off?

He shuddered so hard that Winter looked over at him. As
if she was able to read his mind, she wiggled her nose. Maybe
just to assure him that it was real?

"That could be one of the reasons for the submission,"
Autumn was saying. He refocused on the conversation. "If
she's wearing a wig or makeup or a prosthetic as we've
discussed, making sure the man was unable to touch her
could be more than a Dominant move. It could be tactical as
well."

Mazur clapped his hands together. "What do we do to
catch this woman?"

Autumn compared the images of the two women again.
"Why not set me up as a woman looking for a sugar daddy? I
could try to find these two women at group events."

Sun scooted her chair closer to the table. "I'm familiar
with online dating sites."

"From personal experience?" The question was out of
Noah's mouth before he could clamp his teeth closed.

Instead of verbally fileting him, Sun only shrugged. "A
couple of times in the past. It's easier to find introverted,
intelligent men that way. Men in person are so..." she shot
Aiden a look, "tasteless."

Bree clicked a key on her laptop. "Zing."

Aiden held his hand out, and Noah worked hard to
suppress a smile. It wasn't a secret that the SSA and Sun once
had some hot and heavy times together. And from the way
they sometimes tiptoed around each other, the ending of the
relationship hadn't been mutually agreed upon.

Winter took the photograph from in front of Autumn and studied it. "Well? What does everyone think of Autumn's idea? I like it."

Noah gave Autumn a thumbs-up. As long as it wasn't Winter, he was just fine with the idea.

Miguel shrugged. "It sounds like a lot of work, trying to flirt with some old guys. But I wouldn't be doing it."

Bree waved a hand. "Go for it."

Aiden rubbed his chin.

"Well?" Autumn asked.

His eyebrows pinched together so hard they met in the middle. "I see...some merit in the plan. It would be the logical step. If we can find some way to keep you safe, that is. You'd be going into a situation where you could be targeted by a serial killer."

"Not targeted," Autumn said. "I don't own the appropriate body parts for that."

Aiden gave her a sour look. "In competition with a serial killer then."

Noah tossed his pen onto the table. Time to sow some chaos to keep Aiden off-balance. "Sending Autumn in for surveillance is a good idea, but what happens if we do identify one of the girl gang? Wouldn't it make more sense to bait the scene with an..." he waved a hand at the SSA, "older man."

Sun snorted. Bree laughed under her breath. Winter gave Aiden an assessing look while Autumn frowned. Miguel popped another candy in his mouth and chewed vigorously.

Aiden just stared at him in stony silence. "How old, exactly, do you think I am?"

Noah shrugged, struggling to keep his face carefully blank. "Older than me and Miguel, and the chief is out because he's from this area. It's you or nothing."

Aiden, his gaze still glacial, looked around the room. "What other options do we have?"

Silence.

Noah shrugged again. "You could go to the same events and keep an eye out for Autumn, as well as be our point man for confronting these women. Sun could set up everyone online, fake names and all. No problem."

Aiden sniffed. "No problem? No *problem*? I'm not seventy years old, thank you very much. I'm thirty-nine."

Inside, Noah was practically giggling in glee. He'd managed to get under Aiden's skin *again*.

Meanwhile, Sun ran with the idea. "Your birthday is coming up, isn't it?"

"Fine!" Aiden's nostrils flared. "I'll be forty soon. That's still *thirty years* too young for this shit."

Sun took her phone out of her pocket, aimed it at Aiden, and pressed the photo button with her thumb. She bent over the phone screen, swiping and pinching and jabbing. "Technically, you only have to look like you're, oh, sixty or so. That might not be too much of a stretch."

Aiden crossed his arms over his chest. "That would still make me *twenty years* too young for this shit."

Sun gave her phone screen a few more swipes and turned it around to face Aiden. At first, Noah was sure that he'd refuse to look at the screen, but once he did, he moved closer. "What about the in-person events?"

Bree frowned at her laptop screen, clicking the keys. "Grow a beard. Men's beards are always a little grayer than the rest of their hair."

"My beard is not gray." He stroked his chin, which barely showed any stubble. "Not *that* gray."

Autumn, who almost looked as amused as Noah, held up a finger. "It's not a requirement to be sixty or seventy years old. Your profile just has to be set up so it looks like you've recently suffered the loss of your wife in less than a year, have enough money to make it worth the women's time, and come across as easy to fool."

"Yeah, men can be stupid at any age," Sun added, still staring at her laptop screen.

Aiden lifted both hands in surrender. "All right. I'll only do it if I can be a distinguished fifty. I'll just imagine I'm writing reports. That should age me ten years all by itself, right? But do we really need Autumn to either infiltrate or compete with these people? I should be able to handle this all by myself."

Winter caught Noah's eye and lifted an eyebrow. Shit. Without a word between them, he knew exactly what she was going to do next. She was going to walk calmly into whatever direction there was most likely to be danger. He had long since given up trying to "save" her from her own competence.

Out of Aiden's view, he gave her a small thumbs-up.

"I'll go undercover with Autumn."

Yep, that was exactly what Noah'd thought Winter was going to say.

Aiden studied her thoughtfully. "Go on."

"Four eyes are better than two, and six eyes are better than four. Autumn's strength is her ability to adapt and quickly pick up on the emotional tone of any situation. I have the training to have her back if needed while you focus on courting the ladies." When he started to argue, she held up a hand. "Trust us women. We know when a man isn't focused on us, and trust us…we don't like it."

Aiden, Noah, Miguel, and Mazur took turns looking at each other. None of them could argue with that logic.

Still, Aiden didn't appear to be completely convinced. "She hasn't had the full training yet."

Winter gritted her teeth. "Which is exactly why I'll be

right there. Autumn does have a tendency to run in where angels fear to tread. I'll admit that. But if you keep trying to stop her from doing what she does best, then you'll have no one else to blame if another team swoops in and hires her away from you."

Parrish winced a little while Autumn sat in her chair, perfectly composed. If Noah hadn't noticed the small hint of tightness at her mouth, he would have thought she was enjoying the exchange. Instead, she was pissed.

Not that he could blame her.

Being coddled wasn't what any hot-blooded FBI agent would have wanted. And even though Dr. Autumn Trent wasn't officially on the Feds' payroll yet, she was one of them. An important part of them. He knew it. Hell, the entire team probably knew it. Everyone would cheer the day her hiring became official. Well, except for that prick, Chris Parker, but that was because the little twat had brain envy. Balls envy too, since Autumn's were at least two sizes bigger than his.

Parrish raised both hands. "When is the next speed-dating ev—"

"Tomorrow night at eight." Sun's fingers hadn't stopped clicking.

Parrish frowned. "Does that give us enough time to 'old man' me?"

Sun snorted, still not looking up. "Won't take long."

Aiden's ego wasn't holding up to the punches it was taking with this case, and Noah loved it. He opened his mouth to say something, but Bree stepped in. "When I was working undercover in Chicago, I had to change my appearance several times. I actually got to work with the CIA's famous Master of Disguise a couple times. I picked up some tricks."

Noah was impressed. Aside from Winter and Autumn,

Bree Stafford was one of the coolest women he knew. With a little over twenty years in the Bureau, she normally didn't talk about the cases she had worked or the people she had saved. She just did her job, somehow looking like an African goddess each and every day.

Parrish tugged at the knot in his tie. He really was nervous.

Noah leaned back in his chair. "I'll go buy a cane and whatever old man detritus you need."

Parrish's cold blue eyes fastened on him. "I don't need a cane."

"Actually, you do," Bree said, standing up and circling the SSA. At six feet tall and in the heeled boots she wore, she was taller than their boss. "We'll put a stone in your shoe to change your gait, which will necessitate the cane. I'll add more gray to your hair, create more fine lines with makeup. We'll need to lose the tailored suit and buy one that doesn't scream law enforcement."

Noah covered his mouth to hide his smile. "What about a beard?"

Bree studied the SSA's face. "It depends what types they have available locally. If they aren't high quality with good adhesive, it's better to not use them." Abruptly, she turned to study both Autumn and Winter. "New clothes for you both. Flirty clothes that you would wear on a date."

Winter and Autumn both looked down at the professional suits they wore and didn't even attempt to disagree. Winter raised an eyebrow. "The Bureau is covering the cost, right?"

Parrish was practically snarling by now. "Of course."

Both women stood as if pulled up by the same puppeteer's strings. "Then I say we get to work," Winter said. "Bree, give us a list of what clothes you need for Aiden, and we'll grab them while we're out."

Sun finally looked up. "I'm creating online profiles for the three of you. I'll need photos ASAP."

Miguel popped yet another piece of candy into his mouth. "I used to work in the theater department locally. I'll help Bree with the disguise."

Parrish just stood there. For his credit, the man knew when he was beaten.

But Noah wondered if the seriousness of the situation had settled on the SSA's shoulders yet. Whoever was killing the widowers of Passavant Hills knew what she was doing. The woman or women had skills, an apex predator hunting fresh man meat to slaughter.

SSA Aiden Parrish was used to being on the top of the food chain.

Not the main dish.

10

George Marsh had promised himself that he would spend an entire year mourning his wife before even thinking about moving forward with his life.

He joked about it with himself in the mirror as he checked his throat and cheeks for little nicks from shaving. He was getting ready for his first date after her death. What would the neighbors think? They would surely be appalled.

On the one hand, he had nothing but disdain for the forced morality of the world, the standards that had little to do with good or evil, and everything to do with keeping appearances.

On the other hand, he often found himself self-conscious about breaking society's little rules.

He splashed on a generous helping of aftershave, gave himself one last look over, straightened his cuffs, and marched toward the front door to put on his shoes.

A few months ago, when he had posted his profile on an online dating site, he felt daring and rebellious. He hadn't expected to get a single response. But when an attractive young woman, Karen Nelson, had contacted him for a casual date, his heart fluttered in his chest. He had actually panicked at first.

He soon realized what the setup was. It wasn't about love. It was about opportunity.

Karen had flirted outrageously with him online, making suggestive comments that had somehow led him to confess several secret fantasies he'd never been able to carry out with his wife, Joyce. God rest her soul. She was a sweetheart, but she didn't wander far from the missionary position in bed.

Still, throughout the online chats, there had been a calendar in George's head that made him question himself. *What are you thinking? Your wife hasn't even been gone a year. Didn't you promise yourself that full year?*

He had less than a month to go when Karen had outright propositioned him.

"Imagine being tied down and blindfolded, not knowing what to expect next."

In fact, having Joyce be the aggressor had been one of his upmost fantasies over the years. His wife had seldom turned him down when he wanted sex, but she'd never been the one to seduce him.

The idea of a young woman with tight skin and body parts that gravity hadn't savaged was appealing indeed. Even if she was using him in the attempt to get some of his money, wasn't he using her in return?

A business deal of sorts, he'd told himself several times.

He wasn't cheating on his dead wife's memory. He was offering an exchange.

Which sounded more and more like prostitution if he allowed himself to think about it too much.

So, he'd stopped thinking and surrendered to the seductive wiles of Miss Karen Nelson.

She'd use him. He'd use her.

A fair trade.

Glancing at his watch, he picked up his keys, wallet, and phone, checked for messages, and stepped out to his Lexus. If he wanted to be at the restaurant early, he could not delay a moment longer.

Surely, he had thought, the young opportunistic lass would wait at least a month for a well-off gentleman who was likely to reward her handsomely. He had been wrong. He had tried to explain the situation to her over a phone call, but she had interrupted him, saying that she was only going to be in town for a limited time, and that if he wanted to see her before another three or four weeks had passed, it had to be that weekend.

George had excused himself and told her that he would call her back. He had taken a good, long look at himself in the mirror after that call. He wasn't young, that much he could admit to himself. He didn't have a young man's jowls, and he didn't have a young man's hair. Everything on the top of his head had gravitated downward, growing thickly out of his ears and nostrils, so he had to carefully trim it down.

But, on the plus side, he still had a devilish air, with arched eyebrows and a thick, well-trimmed goatee. He was overweight, but not by much, and he was still fit under the added paunch. He worked out regularly and had a resting heart rate that would put many younger men to shame.

Did he really care what society thought of him?

No, he decided. He had called Karen back and accepted, saying that he would like to take her out to Sander's Steakhouse, a place that was expensive but not exorbitant, for a nice meal. She had agreed to meet him at seven o'clock.

He indeed arrived at the restaurant early, his wallet stuffed with cash. He wasn't sure how to handle the evening, but knew that somehow, more or less delicately, Karen would let him know what she wanted.

And how much.

Sander's Steakhouse was in a nearby town, Drexelville, that featured a quaint downtown made of cream-colored brick buildings that had been built in the late nineteenth century. He found a parking spot and walked past a small women's boutique, a shared dental office, and a massage therapist called "Healing Hands."

He chuckled to himself. The sort of healing hands that he had in mind probably would leave the massage therapist somewhat aghast. He stepped inside the restaurant and was seated almost immediately at a romantic dining nook for two at the back of the restaurant, away from the other tables. He ordered a glass of house red and found it very good. He would order an entire bottle after the lady arrived, if she had no objections.

A minute or two after seven, Karen arrived.

She wasn't tall or beautiful the way some women were beautiful, with a flawlessness that spoke to an essential lack of confidence. She was instead beautiful in the way that a woman is when she knows that beauty comes from within. Her features were far from traditional, with a wide mouth, a slightly crooked nose, and long hair that was so blonde it almost looked silver. Her jaw was a little too square and stubborn, but the delicate arch of her slightly darker eyebrows balanced it out.

Her body was draped in a simple dress that was ostensibly modest. It almost could have passed for a long t-shirt, but it clung to every curve until it reached her thighs, where a slit on one side revealed the powerful muscles of her legs. She carried an enormous black leather bag, wore a slim diamond bracelet, and delicate black boots with heels that added at least three inches to her height.

"George?" Her voice was husky and rough.

He rose from his seat, hoping the shaking of his knees

wasn't too obvious, and took her hand, kissing the back of it. "Karen."

She gave him a broad smile. "You're quite handsome. Even more so than in your profile pic."

He suddenly wished that he had asked for a proper table instead of a booth, just for the pleasure of holding her chair for her. Instead, he watched her gracefully slide into the booth, tucking her purse away under the table.

He sat across from her. "It wasn't a good picture, of course. I was very nervous."

"Nervous?"

"I'm too old for this." He waved a hand. "For romance."

Karen laughed. He wasn't sure whether she was laughing at him for thinking that he was old—or for calling it a "romance."

She brushed her hair back from her face, showing a small, delicate silver hoop at her ear. "We're never too old for romance. Actually, I was worried that you would take things the wrong way. Professionally, I mean."

George found his face turning hot. "Of course not."

"Good. I've had a strange life, but never *that* strange." She laughed again, the sound so sweet that it stirred things that didn't need to yet be stirred. "I'm too forward for most people. Too aggressive? Too something."

"You're not aggressive," George told her, reaching across the table to place his hand on hers. "Aggression is when you attack someone. You're assertive. That's when you assert what you truly want. And I can only admire that."

"Really?" She flashed him another big smile, but this one showed a little more vulnerability than the last. "You're not just saying that?"

He shook his head. "I struggle with the same things. Society tells you to reach for the stars, for what you really want in life. But as soon as you do, that same society lashes out for overreaching."

She leaned forward, suddenly serious. "Right?" She spoke in a low and secretive voice. "Just between you and me, those prudes are nuts. How long do we have in this life, anyway? Not long enough to worry about what other people are thinking."

George found himself losing his nervousness. He was excited—*very* excited—but he was no longer afraid. He *had* taken Karen's intentions the wrong way. He had done it on purpose, he realized, in order to defend himself from the idea that she might actually be interested in him rather than his cash.

He thought of Joyce.

Beautiful, wise Joyce, who had taken the wild, tasteless, uncultured young man he had once been, and raised him into the sophisticated, well-controlled but still devilish man he was today.

He mentally raised a toast to her memory.

Karen tilted her head to the side. "You're thinking about something."

Guilt forced him to move his hand away. He cleared his throat. "I was just thinking that you're even more beautiful than your pictures."

Her smiled faltered a little. "Oh, I thought you might have been thinking of your late wife."

Her insight into his thoughts startled George a little, and in his shock, he waved a dismissive hand a little too vigorously. It wouldn't be a good idea to speak of former love with a future one, would it? At least he didn't think so.

But what did he know? He'd been married for the majority of his life. When he'd last gone on a date, there were no such things as cell phones or the internet.

"Not at all." He met her eyes directly, ignoring the sting of guilt the lie created. "My attention is only on you."

Her eyes slid away from his. Did she look disappointed? Did he say or do something wrong?

Before he could ask, the waiter arrived, and George turned to him with gratitude for the man's perfect timing. He'd changed his mind about the red, this called for a celebration. "I'd like your best bottle of Moët, if you please."

"Yes, sir." The waiter backed away from the table, quickly reappearing with an ice bucket and stately bottle of Impérial Brut. The waiter cut the foil, loosened the wire cage, and slowly eased the cork out with a hiss. He presented George with a small taste, and George nodded his approval.

Karen smiled at him, her full lips seeming to spread from ear to ear. She seemed happy again, and George let out a long breath as the waiter poured for her, then for George. He left the champagne capped with a bottle stopper in the ice bucket and disappeared.

The rest of the restaurant seemed to retreat. It was just the two of them.

George lifted his glass, and Karen lifted hers too. Her smile seemed to have already worked its way into his heart because his organ quickened at the sight. He tried to think of something witty, urbane, and sophisticated to say, but his mind was a complete blank. Only his heart could speak now.

"To the days to come."

She licked her lips before touching her glass to his. "To the days to come."

11

I sat back from the table. "Excuse me, George. I simply must find the ladies' room."

He was on his feet before I could slide from the booth. What a gentleman, wanting to score points for the young thing he wanted to screw. "I shall eagerly await your return."

After giving him a slow wink, I picked up my purse and left, looking seductively back over my shoulder at him. Yes, he had been watching me walk away. I could practically feel his lecherous gaze on my legs and ass.

Most women didn't drag enormous tote bags along with them on a first date, but I had my reasons. And I didn't feel comfortable leaving it under the table in case George was the nosy type.

I needed to be prepared because this first date would be different.

Normally, I liked to go out with my targets a few times, string them along, make them pant for me, yearn for me… but time was no longer my friend.

Although I felt safe from law enforcement discovery, I also felt a pressure to hurry things along. And though it gave me great satisfaction to watch these mongrels drool at my feet, that part wasn't absolutely necessary to achieve the end results I wanted…their money. And something even more important. I wanted, even if it was miniscule, a sense that they cared for their late wives.

That was becoming more and more important to me.

Peter, the sweetie, had spoken about his love for his beloved wife on our very first date. His devotion had touched me deeply. Not enough to turn away the money he'd handed over so willingly, but enough to keep the blade out of his back.

Brice…Edwin…Allen…those three had needed to be taught the lesson of devotion.

Would sweet little George need to be taught the same?

I hope so.

The voice surprised me enough that an audible gasp escaped my lips, and I was glad that the ladies' room was empty as I covered my mouth.

I wasn't supposed to hope for such things.

What was wrong with me?

And why now?

We were so close to our financial goals. So close to fleeing the east coast, and maybe even the States.

You want to get caught.

I pressed my hands over my ears, forcing the voice away.

I didn't. Not at all. Only a crazy person would want to get caught for murder.

The voice in my head laughed loud and long. *Bingo*, it taunted.

"I'm not crazy!"

The words bounced around the tile of the room, and I was once again glad that I was alone.

The bathroom was moderately fancy, with granite countertops and swinging wood-paneled doors instead of cheap bathroom ones. Baskets of cotton towels sat beside the sinks. That was how a girl knew that her date was really invested. Cotton towels instead of paper ones in the bathroom.

I took cover inside one of the stalls and peeled the blonde wig from my head. It was *awful*. I hadn't used this brand before. After that night, I intended never to use the brand again. I tried to scratch my scalp gently through the cap, but I just couldn't scratch hard enough to bring the relief I desperately needed. The itching was almost as bad as burning my scalp with hair bleach left in too long. I peeled off the cap, half convinced I'd discover that all my hair had fallen out, leaving nothing behind but a bloody mess.

My hair used to be long, nearly down to my waist. It wasn't long and beautiful anymore.

I scratched my short, blonde pixie cut. I used to love to play around with my hair, growing it out, cutting it back, dying it a variety of colors, but then everything changed. I'd started pulling it out, one strand at a time. It had gone from full and thick to brittle and patchy, all in under a year.

When I finally just shaved it all off, that was the moment I first felt free.

He…the bastard…had been so mad. That part had made it all the better.

It had grown out a bit, and I kept it too short to pull out. Plus, it helped with the frequent change of wigs. A win-win, I'd call it.

You're insane.

I scratched harder. No. I wasn't.

An insane person couldn't keep it together enough to slip into and out of the wide variety of feminine personas I was forced to maintain. When I was my own "self," I wore baggy t-shirts and sweats, went without makeup, and didn't bother to smile.

It didn't quite match what I felt inside, but it came closer than the other personas I was forced to wear. If I dressed the way I felt, I would have been a witch or maybe Lady Macbeth.

Or Dracula.

Ignoring the mental taunt, I dug my enameled fingernails into my scalp, scratching so hard I almost snapped a nail. Forcing my hands away, I took a few deep breaths to steel myself before pinning the skull cap back in place. Most women wouldn't have done so without a mirror; I could have done it in my sleep.

Although I loathed to do so, I put the wig back on and lightly tacked it down with the clips I'd strategically sewn in. I'd have to redo the adhesive glue around the edges, but that would only take a moment at the mirror. Not that I was worried about the time.

I refused to hurry because rushing caused one to make mistakes. Besides, women were infamous for taking a long time in the toilet. I'd asked George to order for me, telling him that I would eat anything as long as it was rare, so I wasn't worried about how long my bathroom journey was taking. And being able to scratch away the itch that had been building had been so, so worth it.

At the mirror, I rummaged around in my purse for the adhesive glue. I sighed fondly as I touched the handcuffs, whip, and vinyl bodysuit tucked in the bottom, and wondered how the night would end.

In our messages, I'd been able to pull George into a conversation about his fantasies. The targets always played coy at first, but after a little prodding, these horny old men always shared their deepest desires. George had suggested to me that he was interested in bondage play. Thanks to my father, so was I. I had *so* enjoyed my time with Allen Newhouse—until we had been interrupted so abruptly.

Men loved their fantasies of dominance, violence, and

control. I was finding that I also enjoyed mine. Just because they weren't quite a shared fantasy was irrelevant.

They got what they wanted, and I got mine.

You're crazy.

I glared at my reflection. "Stop it," I muttered, the words coming from between gritted teeth. "Just stop it."

Not until you do.

"I can't."

Taking a handful of water from the tap, I tossed it at the mirror. My reflection blurred immediately. Better but not good enough. I raised my hands to cover my face but remembered just in time the adhesive strips that were strategically placed to change the shape of my eyes. I didn't want to touch that.

I'd been able to avoid facial putty this time, and it was nice to not worry about the wax or fixative shifting and giving my change of appearance away. Instead of putty, I'd used nasal clips to change the structure of my nose from the inside. A little contouring with strategically placed makeup changed my jaw structure too.

After making sure my face and hair were perfect, I washed my hands, then grimaced. My scalp began to prickle again, longing for my fingernails. This time, it would just have to wait. I would need to dig deeply into my well of control.

Not like I had with Edwin. I was still ashamed about that.

Leaning closer to the mirror, I examined myself closely.

My father had always dismissed my mother as boring and plain, but I remembered her teaching me how to apply makeup, from foundation and contouring to the longest, most seductive false eyelashes. I had learned that my mother had known exactly how to become beautiful for a man—and had chosen not to do so for my father.

Because, for my father, beautiful was never good enough.

Nothing was good enough, it seemed.

I wondered what he'd say if he could see me now. The bastard.

Forcing my thoughts away from one old man, I turned them back toward another. I pulled out a darker shade of red lipstick and deepened the color on my lips. The brand was a particularly good one, and I knew I'd be able to both eat and lick my lips seductively without worry.

I smiled into the mirror. My reflection wasn't my own. It was the reflection of the woman my mother would have been, if not for my father.

"This is for you, Mom," I told the woman staring back at me. "This is for every woman who went unappreciated in life and was forgotten as soon as she was gone."

The woman who looked back at me smiled. She was *very* pleased with what she saw.

Karen—my current persona—returned to George's booth, sliding into the seat, almost purring with pleasure.

His gaze dropped to my breasts before jerking back up to my face. "I hope you don't mind filet mignon. Rare."

"Rare is perfect. The bloodier the better." I used my most sultry voice. "But I hope you didn't order dessert."

He lifted an eyebrow.

I reached across the table and placed my hand over his. "After our meal, I have something *far* more delicious in mind."

Aiden, as usual, found himself fully awake first thing in the morning, well before sunrise. The hotel room was part of a national chain that he generally used while on travel, so he had had no trouble sleeping.

He went down to the exercise room and spent an hour working out in the adequately equipped gym. When he was done, one glance at the continental breakfast area had him deciding on the Badger's Sett Cafe. The advertisement on his phone proclaimed that he could find their famous five-cent coffee and big breakfast plate for ten dollars plus tax, satisfaction guaranteed, and extra strips of bacon fifty cents each. A cheesy cartoon badger logo grinned at him from his phone screen.

Perfect.

He arrived just after they opened, at six-thirty, and was greeted by waitresses who called him "hon." He ate well, left a big tip, and swore that he would eat there every morning while in Pennsylvania.

He arrived at the Passavant Hills Police Station at twenty after seven.

An officer let him in early. "We're not supposed to open up early, sir."

"Thanks for the favor this morning. I'll keep it in mind."

Aiden went to the conference room and found Sun already there, in the same seat as the day before, working on her laptop. If not for the different shirt, he would have thought she'd spent the night in that chair.

She glanced up before hunching back down over her keyboard. "People suck. I mean, they really, really suck. I thought I knew how much people sucked. I thought I knew how much people on online dating sites sucked. But really, I did not know how much they all *actually* sucked until I researched dating sites that specialize in setting up people over fifty-five."

It was rare to get a speech from Sun. Usually, she restrained herself to the bare minimum of words necessary to make her point.

What she had said probably related to the case, so Aiden decided to inquire further. "How so?"

"The people on those sites? They're not lonely hearts. None of them are actually looking for love. They're all either predators or gold diggers. Like, even the ones who are seventy years old. I dug a little deeper into some of their online footprints, and it's all one or the other. No wonder I'm not having any luck finding good guys on dating sites. I should just never date again." She picked up a bottle of water and gulped from it. "Ack. I even have a literal bad taste in my mouth."

He checked the coffee pot. No one had made fresh coffee yet. He cursed under his breath.

Sun peered at her screen. "Sorry, what did you say?"

"Just that it can't be *all* of them. You did some online dating, didn't you? You're no predator."

She shrugged. "Okay, maybe there are a few naive souls

online who have good intentions, but they're gonna get screwed. The odds are against them."

"People searching for companionship is understandable."

Sun turned her head toward him slowly, one eyebrow lifted. "Aiden, seriously? There's an expiration date on these things. At some point, it's time to just let things go."

It was a cold statement, but Sun was a cold woman. Aiden needed to maneuver away from this topic. "Are you collecting any takers on my profile? What's the name again?"

"Roger Applegate." She clicked a few things using her touchpad. "And yeah, I got you some potential dates. Not as many as I would get if I were posting my own picture and information, but not, like, none. I've been talking to them and pretending to be you. Surprisingly, I haven't managed to scare them all off."

Aiden decided not to ask her whether she meant that she was proud of herself, or somehow insulting him. It was Sun; she probably meant the latter.

But he did wonder if she'd gotten any useful information from the women. "Have you asked them any questions?"

She shook her head. "We're still in the 'tell me all about yourself' phase. After you're done talking about yourself, that's when you start asking questions. But it'll be soon."

Aiden poured water into the pot. "We'll have to be smart about our questions. We're not trying to identify a normal woman. Or even a normal gold digger. We're looking for a woman who's prepared to kill." He added a heaping scoop of coffee. "Sun, tell me the truth. Blurry profile picture aside, am I really what these women are in the market for?"

She closed the lid of her laptop with a snap. She considered his question for so long that his testicles started to sweat. "With the right costume and props, you could give off an old man vibe in a pinch."

He frowned at her and stabbed his thumb on the start button. "You seem awfully sure of your response."

She was teasing him.

He was pretty sure she was teasing him.

"Isn't that why we picked you in the first place?" She blinked at him, her eyes wide. "You always come across as older than you look."

Aiden put a hand over his face. He wasn't sure whether to laugh or to cry. Older than he looked? What? He wasn't even *forty* yet!

She had to be teasing him.

It didn't matter. If he presented himself as being older than he really was, that was how it was. Arguing about it now wouldn't do any good for Sun's ability to get the job done, or the case as a whole.

But when he got back to Virginia…it might be time to get his hair dyed.

13

Autumn had been researching dating profiles for hours, focusing on the local dating sites and hookup groups. After that, she would start on the huge match-making sites. She hoped with all her heart that it wouldn't come to that.

This was depressing.

Not the lonely people looking for love. That was normal. What wasn't normal—or shouldn't be—were the absolute perv profiles she'd read. Some of the profiles had been pulled from the local speed-dating company, Heart to Heart, and some of them were from the GoSteady website. The spider had used both local sites to find her prey.

Autumn had been so focused that she barely noticed the world around her. A breakfast sandwich had appeared beside her at some point as did a hamburger for lunch. Coffee cups appeared and disappeared. Even so, her stomach was rumbling again.

Autumn could feel herself turning into Sun...cranky, disillusioned, and on the verge of becoming a hunchback as she crouched over her laptop.

Without warning, Bree threw a pencil at her. "Earth to Autumn."

Picking up the pencil, Autumn attempted to toss it back. It landed a good three feet from her target. She pointed a finger at Bree. "Don't you dare laugh."

Bree pressed her lips together, but her eyes were shining with humor. "Why don't you stand up and stretch for a minute? That little pinch mark between your eyebrows is getting redder and redder. You're going to pop a blood vessel in a minute if you don't stare at something else."

Autumn leaned back from her laptop, her spine popping, causing her to groan. Beside her, Sun was tapping away at the keyboard, digging deeper into the profiles Autumn had flagged as possibles. She seemed immune to the multiple aches and pains that occurred when a person sat too long.

She tried to relax her face. "Sorry, Bree, I still have six women to go over."

"Take five minutes. Let's go outside and walk around the building just once. You'll regain your focus, and the rest will go faster. I promise."

Autumn snorted and tried to rub away the spot in the middle of her forehead, but the pain there only moved to the back of her head. When she rubbed that spot, the ache moved to her temples. "Ever thought of being a therapist?"

Bree guffawed one of her belly deep laughs. "I'd punch someone in the face the first time they whined that their mommy didn't give them enough attention."

Autumn rolled her shoulders and followed Bree from the building, pulling on her jacket along the way. The day was cold, but the sun was bright in the blue sky.

"How's it going?" Bree asked.

"Frustratingly slow," Autumn admitted. "This isn't like the work I do at Shadley and Latham. I'm used to working with organizations that track data professionally. Schools have their educational records. If kids have trouble in school, it shows up. Police departments collect evidence. Companies collect all kinds of records in their human resources departments. But online dating sites? As far as I can tell, they mostly collect lies."

Bree chuckled and stuffed her hands in her pockets. "You're starting to sound like Sun."

"I'm starting to understand why Sun sounds like Sun. The number of absolutely disgusting perverts, both men and women, on these sites have nearly made me lose faith in our world."

"That bad?"

Autumn shivered, and it wasn't from the cold. "Let's just say that I'd prefer to stay happily single than face the online dating scene."

Bree kicked a rock in the middle of the path. "How many views does Aiden's profile have?"

"When I last checked, he had almost thirteen hundred views and thirty-seven messages."

Bree gaped at her. "Already? He's just been up a day."

A deep sense of foreboding settled on Autumn's shoulders. Could one of those women be the spider? Was she, right this second, spinning her web?

"Most of the women who messaged him are in their twenties and early thirties, with only two in their forties and one in her fifties."

Bree kicked the rock again. "Can you tell if any of them are bots?"

Bots were the bane of the internet. These automated programs had capabilities ranging from spamming to data scraping to cybersecurity attacks. Not all bots were bad, of course. Some were created by the companies themselves to provide services that users might find useful. Malicious bots, though, could easily manipulate a user into doing things like buying a paid membership in order to send a message to a profile that wasn't even real in the first place.

Autumn lifted a shoulder. "Not yet, but the cyber team is working on it." She kicked Bree's rock. "It's just so sad. Real people looking for love are being preyed on so badly. Maybe not as drastically as the spider, but they deserve better than to become targets to people wanting to make a buck."

Bree sighed. "I'm so glad I've got Shelby."

Autumn smiled at the agent. "I'm glad you do too. It's funny. Well, funny in a sad way, but I expected it to be men who poised the danger in dating sites like this. And, don't get me wrong, there are plenty of them who are just nasty, but they're nasty in a very open way."

Bree grabbed herself between the legs and spit in the grass. "Ladies, come get ya some of this."

Autumn bent at the waist from laughing so hard. "Exactly." She wiped tears from the corners of her eyes. "Most were honest like that. Some are even upfront that they are in a relationship and just want some side action. The women, though…" Autumn tried to think of something kind to say.

Bree felt no such need. "Manipulative, passive-aggressive liars?"

"Pretty much. Anyway, I was expecting that it would be the men who hustled for dates, that all the women would have to do is sit back and let the men do all the work."

They came to a shady spot, and their shoes crunched over a thick layer of salt. Bree shrugged. "Maybe women who want actual dates, either for a connection or just for a one-night stand, don't have to hustle. But if you're looking for an actual sugar daddy, sometimes it pays to put yourself forward before your competition can make a catch."

Autumn smiled at her. "So, anyway, I went through a bunch of the online profiles in more detail, thinking I'd work out a quick system for identifying which women were prostitutes, either amateur or professional. Women looking for a sugar daddy don't want their money up front so much as they want an ongoing income, right?"

"More or less." Bree rolled her head on her neck and yawned. "Sometimes, the definitions get a little vague, I'm sure."

Autumn nodded. "I found a code the pros used to ask for money up front. Roses."

Bree got it right away. "As in…hey honey, bring fifty roses with you tonight."

"Exactly. That let me identify a number of them right away, narrowing the list a little. I was hoping to get the dating sites finished before the speed-dating event tonight. After that, I'm sure there will be more women to research." She sighed. "More women to worry about."

Bree stopped walking and pursed her lips. "Autumn, you can worry all you want about protecting Aiden to the best of your ability. We're all trying to make sure he's safe tonight. But don't push yourself so hard that you have a crisis of faith in humanity. Aiden can take care of himself. I know you're trying to make sure he doesn't have to, but that's not the way this is going to work. Even if you identify the serial killer, he'll still need to talk to her."

Autumn said what Bree didn't. "He'll still need to walk into her web."

Bree started walking again. "Yeah. You and Winter will be walking into it too. That's what we do, Autumn."

The two were silent for a long time. Autumn broke the silence first. "Have you ever been to a speed-dating event before? Any idea what I can expect?"

Bree snorted. "You'll probably want to dumb yourself

down a little, say things like, 'I love to travel and go on long walks.' Focus most of the conversation on the man. Compliment them. Act genuinely interested." She stopped and touched Autumn's arm. "I know I don't need to tell you this, but…be kind."

The advice made Autumn like this agent even more. "I've already thought about that. About how nervous some of the guys will be. They could be afraid of opening their hearts, and just because I'm on a mission of sorts doesn't mean that I can forget that."

They started walking again, and this time, Bree hooked her arm in Autumn's. "You'll be all right. Just don't let the bots and the trolls and the greedy, bitchy and pervy bastards rid you of your humanity. Sun may be able to live with that constant sense of cynicism, but I don't think you're cut out for it."

For a moment, Autumn worried that Bree was trying to tell her that she wasn't cut out for the FBI. "You don't?"

Bree seemed to be able to read her mind. She patted Autumn's hand with her gloved one. It was a motherly gesture that warmed Autumn's heart. "You're cut out for so much more, so tonight, you're going to focus on cleaning up humanity's current messes so it can make some brand-new ones."

Autumn smiled. "Humanity is good at making messes."

"We wouldn't have a job if they weren't. Just remember, even those who aren't the purest deserve a little justice in their lives. Focus on that, not on the fact that a bunch of dirty old men are milking the game just as hard as the young women are, or that nobody comes out clean." She chuckled to herself. "You leave that to Sun. She doesn't actually *like* people the way you do."

Autumn drew in a breath, held it, and exhaled it up toward the bright blue sky. "Thanks. I think I will."

Bree yawned so wide her jaw popped. "I'll be glad for the season to turn again. I'm tired of all these cold days. Ready to head back inside and hit the profiles again?"

Autumn wrinkled her nose but nodded. "The clock is ticking, so I guess we have no choice."

Bree laughed. "Well, you could always help me 'old man' Aiden. Maybe you can talk him down from the ledge."

Autumn reached the door first. "I think his ego can handle it, but I'm excited to see your magic."

They stamped their feet on the rubber-backed rug just inside the door, nodding at the officer at the front desk, and reentered the hallway. When they returned to the conference room, Noah was just setting a mound of fast-food bags on the table. Autumn inhaled deeply. "Is that Mexican?"

Noah held up a burrito before taking a huge bite. "Delicious," he said around a mouth full of food.

She grabbed one of the bags. "You're a lifesaver."

Bree tutted and shook a finger at Noah. "Aiden's going to complain."

Noah made a mock-surprise face. "Is he? Whatever for?"

Bree snorted. "You know very well whatever for."

Noah reached into a pocket of his jacket and revealed a box full of breath mints, which he rattled and stuffed back into his pocket. "How does the search go, Autumn?"

She bit into a steak burrito filled with several kinds of cheese and moaned. She refused to answer until she'd chewed and swallowed. "Six left."

"Any crazies?"

Sun snorted as she grabbed one of the bags. "A whole lot of crazies, but do we have a spider?" She shrugged. "A few possibles so far."

Which reminded Autumn that she needed to get back to work on her six. Taking her bag of food to the laptop, she went back to the site, and frowned. Aiden—Roger Applegate —had received a new message.

Hey, handsome! Wanna go out? Grab your bottle of Viagra 'cause you're going to need it.

Autumn groaned and took another bite of her burrito.

It was going to be a very long afternoon.

14

Winter eased the rented red Charger over a speed bump in the middle of the Passavant Hills Community Center parking lot. She freaking loved this car. It was so much better than the huge SUV she had been given before. The team had decided that, to completely look their part as young women on the prowl, she and Autumn needed a vehicle that didn't scream soccer mom or federal agent.

But speed bumps weren't as fun with a car this low to the ground. She wondered if she could get this baby to jump one of them later.

Autumn gave Winter a double take. "You're smirking. Something funny?"

"Just remembering driving around in parking lots in high school."

"With boys?"

"Boys?" Winter snorted. "Boys were aliens who liked to snap my bra when I was that age." She pulled smoothly into a parking spot, giving the powerful engine an extra few hits of gas, just for the thrill of it. "I just liked to drive fast. Even back then, I was a little bit of a thrill-seeker."

"I can see that." Autumn considered the rest of the cars in the lot. "A lot of Lexuses. BMWs. Mercedes. Great place to pick up a wealthy date."

The community center was two stories tall and made of a patchwork of different types of red brick. One wall had a scaffolding against it, half-covered in a blue plastic tarp dripping with icicles.

Autumn stepped out of the car. Under her black peacoat jacket, she wore torn blue jeans and a silky black shirt that bared her shoulders, along with a vibrant red lipstick that should have clashed with her red hair but somehow didn't. She looked totally different than the image she projected as Dr. Autumn Trent.

Winter looked down at her own torn jeans and the bright blue top that matched her eyes almost exactly. She'd applied more makeup than normal and had left her hair long instead of in its usual braid. She was just glad she hadn't been forced into one of those sequined dresses that ended mid-thigh. That had been Noah's suggestion, of course. One hard glare had him agreeing that jeans and a flowy shirt would be perfect.

The sweetheart.

At the community center doors, she and Autumn stepped inside to a blast of warm air, the sound of cards being shuffled, and the chatter of voices. Spoons clinked inside coffee mugs as they stirred in cream and sweetener. Going into the building was like stepping into an old-fashioned school.

Past the front entry, where they both hung up their coats, was a big open room surrounded by tall windows, now dark from the early January sunset. The center of the room was occupied by two rows of square wood tables. Around the edges were a few separate ones, filled with old men playing cards or checkers or chess, or just watching the main event.

The two rows of tables in the center of the room were set

up with name tents made of folded paper. Chairs sat on either side, but no one was sitting in them yet. They were early, and the organizers were still setting up. About forty men and women—half and half—were standing around, drinking coffee or beer or wine out of disposable stemmed glasses.

Aiden was one of them. No...*Roger Applegate* was one of them.

Bree had done a brilliant job of aging him. His normally light brown hair was now a distinguished mixture of gray and black, as were his mustache and eyebrows. With some makeup magic, he now possessed deeper wrinkles at his eyes and mouth. He looked very distinguished, except for his clothes.

Instead of his usual expensive suit and silk tie, Roger Applegate sported a pair of sharply creased khakis and a button-up shirt topped with a houndstooth jacket that was a size too big. Gold-rimmed glasses perched on his nose were the right addition to give him a "retired exec" vibe.

Flesh-colored hearing aids were barely visible inside his ears. Autumn had worried that adding them took the charade a little too far, but when Bree explained that they were actually covert listening devices allowing Aiden to be in communication with Noah and Miguel, she'd seemed relieved.

Winter smiled at how incredibly uncomfortable the SSA looked. Which, after inspecting several of the men, seemed to make him fit right in, cane and all. The ladies surrounding him didn't look uncomfortable in the least. In fact, they were closing in on "Roger" like sharks to a wounded seal.

Not wanting to be caught paying the SSA too much attention, Winter wandered over to a table filled with delicious looking hors d'oeuvres. The fruit looked fresh, which was a trick during these bitterly cold months. Crystal serving pieces and fresh flowers gave the table a touch of elegance. She wasn't sure what she had expected, but class and dignity hadn't been one of them.

Piling a tiny appetizer plate with fruit and cheese, she eyed the selection of wine but chose a glass of punch instead. She knew that she should mingle with the other participants, but flirting wasn't in Winter's wheelhouse. She'd probably end up popping some old geezer in the mouth the first time he leered at her breasts.

Spotting Autumn looking as much as a fish out of water as she was, she sauntered over to her friend and held out her plate. "Want anything?"

Autumn snagged a strawberry and popped it into her mouth. "Thanks. My stomach hasn't been happy with me since the burritos."

Winter was immediately concerned. "Are you okay?"

"Yeah, just nervous, I guess. I keep looking at the women, wondering if one of these smiling faces could be our spider."

Against her wishes, Winter's gaze swept around to find Aiden again. He was talking animatedly now with two women, both of whom were touching his arms. One was blonde, the other a redhead whose hairstylist had gone a little too far on the purple side of the spectrum.

Aiden said something, and both women laughed hysterically, the redhead nearly leaning against him.

"Are our spiders a tag team?" Winter asked, forcing herself to look away from where Aiden stood. "Fulfilling men's fantasies in more ways than one."

Autumn made a very unladylike sound with her nose, and said something that sounded like, "Bitches."

Winter faced her friend, her mouth agape. "Are you jealous?"

Winter got a double middle finger in response and lost another strawberry to her friend.

Before she could say more, though, a honey-blonde with a golden complexion clapped her hands together. In a surprisingly loud voice, she shouted, "Good evening! I'm Heather Novak, and I welcome you to our speed-dating event. I love how eager each of you are to meet your perfect match, but we still have about fifteen more minutes before we begin." She waved a hand at the table Winter had already partook of. "Help yourself to appetizers and drinks and be sure to mingle." She smiled brightly. "I'll let you know when we're ready to begin."

The fifteen minutes went by quickly, with both Winter and Autumn dealing with unwanted male attention. It was interesting. The guys were older while the girls all seemed to be around her same age.

Did younger men find speed-dating lame?

"Your eyes are in competition with the heavens on the clearest day," a silver-haired man named Oliver proclaimed to Winter. "A perfect match to the black hair. Night and day. Light and dark. A juxtaposition that creates a beauty that is more rare than the witnessing of a corpse flower bloom."

Beside Winter, the great Dr. Autumn Trent giggled. Yes, giggled. The sound was so unexpected that Winter found herself giggling too, even as she forced her mind to remember that a corpse flower only bloomed every seven to ten years and emitted a stench so foul, it smelled like a dead body.

Winter batted her eyelashes just to see if she was capable of carrying the gesture off. She was, though it made her a little dizzy. Perhaps, she batted just a little too much? She'd have to work on that, or she'd find herself walking into a wall.

Oliver clearly took the trilling laughter as a sign to go on with his flirty pontifications.

He turned to Autumn. "And you, my dear, are a sublime combination of rubies and emeralds, more precious than—"

Oliver was interrupted by the clapping hands of Heather Novak, and Winter groaned in bitter disappointment. It had been a joy to watch Autumn's cheeks flush a rosy red.

"Take your places," Heather cried. "Love is in the air, and it's time for you to meet your perfect match."

Winter mentally scoffed. Even if she didn't have Noah in her life, she hoped she would never be so desperate as to pay good money to attend an event like this.

She immediately felt bad for being so critical. These people seemed perfectly nice, and as she winked back at a sixty-ish man who'd winked at her, she found herself hoping that he did indeed find someone to enjoy life with. That they all did.

And they stayed safe from those who would do them harm.

Winter had no trouble finding her table as it was clearly marked: *Winter #17*. A stack of index-sized cards sat at her reserved seat. On closer examination, she spotted a place for her name and number and then the name and number of each of her "dates." There was also a section for her to write notes.

Notes?

This dating stuff appeared to be serious business.

At the bottom of the card were two checkboxes: *Date Again? YES / NO.*

Had she stepped into a time machine and found herself back in high school?

Heather was clapping again, providing instructions about the cards. Winter began to jot down her name, then stopped when she almost messed up.

To prevent making too many mistakes, Winter and Autumn had registered using pseudonyms that were fairly close to their real names: Winter Miller and Autumn John-son. It was slightly better than Smith and Jones, but their identities didn't need to be too sophisticated. They weren't *actually* trying to pick up dates and steal their financial information.

Autumn's table happened to be on the opposite side of the room, while Aiden was standing with the men, waiting for their turn to be seated.

Next to Winter sat a woman with curly, dark hair, a cute button nose, and a smile so sweet that she would have made a great Hollywood-style love interest. Her table tent read *Connie #16*. She gave Winter a friendly wink.

Winter gave her a friendly wink in return. "Good luck."

Connie #16 beamed. "You too. Isn't this exciting?"

Winter was saved from lying by more clapping. Heather Novak, still beaming, said, "Ladies, are you ready?"

Winter almost jumped as the women around her practi-cally screamed, "Yes!"

Looking very pleased, the organizer held her hands up in the air, almost like she was starting a race.

If she tells them to start their engines, I swear—

"Gentlemen, if you'll take the seat opposite your first date, we can begin when the timer sounds! Seven minutes, so make each and every second count!"

The men scattered to their assigned seats, and Winter found herself opposite a wiry man with a crew cut, wearing a striped button-down shirt and skinny jeans. There was only a little gray at his temples. His stick-on nametag read *Woody #17*.

"Time!" the woman called.

Woody stuck his hand out and Winter gave it a hard shake. "Hi! I'm Woody."

"I'm Winter."

He bobbed his eyebrows. "Woody and Winter…at least our names seem made for each other."

In spite of herself, Winter laughed just a little. "It seems so."

He got down to business. Apparently, Woody took speed-dating very seriously. "We don't have a lot of time to get to know each other, so I'd like to ask you some questions. First, what color best describes your personality?"

A painful pinch formed over the bridge of Winter's nose. "Blue." Before he could ask her what kind of blue, she added, "A lighter blue. The color of my eyes."

Woody smiled, showing a crooked front tooth. "I'm more of a dark blue. Not navy, but more of a midnight blue. Next question, would you rather fix your own plumbing or call a plumber?"

Winter wished she had been taping the conversation. She was finding it rather strange, but she could only imagine how hard Noah would laugh if he could hear it. "I'd rather call a plumber. I've had to fix plumbing before. It's a pain and never goes the way you think."

His eyes widened. "It's impressive that you even attempted to do it yourself. Do you do much DIY?"

She held out a hand and made a *so-so* gesture. "Do I get to ask you questions?"

Woody put down his dating card on the table and adjusted his cuffs. "People tell me that my questions tell more about me than any answers I could possibly give."

Winter couldn't help but chuckle. "Okay, that's fair. What else have you got for me?"

"Third question. If you could live anywhere in the world, where would it be, and why would it be in the Rocky Mountains, specifically in Colorado?"

Winter finally gave in to the laughter that was threatening to escape. Noah would *love* this guy. "I'm so sorry. I would rather stay on the East Coast. I'm not much of a country girl."

His hand slammed into his chest. "Aw, that's too bad. You're breaking my heart."

Winter got the sense that he had already sized her up and decided she wasn't for him, but because he was a nice guy, he wanted to be friendly and entertain her anyway.

She patted his hand. "There are always other fish in the sea. But since we have a few minutes, tell me, why Colorado?"

He drew back in comic dismay. "Why *Colorado*? Don't you know that the Rocky Mountains are the finest place on earth? And that of all the states that contain them, Colorado is best?"

She looked at him curiously. "If that is the best, why do you live here?"

He leaned forward conspiratorially. "Because I can't leave for another couple years."

"Why? Your job?"

A shadow fell over his face, but the grin replaced it quickly. "Just, um, family obligations."

Winter leaned in a little, watching his face. "What about your family? Have you been married before?"

The smile melted away, and Winter immediately felt a stab of guilt. She wanted to reach out to him, to change the subject, but she couldn't. She had to know.

He cleared his throat by coughing into his hand. "My wife…" he cleared his throat again, "passed a year ago."

A year?

That was outside of their victim parameters. Or was it? He could have simply been rounding up. She would need to do some research on that. It wasn't like she could ask for a specific date of his late wife's death.

"I'm so very sorry." She squeezed his hand, hoping he

could see her genuine regret. "That's so terrible."

He squeezed her hand back. "You don't think it's terrible that I'm here now?" He glanced around at the chatting couples. "Looking for a date so soon?"

He'd just given her an opening she had to take. "You said a year, right?"

He nodded. "A year, a week, and two days, to be precise."

Winter smiled at him. Outside the parameters, unless the Black Widow widened that gap for some reason, or unless there were unknown victims who laid outside those parameters too.

"I'm sure your late wife was very wonderful, and I'm even more sure that she would be glad that you are allowing happiness to come into your life."

He brightened. "She always said that...for me not to mope around after she was gone."

Winter thought about that, about how hard it must be for either the man or the wife. If she were dying, would she want Noah to find happiness with someone else or would she threaten to haunt him from the grave?

The grave. Yeah. The grave.

"What's so funny?"

Winter didn't even realize she'd been smiling until Woody's gentle prompt. "I was just thinking about heaven, I guess. If it is everything we hope it is, then your wife is happy up there. So why in the world shouldn't you be happy too?"

The smile reappeared. "I usually tell people that I want to go to the Rockies because there are no mosquitoes there, but that isn't the real reason." He leaned in closer. "The real reason is because it's the highest I could get to heaven here in the States."

Winter's heart tugged, and a flood of warmth for this man filled her spirit. Before she could say anything else, the organizer's loud voice echoed through the space. "Time."

Woody extended his hand as he rose. Winter took it and stood as well. He pressed his lips to the back of her hand. "Thank you, my Winter angel."

He moved on before she could think of a response, but as she sank back into her seat, she looked at Woody's card. Next to *Date Again?*, she checked "yes." This kind man was just a few days outside of the parameters, and her gut told her to keep an eye on him. Whether he checked "yes" in return didn't matter.

The next person to sit across from Winter wasn't *nearly* as entertaining, but she managed to muddle through. She jotted notes about each "potential mate" and whether he might make a good target for their specific con artist. The evening moved along slowly, with Winter almost counting down the seconds until the next time the timer would ring.

At the halfway point, Heather shouted that they would take a break. Everyone made a beeline for the ham sand-wiches on little plates with small servings of potato salad. Heather was cutting more of the ham slices off with quick, smooth sweeps of the knife, and depositing the extra ham on people's plates.

Autumn approached, holding one of the little plates. "You have *got* to try this ham." A younger man, college-age or so, came by with a platter of small punch glasses and Autumn snagged one.

"You must be feeling better." Winter grabbed one too, gulping down the overly sweet liquid. "Did the Bureau really pay a hundred bucks a pop for us to attend this thing?"

Autumn moaned over another bite of ham, her eyes nearly rolling back in her head. "Worth every penny."

Unconvinced, Winter eyed the buffet, but after her conversations with these men, it was now her stomach that was feeling a little off. Even the thought of eating anything at the moment sent bile surging into her throat. Turning away from the smell, she perused the room, focusing back on their purpose for being there. "Did you learn anything?"

"Not much. One widower, but he lost his wife nearly five years ago. I got some pretty good financial clues on most of them and put stars down by the names of the ones who might make good marks, but none of them were widowed within the past year. I tried to talk to the women on either side of me, but there wasn't enough time between dates to really get a feel for who they were."

Winter looked around the room again. She noted some of the men and women gravitating to each other while a few others stood to the side, looking like proverbial wallflowers. Aiden looked to be having the time of his life as the nearly purple-haired woman clung to his arm again.

Shaking her head, Winter continued to peruse the room and spotted the organizer speaking to one of the women. Connie #16.

The pair clearly knew each other, which wasn't unusual. Connie could be a serial speed-date attendee, or they could have known each other from school or church or a hundred different places. Passavant Hills wasn't a huge city like New York, but it wasn't a small town either.

The organizer, Heather, appeared to be annoyed by something the other woman was saying. Instead of responding, though, she looked at her watch. "Look at the time," she called in her loud voice. "Everyone, please return to your seats!"

Autumn ate the last bite of her ham sandwich and gave Winter a little wave before heading back to her seat. Winter returned to hers, wondering if the night had been a waste of time and self-esteem.

As she talked yet again to more "potential mates," she decided that regardless of whether they got any leads that night, it wasn't a waste of time. They were collecting names and information about potential victims, establishing a cover identity among the community, and getting a feel for how people met others in the area.

But the idea that she and Autumn might have to do this *again* wasn't pleasant.

When "Roger Applegate" was in the seat across from her, Winter had to focus and work hard to keep her expression from giving her away. They politely shook hands and bantered, and while Winter was tempted to ask him if he had any suspects, they were too close to other couples for that type of conversation. It would have to wait.

When their seven minutes were over, she relished checking "no" in the box next to *Date Again?*

Finally, they reached the last date of the night, and Winter noticed that Woody #17 was now chatting with the young woman with the Hollywood smile, Connie #16. She was clearly charming his socks off.

Winter struggled to pay attention to her own date. Something felt off about Connie, although Winter wasn't sure what. The woman wasn't the only one in the place to wear false eyelashes, but did her hair look natural or could it have been a wig? Or extensions?

"Hello?"

Winter whipped her attention back to her annoyed looking date. "I'm sorry. What did you say?"

Cecil #18 sniffed. "I asked you what do you do for a living."

"I *love* Colorado!"

Winter barely contained her eyeroll at Connie #16's pronouncement. Instead, she smiled at her date. "I'm a consultant. What about you?" She made her smile wider. "You seem like an executive or president to me."

Bingo!

Now that she'd stroked his ego, Cecil was happy to go on

about his job. With one ear, she listened to the conversation beside her while maintaining eye contact with the man yammering on about the importance of properly applied insulation.

"I've always wanted to move there," Connie #16 was saying. "Do you know that the cheeseburger was invented in Denver? It's true. It was at a Humpty Dumpty restaurant."

"Is that right?" Woody's eyes sparkled. "I didn't know that."

"It's closed now, but there are a million interesting things about Colorado. I've never actually been there. It's probably really ordinary in reality. But ever since I was a little kid, I used to dream of going there."

Woody put his hand over hers. "I'm sure it would be interesting if you were there."

"...you should really look into buying stocks in my company right now." Cecil leaned closer and lowered his voice. "There will be a merger soon, and—"

Winter's attention whipped back to her date, and she held up a hand. "Whoa there. Isn't that insider trading?"

Cecil's eyes widened, and he scooted his chair back a couple inches. "N-n-no...of course not."

Winter immediately realized her mistake. She smiled and made herself giggle. "I'm just kidding." She batted her eyelashes again, hating herself to her core. "It's just that every time I hear anyone talking about buying stocks, I think of that poor Martha Stewart. I just don't understand what the crime was." Bat-bat-bat. "I bet she just hated wearing orange. It's so not her color."

Both she and Cecil were saved from having to say anything else when Heather Novak yelled, "Time!"

While Cecil scurried off, Winter noticed that Woody and Connie hadn't moved. They were gazing deeply into each other's eyes, their hands linked together like genuine lovers.

Which made Winter immediately suspicious.

"Time to review your cards and prepare to return them to me. If there are two 'yesses,' one from each of you, then I'll send you both a message containing the other's email. From there, you can decide whether to continue your budding relationship on your own."

As everyone rose from their seats, Winter noticed that Connie jotted something down on the corner of her dating card, tore it off, and handed it to Woody. As far as Winter could tell, both of them seemed to have stars in their eyes.

Winter shook her head in wonder. Who would have believed it? Love at first sight...at a speed-dating event. Either that or Connie was an *extremely* good actor.

A good con?

A good spider?

Now, if she could manage to pull out her phone and take a picture.

Pretending she was concentrating on her cards, Winter pulled her phone from her bag. But as she clicked the button, Connie #16 turned her head. Crap.

From the corner of her eye, she spotted Autumn heading her way, Heather Novak at her side. Winter tucked her phone away just as the pair reached her.

"Hello, it's so good to finally meet you," Heather gushed, taking Winter's hand. Beside her, Autumn looked pale, and Winter couldn't help but wonder if her intuitive friend had read something eerie from a similar introduction. "I was just talking to your friend and learned that you're both new to town. I'm sorry I didn't have time to talk to you earlier, but it's been a *day*."

She had pretty blue eyes, friendly but not naive. Winter would have put her age at about thirty. She wasn't wearing a wedding ring.

"No worries, Heather. Winter Miller."

"I remember from your registration information." She stepped closer to include both Winter and Autumn in the conversation. "And you're...Autumn Johnson? I'd ask if you were sisters with names like that, but you don't look too much alike." She laughed, the sound as boisterous as her voice. "Of course, in today's age, family can come in all kinds of shapes and sizes."

A little color seemed to enter Autumn's cheeks. "Our names are actually why we're friends," she told the organizer. "We were at the same restaurant, and when I heard someone call out her name, I knew I wanted to meet someone else with a seasonal name. A friendship was born."

Heather flashed a smile. Heather Novak had many smiles, Winter noted. Some warm and genuine, some quick and obviously superficial. Autumn had rated the latter. "How did you do tonight? Any luck?"

Winter nodded toward Connie and Woody, who were standing very close together, grinning as they whispered sweet nothings to each other. "Not as much as they had. I had fun, even if I did mostly strike out this time. I'm fine being a bit more selective until the right one comes along."

Autumn shrugged. "I just want some fun. I had a couple of maybes I marked down."

Someone called for Heather from the kitchen. She sighed, the fake smile jumping back to her face. "I have to get back to it but thank you for coming. I hope to see you again soon." She turned to face Autumn more fully. "I'll send your contact information on the maybes by tomorrow afternoon, if that's all right?"

She held out her hand to Autumn, and the moment their palms touched, Autumn shuddered and gripped a nearby table to keep from stumbling.

Heather put a hand on her shoulder, clearly concerned. "Are you all right? Do you need a seat?"

"Are *you* all right?" Autumn's face had grown very pale. "I can feel your anxiety and tension, and…your fear. Your anger."

Heather jerked like she'd been struck. "What? How…" Her eyes flew to Winter, but Winter was just about equally as stunned. "What are you talking about?"

"It's nothing. She gets migraines sometimes that come out of nowhere." Winter took Autumn's arm, concerned for her friend. They needed to get out of there. "Come on, Autumn. It's time to go."

But instead of following Winter's lead, Autumn shook her off, tears springing into her eyes. "I'm sorry. I shouldn't have said anything. But…but I have a touch of the…" She tapped her temple with an embarrassed little laugh. "I have an Irish grandmother."

Winter grabbed her arm again. "Autumn, it's time to go."

Autumn didn't move, her eyes nearly drilling a hole in Novak. "What are you afraid of, Heather?"

Heather just stared back at her, her eyes so wide that the surrounding whites were clear to see.

Winter put her arm around Autumn's shoulders, trying to steer her away, but Autumn stepped toward the stunned organizer. For a second, Winter thought Autumn was going to hug Heather, but instead, she took her hand. "We just want the murders to end too. Please believe me. We can help."

Heather took a step back. Her blue eyes flew back and forth between them. "Why are you really here? Did someone send you?"

Winter more forcibly took Autumn's arm. "I'm sorry. My friend is clearly not feeling well. The migraines…they're neurological. Sometimes she talks crazy, and sometimes she can't speak at all."

Which was what Winter desperately wished would happen right now.

Heather's face softened slightly. "That sounds terrible."

Over Heather's shoulder, Winter spotted Aiden staring in their direction. Shit. She focused back on the organizer, her hands tight on Autumn's arm.

"I'm going to get her home." Autumn was leaning heavily against her as she headed toward the door.

"Do you need assistance?" Heather asked.

Winter gave her a small smile. "No, I've got it. Thank you, though."

Autumn seemed dazed, her eyes fixed on something she couldn't see, until Winter pulled her into the foyer. She managed to get her friend's arms into her jacket and then led her outside to the car.

It wasn't until Winter had the vehicle started and the heat blowing at full blast that she turned in her seat. "Are you okay?"

Autumn blew out a breath and lifted both hands to cover her face. "Yes. I'm so sorry. I nearly blew our cover."

Nearly?

Winter wasn't sure that word applied to this situation. But right now wasn't the time to think of that. She needed to understand the situation.

"What happened? What did you feel?"

Autumn turned in her seat. "I'm not sure, but what Heather was feeling...it was like being tossed into Hell. *Something* is going on with her."

"Did you pick up any clues as to what that 'something' might be?"

Autumn pressed her fingertips to her temples. "No. I was too overwhelmed with her emotions. It was like being covered in boiling hot blood."

Winter winced. There was an image of Hell, all right. "Do you think she's the spider?"

"I don't know. I can't tell. But something is wrong, that much is clear."

Winter stared at the front door of the community center, wishing she could take a peek inside the woman's head—or at least her private emails and phone records. "Let's put her on the radar. I'm sure you're right. I just wish we knew whether it was related to the case or not." She sighed.

"What is it?"

Winter leaned against the headrest. "We need to tell Aiden that our cover might have been compromised."

Autumn blew out a long breath. "I know."

Reaching over, Winter squeezed Autumn's hand. "Trust me, this won't be the first and it won't be the last time an agent's cover is blown." She laughed. "Well, maybe the first time a potential suspect mentally punched an agent, causing her to compromise her cover."

That got a little smile. "It did feel like a punch."

Speaking the SSA's name caused him to appear through the community center door. Still on his arm was Miss Purple Hair. As they walked closer, Winter caught the woman's name. Nicole #5.

Aiden mouthed, "Dinner," when he was close enough for them to read his lips.

Winter nodded, and both she and Autumn watched him lead Nicole to his car. A few minutes later, he was pulling away. Winter blew out a relieved breath when a black SUV containing Miguel and Noah followed them.

When they were gone, Winter revved the engine of the powerful car a few times before backing out of the space. "Well, if Heather Novak turns out to be our spider," she put the car in drive and hit the gas, "I'll let you punch her back."

15

The lights in the main room of the community center were off. The chairs were upside-down on the tables, the floor had been swept, and the kitchen was clean.

But the night was never over until the information was in the computer. Because if she didn't email the eager boys and girls by the morning, they'd be stomping their virtual feet, demanding refunds and other such nonsense.

So pathetic.

Heather rubbed her temples. Normally, she wasn't this cynical, but tonight, she had a screaming headache. She rummaged around in her bag and pulled out a bottle of extra-strength ibuprofen. After shaking three of them into her hand, she swallowed them dry.

Grace Henderson, a happily married, fifty-year-old grandmother with apple cheeks, stepped into the tiny office she let Heather use on nights like this. Grace had been running the community center for over twenty years, and from what Heather could tell, the woman loved each and every brick of the place.

Grace put a key ring onto the desk. "Kitchen's all locked

up. Unless you need me for something else, I'm going home for the night. It was another good one."

A good one?

After that scene with Autumn Johnson and Winter Miller? Hardly. But she had to keep things running smoothly, no matter how difficult.

She laughed nervously, feeling more than a little off-center. "A full house, indeed, and everyone liked the ham."

Grace frowned, and Heather could tell that she wasn't doing a good job of covering her anxiety. "What happened with those two new women at the end there?" Grace asked, concern darkening her features. "Did they say something off to you? You seemed upset."

In addition to knowing every single person in the community, Grace was a busybody who enjoyed gossip as much as the tea and cake she served with it.

Heather looked Grace straight in the eye, putting on her most confident face. She had always been good at covering up the truth. "They were just new and wanted their notifications right away. I told them that I'd get the information to them by tomorrow afternoon. They were a little disappointed but understood."

Grace smiled, showing dimples. "That's good." Her dimples grew deeper.

Heather raised an eyebrow. "What?"

Grace clasped her hands over her heart. "That sweet Woody Waller." She sighed, deep and long. "He is just the nicest man, and to see that pretty Connie girl take to him like she did…" She sighed again. "They were just so adorable together. I hope things work out."

A twinge of guilt ran through Heather, but she refused to let it show on her face. "I hope so too. Everyone deserves love."

Not everyone.

She ignored the voice in her head, keeping her smile in place. "Well, goodnight, Grace. Have a safe drive home, and thanks so much for helping me tonight. I don't know what I'd do without you."

Grace beamed. "It's always my pleasure, dear. You have a good night too." Grace waved goodbye, and a few moments later, the back door closed behind her.

Heather dropped her forehead to the desk, enjoying the feel of the cool wood against her heated skin. What was she going to do?

That evening's event had made a tiny bit of profit, but not enough to shove her bottom-line numbers from red to black. But business numbers weren't what was weighing so heavily on her shoulders.

That Autumn woman had looked at her so closely, almost as if she could see into Heather's mind. Which, right now, wasn't a good place for anyone to inhabit.

Not a good place at all.

Forcing herself away from the well of self-pity, Heather straightened and ordered herself to finish the night's business. She chewed a thumbnail as she set up the emails for Connie and Woody to exchange information. These types of messages always contained suggestions on setting up a first date. She remembered Connie exclaiming about loving Colorado and typed in another line on Woody's email.

Don't forget that Denver is famous for their Denver-style omelets! Good luck!

She was just about to press send when her phone buzzed on the desk. She tapped the message app.

In case you didn't know, Connie is about to show Woody a real good time.

Heather scowled at the screen. She gave herself a moment to calm down before typing: *I wonder what the rush is? We're not in that much of a hurry.*

The phone immediately buzzed again. *Don't ask so many questions.*

Heather closed her eyes and waited for another melodramatic message to come through, but apparently, that was all for now. Giving herself a mental shake, she refocused on the tasks yet to do.

She hit send on the emails to Woody and Connie. After all, she didn't want it to look like she already knew they were hooking up so quickly.

Once that was done, she hurried through the other matches before closing the email program with a weary sigh. The spreadsheet with all the participants' contact information filled the screen.

Heather bit her lip as she scrolled through to Autumn Johnson's number. Should she call her sister and tell her about her run-in with the strange woman?

"I can feel your anxiety and tension, and...your fear. Your anger. What are you afraid of, Heather?"

Whether the woman had psychic abilities or not, she was right about one thing. Heather *was* worried.

About so many things.

16

The Busy Bee Bistro wasn't the kind of place Aiden would normally take a date, but his date had insisted that it was her favorite restaurant, so there they were. He was nearly blinded by the bright yellow and black stripes on both the walls and the ceilings. The yellow tables and black chairs made him want to cover his eyes and scream, but that meant he would need four hands because he also wanted to cover his ears.

Nicole Beyer hadn't stopped talking since they first got into his car. She was a pretty young thing. Twenty-four years old, about five-nine with her three-inch heels strapped to her feet. Deep brown eyes complimented dark red hair that turned purple in certain light. But that mouth…

He wanted to stuff his meatless meatball sub into it just to shut her up.

And yes…a meatless meatball was not only a contradiction in terms but should have also been a sin. But, after perusing the menu, it was the only thing he'd felt brave enough to try. He just wished it didn't come with Moroccan spices and pickled vegetables.

And he wished he'd eaten some of that ham at the speed-dating event instead of flirting with the ladies. Of course, he had no idea at the time that Nicole had additional plans for him.

"…and so my friend just couldn't believe that I'd be brave enough to really jump." She wiggled her eyebrows. "But you know I did. And let me tell you, once my body left the plane, I wished I could pull it right back in, but after that…it was just so thrilling. Too bad the free-fall part just lasts about a minute, then you're pulling the chute and holding your breath, just praying that the dang thing will open. Well, mine did, as you might have guessed or this story wouldn't be ending by us sitting here right now, now would it?" She flashed him a grin and mimed a jumper splatting the ground with her hands. "So, we floated, I'm not sure how long, but I got some amazing pictures. Want to see?"

And so it went…blah…blah…freakin' blah.

He made the appropriate noises as she slid from one picture to the next while explaining them in every…single…detail. By the time their food came, Aiden thought Nicole Beyer might very well be their spider because she must bore every single man she dated to death.

She giggled. "I still can't get over how fit you are, Roger. I mean, do you workout? Of course you workout. I've always been interested in older men. I mean, I haven't been *exclusively* interested in older men. I've dated some younger men too. They never hold my chair, and they always try to tell me that I shouldn't order whatever I want to order. 'Nicole, why are you always on a diet,' they ask. 'Why are you always at the gym?' I'm a gym rat, although obviously, I don't have the muscles you do. It's all that testosterone you hunky men have. I have to work ten times as hard to get these skinny little muscles. It's like, no matter how much you work, you can only get so much out of your pretty little gym muscles. I was trying to help a friend of mine build a rock wall for her yard the other day and I thought I would *die*. Why do rocks have to weigh so much? I mean, the ones you buy in the store. Couldn't they like, make them lighter or something? But, anyway, after we rocked her yard, we..."

As close to death as he currently was, Aiden knew in his gut that Nicole wasn't their killer. She might be looking for a sugar daddy, but Aiden doubted this woman could stop talking long enough to plan a trip to the grocery store, let alone a murder.

Annoying as she was, she wasn't the one who'd mercilessly stabbed these widowers in the back.

Aiden finished his surprisingly tasty food before Nicole had managed to eat more than a few bites. Even then, she groaned and claimed to be "stuffed" before asking Aiden to get a to-go box for her leftovers.

"Pretty please with a strawberry on top." She giggled and attempted to stuff one of the berries in his mouth. He tried to avoid it, but Nicole and her skinny little muscles was strong and refused to give up until he just opened his mouth and accept his fate. Maybe she'd laced it with arsenic, putting him out of his misery.

She was chugging the last of her skim venti mocha no whip extra shot when he limped back to their table. Having a rock in his shoe was a damn pain in the ass, but now he limped even harder, planning to use gout flare-up or some other elderly shit as an excuse to get the hell away from this place. Sans Nicole, of course.

Then it hit him...she had ridden with him. What in the world had he been thinking?

"I really like your ride," she said the moment they were back in his rented Lexus.

"Thanks," he muttered, trying to remember if he was

supposed to turn left or right. The extra gray and wrinkles were probably making him senile.

"I like you too." She giggled, her hand moving from caressing the leather console to caressing his thigh. "I like you a lot."

Shit. Shit. Shit.

Aiden cleared his throat. "You're a very nice girl."

The hand moved higher, and she leaned closer. Her warm breath caressed the side of his face. "I'm no girl. I'm all woman."

What had happened to the giggling dingbat? What had happened to the motormouth?

She'd changed.

Anxiety raced up his spine, and he glanced over to see her face.

She smiled, her hand now dangerously close to his zipper. Were those...fangs?

No. He relaxed a little. He was just seeing the shadow of the streetlights hitting her face in an eerie pattern, but still... Aiden glanced in his rearview mirror, comforted by the headlights of an SUV thirty yards back.

His testicles squeezed together, caught in an iron grip that was as strong as it had been unexpected. He nearly yelped in surprise and pain, and somehow managed not to drive them into a ditch.

"Easy there," he said and tried to remove her hand. It didn't move. It was like her palm was welded to his groin.

"You like it rough, don't you?" She'd unbuckled her seat belt and was now attempting to climb over the console. "I like it rough too, Roger Woger Doger. Can I call you Daddy?" She pressed her lips to his ear, causing his fake hearing aid to squeal.

In his other ear, Vasquez and Dalton were laughing their asses off.

"Vanilla," Aiden hissed, hoping the mic would pick his voice up. He now better understood why Winter had called it his "safe word." It was really his code word for "danger-danger...get me the hell out of here."

Nicole moaned and licked the side of his face. "I like vanilla too. Want me to rub a big glob of vanilla or maybe some chocolate all over that big fat c—"

"Vanilla!"

She jerked back in surprise as he yelled the word, but only a little. "Okay, okay...vanilla it is. Geez. Don't be cranky...Daddy."

Laughter continued to ring in his ear, and when it became very clear that his cavalry wasn't planning to ride to his rescue any time soon, he did the only thing he could think to do. He hit the brakes, and then, with all the drama he could muster, grabbed his chest with both hands.

"My heart!" he cried, wincing as if in great pain.

Nicole's tongue moved away from his ear as quickly as her hand jerked away from his crotch. "Oh no! What do you need me to do? I know CPR."

"Help!" He half closed his eyes and let his head loll to the side.

Nicole screamed but had her head on straighter than he would have suspected. She thrust the car into park, wailing, "I'll save you," as she climbed onto his lap. As if she was familiar with all the buttons, she reached down and guided his seat back until he was practically laying down.

"Vanilla," he whispered.

Howls of laughter were his only response as Nicole straddled his thighs and began to pump his chest to the beat of "Another One Bites the Dust." He knew the tune because she was singing the damn song to guide her compressions.

Nicole yelped when someone pounded on the Lexus's

window. She kept pumping his chest with one hand while rolling the window down with the other. "Help! Call 911!"

Dalton's face appeared in the opening. He was trying his best to look serious, but the twitching lips almost gave him away.

"I'm a paramedic," he said. "Off duty. My friend will take you home while I take over here."

"Oh, thank god!"

Dalton reached in and unlocked the door, but once it was open, Nicole just stared up at him, looking more than a little dumbstruck. Dalton gave her his most brilliant smile. "If you could, um, get off him, miss?"

"Oh…" She scrambled, her knee sinking right into Aiden's testicles in her haste.

Aiden moaned, for real this time. Dalton, apparently feeling sorry for him by now, reached in and scooped Nicole out of his lap and into his arms.

"Oh, you're so strong? Do you workout?" One arm went around Dalton's neck while the other massaged a thick bicep. "I workout, but I could never get my little bittie muscles to ever get so big."

As if God had reached down and personally delivered Aiden's most fervent prayer, the now simpering voice faded as Dalton walked away. In the mirror, he watched him put her on her feet, then grinned when Nicole launched herself into the big agent's arms, clearly intent on never letting go.

The smile slid away as Aiden realized he'd been effectively dumped by a gold digger in his hour of "need."

Vasquez, whose laughter was still ringing in Aiden's ear, finally got out of the car and gently led the damned woman into the SUV's passenger seat.

"Purse…purse…purse…" Aiden called into his microphone.

Dalton jumped into gear and opened the Lexus's

passenger door. He was still grinning as he grabbed the bag but was gone before Aiden could curse him out or fire him, he wasn't sure exactly which.

The moment the purse was handed off, Vasquez hit the gas, and Aiden inhaled deeply, still laying where Nicole had left him. The car rocked as Dalton climbed in and slammed the door shut.

"Want me to drive?"

Not answering, Aiden reached down and found the button that raised the seat. Equally slowly, he rammed the car into drive.

Beside him, Dalton snickered but was wise enough to keep his mouth shut.

Aiden's ego was throbbing, like it'd taken a lick from a hammer. Worse than that, he felt...molested, both physically and emotionally.

That silent admission came as a surprise, and as he drove back to the police station, he realized just how easy a man could be lured into a spider's web.

If he hadn't been on the job with two bozos listening to everything he said, he would have been charmed by the beautiful woman's attention, and if she'd had the ability to close her mouth, he could see himself easily taking her home with him. And he would have done so even though he'd felt certain she was after him for money.

He suddenly found himself with more insight into how older men were getting pulled into these schemes. What the women wanted sounded harmless at first, a few bucks here and there, but it was all too easy to get one's ego caught up in the situation, even without sex thrown in to sweeten the pot.

At the station, Aiden pulled up to the door, both hands on the steering wheel, eyes forward.

"You okay?" Dalton asked after a moment. The words cracked with humor.

"Get out."

Dalton cleared his throat. "Copy that."

Aiden blinked as the interior lights clicked on, but just before Dalton closed the door, Aiden leaned over and met the other man's eyes. "If you say a word about this, I'll personally make sure that you'll be guarding penguins in the South Pole."

Dalton gave him a little salute. "Case stamped confidential."

Aiden hit the gas, the door slamming from the force. He drove straight to his hotel, went straight to his room, disrobing on the way to the shower.

Half an hour later, after all the makeup was gone and his hair was normal again, he plopped on his bed and did something he knew he'd regret...picked up his phone.

Opening the dating app where his Roger Applegate profile was live, he half expected a message from Nicole asking him if he was okay, but instead, he found a review. The app was one that allowed participants to "rate" each other with a series of hearts.

"Don't do it," he told himself, even as his thumb clicked the button.

Three hearts out of five. Average.

Ouch.

Seriously?

After all he'd just been through? The woman was coldhearted. She...

He tossed his phone away and scrubbed his face with both hands. He needed to get a grip and pull his head out of his ass. But as he lay there in the dark, one thing became clear.

He was no longer worried about the spider taking him down. His pride wasn't going to survive this case.

17

"Your name is Connie. Your name is Connie."

Courtney repeated the reminder over and over as she chewed on the inside of her cheek, watching Woody's taillights ahead of her like a hawk. He was driving slowly, using his blinker about a quarter mile before each turn, and stopped at every yellow light.

Clearly, he didn't want to lose her. He wanted her to follow him home.

He was so sweet. So interesting. So...

She forced herself to swallow, even though her mouth was dry as cotton. She was nervous. She was going to get in so much trouble.

Because sweet and interesting wasn't supposed to matter.

Nothing was supposed to matter except for the rules:

Don't rush things.

Stay in control.

No sex on the first date.

Take them for every penny you can.

And for the love of baby Jesus, don't forget your alias.

With Woody, she didn't want to follow the rules, and she knew that would get her in trouble. Did she care?

She considered the question as she made yet another right turn.

No. Well, yes and no. She did care but not enough to skip this opportunity.

Woody was the most charming man she'd met in a *long* time. He made her laugh. Wasn't that good enough? He liked her, that much was obvious. She had seen Heather roll her eyes at her outburst about Colorado, but every word of it had been true. She had *always* dreamed of going west, of living high in the mountains. It had just never worked out.

Very little ever worked out for her.

When she had burst out excitedly with a random piece of Colorado trivia, her first reaction was to feel ashamed of wrecking a perfectly good setup for a "date," because she'd broken yet another rule. *Be elegant with these older men.*

But her real self had been bottled up for so long—and Courtney was bad at bottling—that it had all come rushing out before she could stop herself.

And Woody had liked it.

Sure, he was much older than her. Nearly sixty years old to her twenty-three, but she didn't mind the age difference. In fact, she quite enjoyed the comfort of being safe with someone so much older and wiser. Maybe a bit of that wisdom would transfer to her.

She smiled, remembering how he had stuttered like a teenager when he'd asked her if she might want to see him again. He'd blushed when she'd whispered, "Yes," in his ear before writing her phone number on the corner of her date card.

When it was time to leave the community center, both discovered that neither wanted to wait another day to meet again. He'd barely made it halfway through his question

—"Would you like to come home..."—before she whispered, "Yes," meaning it with all her heart.

Which had never happened to her before.

Woody's turning light blinked again, and Courtney was relieved to see that they'd arrived at a normal looking driveway, but it didn't lead to a normal looking house. Not even a normal house for the types of men that usually attended Heather's events.

"Holy shit," Courtney whispered, her guts clenching. "Holy shit."

She'd hit the gold mine. Except, with Woody, mining for treasure was the last thing on her mind.

This was both an opportunity, but also a problem. Woody was rich. *Filthy* rich.

"Concentrate," she belittled herself. She needed to stop thinking of fairy tales and happily ever afters because, after everything she'd done...

Happy wasn't in her future.

She took a deep breath. She was being a fool. Maybe Heather had spiked her drink with some potion that made her think crazy thoughts. No, not Heather. Heather was only focused on money. Focused on saving her little business so she didn't end up looking like a failure, which to Courtney's oldest sister, was a fate worse than death.

And Courtney was supposed to help her. She was supposed to help them all, but when would enough be enough?

Enough was supposed to have been two states ago. Then one. Then "soon." Then... "We can't stop until there's enough for each of us to live on for the rest of our lives."

But what "enough" was, Courtney didn't know.

Realizing that her fingers were growing numb from gripping the steering wheel so tightly, she forced her fingers to release, then her jaw, then her shoulders. Finally, she inhaled deeply and made her decision.

She could do this. Go in, enjoy herself, get at least twenty grand out of him, and run. Very, very far away. So far away that she would never be able to remember how safe he'd made her feel.

Safe.

It had been so long since that word was in her vocabulary.

She whispered, "Oh shit," once again as they passed a gushing fountain and then a statue that made her want to get out of the car and touch the stone that had so brilliantly been carved into an angel on the verge of taking flight.

Tears pricked her eyes, unwanted as they were unexpected. Courtney blinked rapidly, praying they didn't spill, giving evidence of her twisting emotions.

They pulled past the front door and toward a side wing with an untold number of garage doors, lined like soldiers in a row. Two of the doors opened, and Woody pulled his Lexus inside the one closest to the main house. Courtney stopped, not sure what to do. When Woody appeared and walked over to her little Corolla, her heart started beating fast.

What if he was as good at acting as she was?

What if he had devious plans for her just as she had devious plans for him?

No one could be that nice, after all. That perfect. That…real.

Charm was one of nature's most powerful camouflages, after all.

Courtney knew that all too well.

"Would you like to park inside?" He stuffed his hands into his pockets, rocking back onto his heels. "It might snow tonight, and then I'd have to come out and scrape the ice off your windows."

Courtney just gazed into his sweet face. He could be a

serial killer. He could have lured silly women just like her back to his castle and tossed them in his dungeon.

Her gaze wandered from his face to the enormous house in front of her. The steep pitch and multiple angles did give the home a castle-like appearance.

"I should have warned you."

She almost asked him why, then understood that he was talking about the extent of his wealth and gave him a teeny tiny nod. "Your home is very beautiful...and large."

He laughed, making the wrinkles by his eyes crinkle up. "It's too much, I know. But..." He lifted a shoulder. "My great-great-grandfather commissioned it to be built, and it's been the home for Wallers for generations."

It clicked. Standing before her was Woodrow Frederick Waller, the fifth. Sole heir of the Waller steel fortune.

Overwhelmed, her eyes trailed to the row of garages, and he laughed.

"Well, maybe I added the garages, and maybe I have a little fetish for restoring old cars."

She swallowed hard. Woody was in a financial league that she didn't need to be playing with. If she were caught, he had an army of lawyers that would see her rot under a jail. And she would go to jail, no question. His family's connections with presidents and powerful political figures was well known.

How had this happened?

She was about to put her little car in reverse and speed away, when he leaned in through her car window and kissed her softly on the cheek. "Don't worry, Connie. You don't have to do anything you don't want to do. I just want to spend more time with a woman who holds Colorado deep in her heart."

She giggled. She couldn't help herself. Tears prickled her eyes, and she forced them back. He was so sweet.

One night.

As she gazed into his eyes, Courtney knew one thing. She couldn't scam this man. She wouldn't. And…if she had no plans to harm him in any way, wouldn't it be okay to allow herself one night to feel cherished?

With a shaky nod, she put her car into drive and pulled into the empty bay. As she stepped out, the rolling door began closing off the cold air from outside. She hefted her purse onto her shoulder.

Another rule: *Always be prepared.*

She decided to add another rule to her list: *Don't get attached.*

Woody took her hand, and she linked her fingers between his. When she paused in front of an ancient looking Porsche, she had to stop and admire its beauty.

Woody beamed at her and moved to the side and opened the car's door. "My very first restoration. It's a 1966 Porsche 912 I saw sitting on blocks in this old man's yard." Courtney gaped at him, and he laughed. "Bought it for a thousand dollars, and it took me nearly a year to find all the parts, then another year to baby it into the shape it is now."

"It's beautiful." Tears pricked at her eyes, and she didn't even know why. Well, maybe she did. "I love that you saw beauty in something old and worn. You didn't turn your back on it, didn't reject it, didn't look for a new model to replace it."

Like her dad did her mother.

Woody wiped her cheek, and it was only then that she realized her tears had spilled over. With that soft touch, Courtney began to cry in earnest.

She found herself wrapped in strong arms, lean fingers stroking her back. He didn't ask her what was wrong, nor did he try to soothe or urge her to hush.

He just held her. No judgement. No rebukes.

When she finally calmed enough to pull her head back, he pressed a linen handkerchief into her hand. She wiped her cheeks, offering a small, embarrassed laugh. "I'm sorry. I don't know what happened there."

"I do," Woody said softly, and she lifted her head to see his expression.

Did he know? Did he know she was a horrible person who preyed on men? Did he know she was a whore and a slut and a thief and a manipulator?

"You have a wise, old soul, Connie."

Courtney closed her eyes. Even her name was a lie.

She couldn't do this. Not with him.

"Woody, I…"

Say it. Just say it.

Her phone vibrated in her purse, the surprise of it making her jump. Making her come back to reality. Come back to her senses.

"What, dearest Connie?" He tucked a strand of hair behind her ear.

Connie.

Yes, she was Connie right now.

She had a job to do.

She had people who relied on her. Needed her.

People she was afraid to let down.

Taking a deep breath, she pulled her shoulders back and smiled. "When you move to Colorado, I don't think this Porsche will get you through the snow."

He studied her face, and for a moment, she didn't think he'd let her get away with the change of subject. Then he took her hand and squeezed it. "That's why I restored this ancient Jeep."

She followed him to where the sturdy vehicle sat. She listened to him talk about the renovation process and how the tank-like truck could now plow through the highest snow.

"Come with me, Connie."

The name brought her back to the conversation, and she realized she'd zoned into another place, another time, another snow.

Don't you dare come back in until the job is finished.

She'd only been nine at the time, the snow shovel almost bigger than her. She was frozen, her fingers numb, but no matter how much she shoveled, the falling flakes covered her efforts back up.

That was the day when she knew her father saw her and her sisters and her mother only for what they could do for him.

The selfish bastard.

"Connie?"

Courtney shook her head, shaking off the memories. He was why she was here now. Her daddy dearest, who'd abandoned them all, over and over and over. And the selfish man had abandoned them without ever leaving their lives.

She smiled up at Woody. "Come where?"

He looked at her funny, and she knew she'd missed something important. To cover up her mistake, she did what she did best…she stepped closer to him, pressing her breasts into his chest. She wrapped her arms around his neck and pulled him down for a kiss.

Their first kiss, and she was Connie…not Courtney.

"Let's go inside," she whispered against his mouth.

He took her by the hand, and she followed him into what in most houses would be called a mudroom, although this mudroom was bigger than most living spaces and filled with boots and jackets and coats of different sizes.

"Sorry for the mess," Woody said. "There's a fancy door in

the front, but I only use it for..." He turned pink again under the fluorescent lights of the mudroom.

"For fancy guests," she finished for him, hurt for reasons she didn't want to think about.

He touched her cheek with the back of his hand. "You're a fancy guest."

Something in her throat loosened. "I'm not. I have *never* once been a fancy guest. I grew up so poor I thought putting peanut butter in our ramen was special."

Not because her father didn't have money, but because he didn't want to waste his "hard-earned money" on them.

She blinked the memory away as he pulled her into his arms again. He began to whistle, and after only a couple of notes, she picked up on the tune, "Wouldn't It Be Nice" by the Beach Boys.

He began to sway, waltzing her out of the mudroom and into an enormous kitchen with an island so big she could have camped on it.

The whistling transitioned to a slower tune. "God Only Knows."

God did indeed know. Guilt wrapped its fist around her heart, and she buried her face into Woody's chest.

She needed to get out of there before she spilled all her secrets to this man.

After what seemed like hours, Courtney took a step back from him. The way he looked at her made her feel so special. She needed to go, run away from this place. But first...

With shaky fingers, she began to unbutton his shirt. Then she was in his bed. Then her body was feeling what her heart had already felt.

A connection.

Afterwards, she lay in a tangle of limbs and sheets, listening to the soft sounds of Woody's breath as he slept. She was physically sated. Spiritually filled.

Emotionally barren.

Because she knew what she needed to do next.

Slipping from the bed, she gathered her clothes and bag. She walked past the vases and treasures that, at auction, would bring more than she could ever steal.

Back in the kitchen, she found the shoes she'd kicked off only a few hours ago.

Her phone buzzed, and she pulled it from her bag.

Ten texts. Three missed calls.

Finding the door that led to her car, she tapped the icon for Heather. The call was answered on the first ring.

"Where are you!?"

Tossing her bag into the passenger seat, she slid behind the wheel. "On my way home." It wasn't a lie completely.

"Did you score?"

Shame closed Courtney's eyes. The word was ugly, compared to how Woody had treated her.

"I don't know how long I can keep playing this game, sissy. It's getting too hard. This guy, he's—"

"Loaded." Heather barked out the word. "That guy is loaded. That's all that matters." Her sister sighed. "Don't forget why you're there. Nothing but lint, Court. You know that."

"I know, I know." She realized the garage door was still down and got out of the car to find the button to send it up. "I'm just tired of it, that's all."

"We're almost done. Don't lose sight of your primary purpose." The phone's screen went dark.

Courtney made a face. She hated being hung up on.

She suddenly didn't feel like being Courtney…or Connie or Candace or Charlotte or Claire or Clara or any name that began with a C.

Courtney was a criminal who used lonely men for their money. Courtney felt sick to her stomach a lot of the time, worrying about her sisters and about getting caught. Courtney felt like she was never going to be able to let down her guard ever again.

Once they escaped, she would change her name. She'd become Eva. Eva meant life, and Courtney very much needed to live. Live out from under the shadow of her family, out from under the shadow of her past deeds.

Maybe she would become Arabella…lovely and elegant.

Or Avery…wise.

The word made her tear up again, and she desperately wanted to leave this garage and crawl back into bed with the very wise man who'd somehow managed to capture her attention and her heart.

Which was stupid!

"Stop being stupid!" she told her reflection in the rearview mirror as she put her little Corolla into reverse.

She'd just had a weak moment because she was worried about her big sisters. Worried that they'd be caught before they could escape.

The back of her hair stood on end as she thought of Katherine.

She'd killed a man. *Men.* In self-defense, sure. Or was it?

Katherine was changing, morphing into a person Courtney didn't recognize.

Maybe that was why she was clinging to Woody. Maybe she wanted to stay with him for a different reason. A reason she was almost scared to name.

Maybe it had nothing to do with Woody at all. Maybe she wanted to stay here because she was afraid to go home.

18

"Nice place." George Marsh didn't hide his curiosity as he checked out my little cottage. "It's got a real Cape Cod feel, and all the way out in the middle of nowhere. Nice. Private."

When he ran out of false compliments on my shithole of a childhood home, I purred, "Why don't you come in?"

He bobbed his eyebrows. "Why don't I?"

As I closed the door behind me, I locked it and smiled. What had happened with Allen Newhouse wasn't going to happen this time.

No relatives banging on the door, taking me by surprise.

No rushing in this little cottage, because here, I could take all the time I needed.

After our first date, I'd broken my own rules and gone with George to his home. I'd let him kiss and fondle me... after giving me a full tour of his six thousand square foot mansion. But no sex.

"Not on the first date," I'd murmured to him.

He'd been panting when he said, "Can I see you again tomorrow night?"

So, here we were. No date in public because I'd promised to cook him a nice meal. Hooking my arm through his, I led him toward my tiny kitchen.

The best way to a man's heart is through his stomach, my poor mother had often said.

She was wrong.

The best way to a man's heart was with a knife.

Picking up a very sharp one, I slashed it down. Again. Again. Again.

George's eyes were wide as he watched me chop the greens for our salad. Perhaps I got a little carried away? According to the spinach and the expression on my date's face, that would be a yes.

Loosening my grip on the handle, I gave him one of my sexiest smiles. "Will you pour?" I nodded toward a perfectly chilled bottle of wine.

He moved quickly to do as I said, and soon, the cool alcohol moistened my dry mouth.

"This smells delicious. Can I help do anything?"

I gave him my brightest Karen smile. "Just keep me company. I just need to toss this, and we'll be ready to eat."

The table I'd already set was tucked into a little nook with wallpaper peeling from the walls in large sections. Candles made the shabby area look less shabby but didn't hide its disrepair completely.

Which was exactly what I wanted... a mixture of humble and proud.

Men ate that combination up with a spoon and fork.

As I chopped the broccoli, I was glad I'd changed the plan.

I'd almost invited George to my little apartment downtown I rented for dates like these. In fact, I'd been meaning to write down the apartment's address to give George when I found that my hand had other ideas. Better ideas.

Downtown, I'd have neighbors to worry about.

Downtown, I'd have to worry about my control slipping.

But here, so isolated and alone, I had to worry about nothing. It was perfect. I could be me and see how it all played out.

But first, I needed to give George another chance to prove his loyalty to his late wife.

As I scooped tomatoes onto the greens, I glanced up at him and asked as casually as I could, "Did your wife cook for you often?"

The smile disappeared from his face, and he stared at me for several seconds before lifting his glass to his lips. He was stalling. Deciding whether to betray or be faithful.

Which would it be?

I had to force my hands to keep moving, adding diced carrots to the bowl. Act as if his answer meant nothing to me at all.

He cleared his throat, then coughed in his hand. "Is that lasagna I smell?"

Interesting. Disappointment mingled with excitement as George changed the subject. Choosing to not answer my question was a choice. Did he not realize that?

Because I did.

Stabbing the knife into the cutting board, I smiled, glad that my acting classes made the gesture appear to be natural. "It sure is. My mama's recipe, in fact."

He still looked uncomfortable as he stood to pour himself another glass of wine. "My mother was a wonderful cook too," he said, topping my glass off as well.

Figures. That's what women did, after all. Cooked and cleaned and pampered the men who did nothing to earn their hard work.

What were women if not slaves?

And what happened when we died?

They kicked some dirt on our graves and moved on, that's what.

"Are you okay?"

Jerking my attention back to my kitchen, I noticed that I was holding the salad tongs mid toss. I needed to focus. Needed to play my role as a sweet little thing instead of the cynical man-hater I'd become.

"Absolutely. It just occurred to me that I hadn't heard back from my, um, roommates about them not coming home too early tonight." I winked at him. "Don't want any interruptions, do we?"

His smile faltered a little. "You have roommates?" He looked around the cottage, almost like he was wondering where any other human could possibly fit.

"Two of them, actually."

His surprise was almost comical. "Two?"

"Yep." I looked down, giving him an embarrassed expression. "Girl's got to do what she's got to do to pay the rent."

Wrinkles furrowed on his forehead. "How big is this place?"

He was judging me. I didn't like to be judged.

Lifting a shoulder, I placed the salad on the table before heading back for the dressing. "Big enough."

"If you don't mind me asking, what is your rent?"

I turned and opened the fridge to hide my smile. This was how it always started, by them wanting to help. But what they really meant was that they wanted to give just enough to make me feel beholden to them. Men were so predictable.

"Rent is actually pretty reasonable, especially since I split everything three ways." Closing the door, I faced him again, salad dressing in hand. I made sure to lean close to him as I set it on the table, brushing my leg against his when I turned back to retrieve the rest of the meal. "It's the student loans that kill me. Even working two jobs, it's…" I put my embarrassed expression back on and grabbed the oven mitts. "Never mind that." I pulled the lasagna from the oven. "Let's eat."

He seemed an equal mix stupefied and embarrassed, and I could practically hear him asking *how can you afford such an expensive dish.* "Uh...that looks as amazing as it smells. At the very least, let me pay for the groceries. A lasagna like that couldn't have been cheap."

Oh...he'd pay for the groceries all right.

"I could never let you do that," I demurred, placing the lasagna in the middle of the table. "I wanted you here." I let my eyes drop to his mouth for a beat, then two, then three. He licked his lips, which was my cue to look away.

His hand covered mine. "Karen, I want to be here too, but not if I'm a burden."

My heart kicked up speed. Dating was like a dance. You stepped closer, then stepped back. You circled close, then circled away. It was time for me to step closer again.

So, I did. Close enough to smell the expensive aftershave he'd splashed on his cheeks. Then closer still.

"You could never be a burden, George," I said softly before lifting his hand until it covered my breast. I moaned when he squeezed. "Are you hungry right now?" The words came out breathy and full of need, even though this seduction scene was such a bore.

He was breathing hard, his pupils dilated into two huge circles. "Yes...I'm starving. For you."

Despite the lameness of the line, I took his hand and led him from the kitchen and into my bedroom. He stood where I told him to stand as I removed each article of my clothing. "If you move, you'll be punished," I told him when I was completely bare. I smiled, nodding toward his pants. "Your turn."

Gravity wasn't as big of a bitch to men as it was to

women. Their bodies held up against the ravages of time better than ours, but his skin sagged in unfortunate places, and he'd clearly never heard of the term "manscape."

Once he was naked, it didn't take much to convince him to let me tie a blindfold around his eyes.

Taking his hand, I led him to stand on a rug I'd already prepared for this moment. Sheets of plastic were layered underneath to catch any spills. "On your knees."

He didn't hesitate, nor did he do anything but moan when I clamped the cuffs around his wrists. He shivered when I dragged the strings of a flogger up and down his back.

Being so secluded, I didn't bother with slipping the ball gag between his lips. Instead, I opened my special drawer and pulled one of my special knives out.

"George, I have an important question to ask you," I said as I knelt in front of him.

His heart was beating hard, evidenced by the pulse throbbing in his neck. He was turned on, evidenced by his...well, his sad little penis pointing straight at me.

Placing the knife on the floor beside me, I leaned forward and pressed my lips to his. His response was immediate, and his tongue plunged into my mouth. Disgust born of painful memories tightened my throat, and I pulled away, wiping the back of my hand over my mouth as I reached for the crop.

I wanted to scream. I wanted to pummel him with my fists. Instead, I stared into his blindfolded eyes. "Time for your test."

"Yes, mistress."

"Have you been bad?"

He chuckled. "Very bad, mistress."

"How have you been bad?"

"I've had lusty thoughts about you since the moment we met."

Forcing laughter into my voice, I swatted his thigh with the crop. "Oh, really?"

"Yes, mistress."

My heart picked up speed. This was make or break time. One last chance for him to redeem himself.

"Do you love your wife?"

His entire body twitched, and the cuffs rattled as he tried to escape their bonds.

My heart was like a rabbit in my chest as I waited... waited...waited...

"I...of course...um—"

Not good enough.

I brought the crop down hard on his shoulder. The skin welted immediately. "Do you?" My voice had a near hysterical edge to it that I didn't like at all. I took a breath deep enough to calm down.

He was panting now, trying to back away from me. "Yes... I, yes!"

I hit him again, even harder this time. "You're lying!"

He jerked back so hard he fell over on his side. "I...I...I want to stop."

I laughed, throwing my head back to give the sound all my volume. "Stop? You want to stop?" I laughed again. "You don't get to just stop. Your wife didn't get to just stop from dying, you know?"

He screamed when I brought the crop down hard on his belly, his chest, his penis. "Don't—"

I hit him again and again, and he was weeping by the time I could make myself toss the crop away.

"This isn't over until I say it's over," I screamed at him, not caring about my voice or the emotion it carried. "These are my rules, my game."

He sobbed harder. "I-I-I'm s-s-sorry."

I scoffed, disgusted by the display. "So, you're sorry now?"

Bending, I picked up the knife. That's when I noticed that the blindfold had fallen from his left eye.

Eyeing the sharp blade, he tried to back away, but with his hands behind his back, he could do little more than roll. "Wh-what are you d-doing?"

With a foot, I rolled him onto his back, then lowered myself until I straddled his belly. Waving the knife in front of his one open eye, I smiled. "I'm avenging your bride."

"Wh—"

The word was lost as I slid the blade across his throat, and a geyser of blood wrapped me in its warm embrace.

George's mouth worked, his body jerking as he desperately tried to move his hands to his throat. Sounds I couldn't recognize came from him. Not words, though. A damaged larynx saved me from the questions I knew were running through his oxygen-starved brain.

I licked my lips. Salty warmth burst over my tastebuds. I licked them again, longer this time.

"Why?" I asked his question for him. "Is that what you're wanting to know? I'll tell you why. You're dying right now because you're a traitor. A deceiver. On behalf of your late wife, I now commit thee to hell."

I was going to say more, but the allure of his blood was too much. I pressed my lips to skin and sucked...savored... not stopping until I'd had my fill.

Power surged through me as his DNA mixed with mine. Fueling me. Giving me his life.

Renewed now, I opened my eyes and pushed to my feet, stepping in his draining life force as I rolled him onto his stomach. This was my favorite part.

Lifting the knife high, I watched as it slammed down, sinking deeply near his spine with a satisfying crunch.

Betrayal. Treachery.

Revenge.

With Brice, I'd enjoyed pressing my body to his where he knelt. With Allen, I'd been robbed of the opportunity to relish this moment because...*knock, knock, knock*...exsanguination interruptus.

Now, I could take my time.

The pulse at his throat still moved in and out, though much slower than before. Needing to watch, I lifted his blindfold completely away from his face and lowered myself to the floor so I could look straight into his eyes.

They jittered in his eye sockets. Tears streaked on his skin.

"So, you'll cry for yourself but not for the mother of your children?"

He didn't answer.

"Are you sorry for betraying her so badly?"

His mouth moved, but no words came forth.

A minute passed as I laid with him, my fingers on his cheek as his pulse grew weaker. Weaker. Weaker.

And when it stopped, I was whole.

19

Courtney sat in her car, wondering what to do. She hadn't seen the text from Katherine until she was nearly home.

Brought a man home. Stay clear.

Stay clear to where?

She didn't have enough cash on her to get a hotel room, and she didn't want to go back to Woody's. She'd been too vulnerable with him. Too needy. She needed to stay away from men like that…period.

So, there she sat, at the base of their driveway, staring at the red light that told her that her gas tank was almost empty. What should she do?

Headlights swept across her car, and she sat up straighter as she realized the vehicle was pulling in. Please don't be the cops. But when the Civic stopped beside her, she realized it was her oldest sister.

Heather rolled her window down and Courtney did the same.

"What are you doing?" Heather called. "Car trouble?"

Courtney shook her head and lifted her phone. "Didn't you get Katherine's text?"

Heather frowned and went digging for her device. Her face lit up as the screen came on. A second later, she was saying something Courtney couldn't hear. Probably a string of curses so nasty they'd make a sailor blush.

"You've got to be kidding me," Heather yelled.

Courtney was about to yell back, but instead turned off her car and circled around to Heather's passenger door. The locks clicked, and she slid inside. She sighed. Heather's heater worked much better than her own.

She shivered and held her hands up to the blowing air. "What should we do?"

Heather muttered another stream of curses under her breath. "We should drive to our house and kick our sister's ass."

Courtney smiled, but the grin faded quickly. "What do you think she's doing, bringing a man here?"

That wasn't the question she really wanted to ask. No, the question on her mind was much deeper and darker than that.

When Heather turned and their eyes met, Courtney could tell that she was thinking very nearly the same thing.

Katherine was losing it.

But instead of speaking directly about the elephant in the room, Heather sank back into her seat. "Something very strange happened tonight after you left with Woody. Which, by the way, you were *not* supposed to do on a first date."

Courtney lifted her chin. "I was following my instincts."

"Fine. As long as everything went smoothly."

She forced Woody from her mind. "Super smooth, but don't change the subject. What happened after I left?"

Heather rubbed her hand, almost as if something had pained her. Courtney examined her big sister more closely. Heather didn't seem herself. She seemed weaker somehow.

"The woman you were sitting next to. The one with the dark hair and those intense blue eyes."

Courtney struggled to bring up a name. "Winter?"

"That's the one. She was there with a friend, a redhead named Autumn."

Winter and Autumn? The names made Courtney smile. "And...?"

Heather rubbed her hand harder. "And Autumn went completely apeshit on me."

"Apeshit how?"

"We were chatting for a moment, and when I went to say goodbye, I shook their hands. Winter was fine, but I'm telling you, the second I touched Autumn, it was almost like an electric shock."

Courtney was confused. "It's cold outside. Static electricity happens."

Heather shot her a droll look. "Not that kind of shock. The woman's knees nearly buckled, and I thought for sure she would fall. Then she started babbling all this nonsense about having an Irish grandmother and being able to feel my anxiety and fear. Her friend, Winter, kept saying it was a migraine, but when this Autumn woman looked at me..." Heather shuddered and crossed her arms over herself. "She actually asked me what I was afraid of."

The hair rose on the back of Courtney's neck. "What did you say?"

"What could I say except absolutely nothing?"

Courtney gave herself some time to think about it. "Do you think she was psychic?"

Heather gave a bitter sounding scoff. "Hell no." She turned her head to look Courtney directly in the eye. "I think the two of them are something much worse?"

What could be worse than a person who could read your mind?

"Worse how?"

"I could be way off, but that Winter woman…she had this, I don't know, air about her. Like a cop air."

Courtney frowned, thinking back to the pretty woman in skinny jeans and flowy top. "I didn't pick up on that."

Heather's lips twisted. "I'm not surprised, but anyway, I think they were fishing for information."

It was Courtney's turn to scoff. "I think you're just being paranoid."

"And I think you're just being naive."

The sisters were quiet for a long while before Courtney looked down at her hands. "What are we going to do?"

Heather's head moved side to side. "I don't know. I tried to research their names. Autumn Johnson and Winter Miller. Did you know those last names are in the top ten of most common surnames in America?" The question was clearly rhetorical because she went on. "Anyway, I found absolutely zero information on those two women."

"Aren't they new in town?"

"Yes, and both their profiles say that they came from Savannah. Guess what? Couldn't find a trace of them there, either."

Courtney knew she wasn't nearly half as smart as her oldest sister, lord knew she'd been told that time and time again. But still, she couldn't understand how that little bit of evidence had Heather accusing the pair of being law enforcement. "So just because you couldn't find information on two women in the, um, two hours you've had to research, that makes them cops here to spy on us?"

Heather nodded, ignoring the sarcasm that went with the words. "I think so."

"Why?"

Wrinkles appeared on Heather's forehead and she gazed up the long driveway to the little house sitting back in the woods. It glowed from light streaming through the front windows. "Because of *her*."

And just like that, Courtney understood. "But...but they were accidents. Katherine got super unlucky with a couple of rapey guys. It could have happened to me too. Or you, for that matter, if someone got fresh with you at one of your events."

Heather looked at her for so long that Courtney felt ashamed. "I would have slapped anyone who got fresh with me," her voice was almost a growl, "not *murdered* him!"

And just like that, the spotlight fell on the elephant they had all been tiptoeing around.

Tears sprang to Courtney's eyes. "But—"

"But nothing, Court. Our sister has killed three men. Do you think she even remembers their names? I do! Carl Jameson, Brice Sutter, and Allen Newhouse. And guess what?"

Courtney wiped her cheeks. She didn't want to know more.

Heather told her anyway. "Edwin Gallagher, yet another target of Katherine's, is missing. Missing!" The last word was nearly a screech.

Courtney licked her lips. "Maybe he just went on vacation or something."

Heather, in that moment, looked exactly like their mother, though the disappointment in her eyes was the spitting image of how her father used to glare at them.

"You know better than that."

She was right. Courtney did know better.

"She *murdered* all three of them, Court. Maybe four. Stabbed them to fucking *death*. Katherine is losing her shit. She has always been obsessed with the idea of screwing these guys out of their money. And now the money isn't enough for her." She covered her face with her hands. "Since we moved back here, she's changed."

Courtney looked back up the driveway to the little house. "We should have never come back here." She reached over the console and grabbed her sister's arm. "Let's leave. We have enough money now. We can pack up, or hell, we can just leave everything." Her voice was pleading, but she didn't care.

Heather covered her hand with her own. It was like a block of ice settling on her skin. "We can't. If we run now, the cops will chase us, thinking we are running from something."

"What should we do?"

Heather pulled her bottom lip between her teeth. "Katherine needs to stop doing what she's doing."

Courtney jerked her hand away. "Are you saying we need to tell the cops on her?"

"I—"

"No!" Tears pricked her eyes again. "We can't do that."

"I'm not saying we call the cops. I'm just saying that she needs help."

Thoughts of straightjackets and electrical shock therapy ran through Courtney's mind. "No. I'll help her. I'll—"

She jumped when her phone buzzed in her lap. Looking down, she expected it to be Katherine on the line, but it wasn't her sister at all. Her stomach flipped. It was her father.

Terrance.

Heather gasped as she saw the screen too. "Speak of the devil."

Devil indeed.

Pissed beyond all measure that her dear old father would call her this late at night, she swiped to answer the call. "Hello, Terrance."

He hated when they called him that.

"Hey, princess." He had a nasal voice and always spoke in a snobby upper-class kind of way, which was hilarious considering he was born dirt poor. But not long after their mother died, he walked into a store, bought a lottery ticket, and did the near impossible…won eleven million dollars. Not that his daughters ever saw a single penny from that winning.

"Courtney, my dear. This is your father. How *are* you?"

He was extra snobby and patronizing at the moment. Beside Courtney, Heather rolled her eyes.

"I'm fine. How is your vacation?" She spoke in a monotone.

"The Caribbean is absolutely beautiful. The sea is green in the shallows, the color of a turquoise bead on a Navajo necklace, and a blue so deep and so clear that it is almost impossible to tell how deep the water is. We're having the time of our lives."

We.

Courtney's nails bit into her palms.

"Yesterday, we went to an island that was so isolated that we had to swim to it. It wasn't far, and it was quite an adventure, and we found you girls a present while we were there. We had to bring our wallets and phones in waterproof fanny packs. And when it was time to go, we had to swim back. But of course, we're both excellent swimmers. It's your mother who couldn't swim well."

Heather growled beside her.

"What's the name of the island?"

"Hmmm…I'll have Deena write it down for me. I have quite forgotten."

Heather growled again.

"How is your girlfriend, Terrance?"

His laugh had a "ho-ho-ho" quality to it. "Girlfriend? Don't you mean wife?"

Courtney was stunned into complete and utter speechlessness. Glancing over at Heather, she could tell that her sister was equally surprised.

"W-w-wife?" she finally managed. "When did you get married?"

"Over Christmas. I *sent* you a notification. On good card stock with gold trim. I picked them out myself. We were married by a waterfall."

The two sisters just stared at each other. It was clear that no gold-trimmed card had arrived in their mailbox. Courtney's lips felt numb as she said, "It must have gotten lost in the mail."

"I'll have Deena send you another."

That pissed Courtney off. "Terrance, I don't want a wedding notification for a wedding that already happened. And I don't really want a present. Because no matter *what* you bring to the house, you're also bringing the woman you married at Christmas, when Mom died in October."

"*Early* October," Terrance corrected her. "You don't like Deena?"

No, she didn't like Deena, but Deena wasn't the real problem. She was a gold digger without much of a personality, but she was only doing what gold diggers did...take advantage of the opportunity Terrance gave her.

He was the problem. He had *always* been the problem.

"I didn't expect to fall in love again so soon, Courtney. Can't you girls understand that?"

Angry tears burned through her sinus cavity. "You 'fell in love' while Mom was on her death bed."

He sighed. "Let's not go through this same old song and dance again. Instead, tell me, how is the house?"

Courtney's eyes followed the long driveway again. After Daddy won his millions, he'd offered his daughters the tiny Cape Cod...and nothing else.

"Falling apart as usual," she said lightly.

"You girls will get it back in shape in no time, I'm sure."

Unlike you did.

Hate was like a boa constrictor wrapped around her heart, squeezing until she could barely breathe. Courtney gritted her teeth against the pain. "Yeah, sure. No time."

"Well, my dear, I better go. We're flying home tomorrow, so we want to enjoy our last evening in paradise. Deena and I will bring your present to you soon."

Tomorrow?

"Sure. Bye."

She disconnected the call with shaky fingers and looked over at her sister. But her sister was staring at her own phone, her mouth dropped open in surprise and...fear?

"What's wrong?"

The phone dropped into Heather's lap, and Courtney snatched it up.

There was a text from Katherine.

It happened again. Please help me.

20

Heather was the first to burst into their home, her little sister on her heels. Her heart was in her throat as she took in the kitchen and little dining nook.

Lasagna and salad…not a bite eaten.

Wine in two glasses, only partially filled.

"Please, God, no," she breathed as she stepped farther into the room. She didn't know what to expect, but she felt sure that whatever she was about to find would change her life forever.

Change them all.

"Katherine!" Courtney called, going around her when her feet seemed nailed to the floor. "Where are you?"

From where Heather stood, she watched her baby sister go down the hall, then scream. Not from surprise or even fright. The scream seemed to rise from the very depths of hell.

Heather closed her eyes. The moment the text appeared on her phone, she'd known what they would find.

But here?

Why here?

It wasn't the most urgent question to consider, but it kept rolling through her mind. It was followed by, *what had Katherine been thinking?* Then, *what were they going to do about it?*

That was the question she most wanted to avoid. The answer would either break her family down further, or it would make her a part of a crime.

You already are!

She ignored the voice of reason whispering in her mind. Yes, the voice was right. She'd known what Katherine had done, and she'd also never told the authorities like she should have.

Katherine was her sister!

Heather had been five years old when her new sister was born. Old enough to remember counting her tiny fingers and toes. Giving her a bottle. As Katherine grew, it was always Heather who got the biggest smiles and longest cuddles.

"She's your shadow," Mom would say, and even though Heather would try to look annoyed, she secretly liked it.

Something was very wrong with Katherine now, and she refused to abandon her sister just because times got tough. Either of her sisters.

She reminded herself of that as she quietly walked down the short hall. "It doesn't matter what Katherine has done, you will support and love her." It was the promise she continued to make...up until she turned the corner and looked into Katherine's room.

Heather had braced herself to find a body. She'd braced herself for blood. But nothing could have prepared her for the sight before her.

Katherine was naked, curled up in the far corner of a room that appeared to be painted in blood. An equally naked man lay on his stomach, a knife protruding from his back.

Courtney had sunk to her knees, her face in her hands, sobbing uncontrollably. "What did you do?"

Katherine said nothing. What could she say?

People said that your life flashed in front of your eyes when you were on the very edge of death, and Heather's life, such as it was, did that now. Was she having a heart attack? An aneurism that would soon make her simply drop to the floor?

No…she felt fine physically, and she knew her life was flashing before her for one reason…because the life she had so carefully planned to create was now over. She was thirty-one years old and had never really lived, but she'd thought she was going to. She'd had such big plans.

Together, the sisters had hatched a plan to take control of their lives, using men now so they'd never have to rely on them again.

Now, she and her sisters would go to prison. Locked in tiny cells with people who told them when to eat, when to shower. They'd rot in there. They'd—

A movement caught Heather's eye, Katherine lifting her head. Heather nearly gasped at the sight of her sister's face. It was covered with blood…even her teeth.

"He tried to rape me."

Heather heard Katherine's words, but her eyes saw something else. Her heart knew the truth.

This man had been bound with his hands behind his back. The handcuffs were gone, but the rings where they once had been were still there. This man had fought against his bonds, that much was obvious. So, if he'd been handcuffed so securely that his skin was broken in places, how could he have attacked her sister?

Courtney was still keening, but she pushed up from the floor. She and Heather's eyes met, and they silently communicated a heartbreaking fact.

They couldn't trust their sister.

Katherine was on her feet now too, her hands held out to them both. "Do you believe me?" Beseeching. Begging. The whites of her eyes looked ghastly against the red everywhere else. Heather had to look away.

Courtney was the first to break. She went to her big sister, took her hand, and gently led her to the bathroom. Moments later, the shower turned on. Heather heard murmurs from her sisters but was unable to process the words.

As they spoke in the other room, Heather gazed at the body a little closer. The man was sprawled on a rug, which thankfully had absorbed much of the gore. Slowly, Heather knelt, and lifted a corner of the rug. She wanted to see how much blood had seeped into the wood.

She found plastic. Two layers of the thick black kind you found in hardware stores.

At the realization of what it meant, Heather backed away, not stopping until her back pressed against the wall. Katherine had clearly placed the plastic under the rug on purpose, which could only mean one thing…premeditated murder. Pennsylvania was a death sentence state.

"No," Heather whispered.

She couldn't let that happen. She couldn't. She just couldn't.

Katherine and Courtney were her responsibility. She was supposed to protect them, look after—

Heather jumped when a hand came down on her shoulder. Courtney was back, looking pale as death. "What are we going to do?" Courtney whispered.

The big sister took in a deep breath. What choice did they have?

"We're going to get rid of the body, then we're going to leave this country and never, ever come back."

Courtney was nodding before all the words were out. "When can we go?"

They needed to find a country with no extradition agreement with the United States. Did they need identifications too? Her mind was whirling, her head spinning. How had it come to this?

In the bathroom, Katherine's pure mezzo-soprano voice began to sing.

"Step into my parlor, I said to the fly."

Courtney and Heather both glanced at the bathroom door, their expressions stricken. "Soon," Heather said in a near whisper. "We need to leave soon. A couple days at most."

"Dance into my heart and let me taste your soul."

Courtney shuddered and leaned closer to her sister. "Did you see her teeth?"

Bile rose into Heather's throat as she nodded.

"Show to me that you are devoted to the one you should miss."

"We need to get her help," Courtney whispered, and Heather fully agreed.

"Prove to me that you will not betray her for the sake of a single kiss."

Heather's mind whirred with a list of immediate things to do. "We need to clean this up first."

Courtney's face drained of what little color it had possessed. "I know."

"Convince me that you are noble."

Heather pulled a blanket from the bed and tossed it over the body.

"Confirm that you have nothing to forgive."

Tears slid down Courtney's cheeks as they began the process of rolling the man into the rug.

"And in return, I'll demonstrate my gratitude to you."

"Sissy?" When Heather looked up, their eyes met, and Courtney began to cry harder. "I'm scared."

"*In return, I'll let you live.*"

Heather took her sister in her arms and whispered close to her ear. "I'm scared too."

21

W inter stifled a yawn behind her hand. She'd had trouble sleeping last night because her dreams were filled with vampires and bats swooping through the air, seeking bites of flesh. Her flesh.

She was also more than a little annoyed with Noah, who'd arrived back to their room with a big smile on his face. When she kept asking him what he was smiling about, he said that it was classified and was unable to tell her.

That didn't go over very well, and she threatened his manhood if he didn't spill. He just pulled down his pants, closed his eyes, and told her to do what she had to do, but that he couldn't break the confidence.

How could she argue with that? A man willing to sacrifice his man parts for a promise was the kind of man she wanted on her side.

The entire team except for Aiden were in the police station conference room. They all looked sleepy. Well, except for Sun. She was looking as bright-eyed and intent as ever, her fingers blurring on the keyboard, her gaze locked on the screen.

"Don't you ever sleep?" Winter asked, noting the half-dozen coffee cups next to her laptop.

Sun glanced up, giving her a smug smile. "It takes practice and discipline to survive the geek life."

"Do you miss being in the field more?" Winter asked, and Autumn's head lifted from the report she'd been reading to pay closer attention to the conversation.

Sun twisted her neck, and the popping of her spine made Winter cringe a little. "Yes and no. I'm happy to fill in while we're short-staffed, and the cyber team is teaching me things I've always wanted to know."

Curious, Winter took a peek at Sun's screen. It was filled with code, so she immediately sat back in her seat. Code wasn't a language she was interested in.

"Learning deeper hacks," Sun explained and then turned her laptop so Winter could better see. The code continued to scroll before Sun clicked another tab. Autumn stood and came to stand behind them. "I won't bore you with how it's done, but I'm using this particular laptop solely to access the dark web with a Tor browser and multiple VPNs to ensure anonymity."

"What are you looking for?" The question came from Autumn, who was leaning between them now.

Winter expected Sun to snap for her to give her space or something equally charming, but instead, the agent clicked to another open tab. Autumn gasped when the image of a bloody man appeared on the screen.

"I've been thinking about the possible tripod marks in Newhouse's carpet," Sun explained. "If our spider did indeed put a tripod there, I started wondering why. If she was taking pictures or videos, would she do so for her own personal pleasure or," she tapped a few keys, "would she, because it appears that she is as money hungry as she is bloodthirsty, use them for extra income?"

Winter felt her breakfast edging back up to her throat as Sun paged through "sample" photos of men in bondage scenes. Some were simple porn, some were more sinister looking, verging on snuff films.

"These are all for sale?" Autumn asked.

Sun nodded. "These are just the ones that fit my search parameters of a male over fifty years old with hands bound." Sun tapped a button and the photos went away and a search engine form appeared in their place. "I was just about to add 'knife in back' to my parameters."

Winter and Autumn were both holding their breath as she hit "enter."

"Hold your knickers, ladies." Sun's smug little smile was back. "It could take a minute or so for the pages to populate."

She was right. It took almost exactly two.

A warm hand circled Winter's upper arm. Noah had come to watch the show, and when Winter glanced back, she realized that the entire team surrounded them.

"Back off!" Sun shouted and reached for an aux cord. "I'll put it up on the screen so everyone will stop breathing their nasty germs on me. It's still flu season, you know."

The hand on her arm gave a gentle squeeze, and Winter shot a smile at Noah before she remembered that she was supposed to be irritated with him. He smiled back, and the irritation completely faded away.

He was a good guy, and she was lucky to have him in her life.

"Stop!"

Winter's attention was pulled away from her boyfriend and to the projector screen. Autumn was pointing. "Go back." Sun clicked buttons until Autumn said, "There."

Winter studied the image and frowned. The guy was naked and yes, there was a knife in his back. His hands were behind him, and she assumed that meant they were cuffed. But his throat was clean.

"I think that's Carl Jameson." Autumn was paging through her iPad. "Can someone get Chief Mazur?"

Noah was on his feet and out the door before Winter could even stand. Since she was already up, she went over to her friend, trying to see.

Even before the chief of police—with Aiden by his side and Noah trailing the pair—stepped into the room and studied the dead man's image, Winter knew that Autumn was right. The person who had killed Carl Jameson had taken pictures after his death with the intent to sell them on the dark web.

Their spider was greedy.

The chief looked sick as he came to the same realization. He looked even sicker when Sun found similar images of Brice Sutter and Allen Newhouse.

"These are screen grabs promoting a video," Sun explained. "Marketing."

"Can you tell how many have been sold?" Aiden asked.

Sun shook her head and moved her cursor so that they could see the view count. Over three hundred thousand views for each. "Just the number of views. Maybe cyber can go deeper?"

"That's so disturbing," Bree muttered.

Winter agreed. "And just imagine how many views little girl and little boy videos get."

The room was quiet for a moment while Sun continued to click through photos.

"Wait," Autumn exclaimed. She had Sun scroll back until she spotted a fully clothed man lying on a rug. "There." They all stared at the picture, trying to see what Autumn obviously saw, and the second she said, "Is that Edwin Gallagher?" it made total sense.

"Shit," Mazur muttered, pressing a hand into his eye.

Aiden grabbed a marker and headed for the whiteboard. "Okay, so it appears that we now have some proof that our unsub or unsubs have a larger body count than we first believed."

"Unsub," Autumn said, looking absolutely certain. "The women might be a team, but only one of them has escalated to murder."

Most in the room nodded their agreement. Except Mazur. "How can you be so sure of that?" He waved a hand at the projector screen. "No BDSM that I can see."

Autumn caught the verbal volley. "Remember when we spoke about Brice Sutter not being our unsub's first killing?"

Mazur nodded just once. "Yeah. Something about stressors and other psychobabble."

For her part, Autumn's expression didn't change. "That's right. I shared how serial killers had gestational phases to their fantasies, and when there is a stressor in their life, the person snaps and kills." Autumn addressed Sun, even though her gaze on Mazur didn't stray from his face. "Sun, can you put all those photos up, side by side."

They waited while Sun did exactly that, and Winter's heart squeezed when the four men's pictures were side by side. It was just so very sad.

Autumn cleared her throat. "If my theory is true, and our unsub experienced a recent stressor, then her first killing would have been an impulsive act. That's why Carl Jameson, the first to die, wasn't posed or left in the same way as Sutter or Newhouse. It's also why she didn't video the murder and took postmortem pictures instead. She most likely didn't mean to kill him, at least that night or in that way."

Mazur scoffed. "So, she just carries a knife everywhere she goes?"

It was a good question, Winter admitted, and like the rest

of the team, her head turned to Autumn like a spectator at a tennis match.

"That's very possible. Our unsub might have an aversion to guns, or she might be fascinated by knife play." Autumn shook her head. "No, I still believe 'stabbed in the back' is her primary theme. These men are being punished for betraying their wives so soon after their deaths."

"So, should we be looking for a woman whose daddy got remarried within a year of her mommy's death?"

Though Winter felt the sarcasm in Mazur's question, Autumn nodded. "Yes. I believe that, if such a thing were possible, it would lead us to our suspect that much quicker."

Winter thought Mazur would argue more, but he simply let out a breath and leaned against the wall. "I just can't believe this is happening in my town." That was where the arguments stemmed from, the chief's lack of control.

Autumn's expression softened. "I know, and I'm so sorry that she's here too, which begs the next question…why here? Why this town? Was her stressor this place? Could this be her hometown?"

Another good question. Beside her, Noah leaned forward. "That's a possibility, isn't it? Let's say she moved or ran away, and for whatever reason started her crime spree farther south but was drawn back home. She started the spree for purely financial reasons, but when she got back home." He snapped his fingers.

Autumn nodded. "This place or someone in this place is her trigger. We just need to figure out what pressed it." She looked back at the pictures on the projector. "Before another man dies."

Silence fell again, then Aiden cleared his throat. "Time to divide and conquer."

Sun glanced up. "There is another speed-dating event

tonight at eight. Do we want Winter and Autumn to try again?"

Autumn groaned, raising her hands to her face. "Please, no."

Winter wanted to whack her friend. This wasn't the place or time to mention what had happened last night. But everyone's attention was on Autumn. "That bad?" Sun asked.

Please don't...please don't...

Autumn opened her mouth to speak, but Winter jumped in. This group wasn't the place to confess her lack of control. "Maybe it would be better to have you and Bree go this time," she suggested to Sun. "Mix it up a little."

Sun looked like Winter had just smacked her while Bree looked equally stunned. "Did you seriously just throw me under that bus?" Bree hissed before turning to the group. "And, in case you didn't notice, I don't fit the 'under thirty' demographic for this case."

Crossing her arms over her chest, Sun turned mutinous. "I refuse. Fire me, I don't care. I'm not doing this."

Winter sighed. Autumn surely couldn't show her face in that place again. She decided to turn the tables on the men. "Is Roger Applegate going to be attending a second night of speed-dating too?"

Noah and Miguel both snickered while Aiden shot death glares in their direction.

The four women as well as Chief Mazur turned curious gazes on them. "What happened with your date with Nicole?" Winter asked Aiden.

Miguel shot to his feet. "I'm going to get some coffee. Anyone want any?"

Noah raised his hand, his entire body practically trembling with suppressed laughter. "Extra large, and could you add a shot of...vanilla to it?"

Miguel barked a laugh. "Sure thing. Aiden, would you like a shot of vanilla too?"

The very tips of Aiden's ears looked like they'd been dipped in red ink. "I'm good," he said through gritted teeth, "but please don't walk all the way to the *South Pole* to get it."

Miguel practically ran from the room, his laughter following in his wake. Noah shook harder, his face striving and failing to be blank.

"Spill," Sun said.

Aiden ignored her and turned his back on them all to begin marking on the board. "Winter and Autumn will be attending tonight's speed-dating event while I—"

"You have a date."

Aiden whirled and faced Sun. "As of when?"

Her eyebrow shot up. "As of this morning. You have a date with an..." she tapped some keys, "Kay Nash."

Before he could argue, Bree stepped in. "I have a list of suspects. I'd like to get out of this building and drive by their homes, get a feel of the territory. See who has close neighbors, that sort of thing."

Winter was alarmed. "By yourself?"

"No." Bree shook her head. "I'd like to head out with one of the locals," she nodded to Mazur, "if that'd be okay with you, sir."

Mazur didn't hesitate. "Don't have a problem with that."

After receiving a nod from Aiden, Bree looked satisfied. "After my scouting, I'll be back in time to 'old man' you up for your date."

Noah snickered again, and Winter thought, come hell or high water, she was going to get the story out of him later.

Aiden's nostrils just flared, but he didn't argue. He just turned his back on the entire group and wrote the new assignments on the board.

22

After the meeting, Autumn followed Winter from the conference room and into the ladies' room. Girls always peed in pairs, so why should being in the FBI be any different?

Winter turned to her as soon as the door clicked shut. "Any clue what happened with Aiden last night?"

Autumn shook her head. "Not a single one, but I would have loved to have been a fly on the wall, whatever happened."

"Me too."

Autumn sighed and went to the sink to run cool water over her hands. "I clearly can't go to the speed-dating event tonight."

Winter leaned a shoulder against the wall. "Have you spoken to Aiden yet?"

Autumn felt her face grow warm. "No. I was going to do that this morning, but he was in a meeting with the chief, so I didn't get the chance." She splashed the soothing water onto her face.

Ripping off a paper towel, Winter handed it to her. "Maybe there's a way we can avoid that."

The brown paper clung to Autumn's skin as she stared at her friend. "No. I just need to tell him that I blew mine if not both of our covers."

Winter held up a hand. "Hear me out. I've given this a lot of thought, and it wasn't just your fault. You got emotionally hammered and reacted the best you could under the onslaught of emotions. I, however, was the imbecilic goose who yammered about migraines instead of scooping you up and running from the room."

Autumn finished with the rough paper towel and tossed it in the basket. "What do you suggest?"

Winter seemed to relax a little. "Can we talk while I pee?"

Autumn grinned. "As long as I can pee too. I'm dying."

They entered stalls and started about their business. "There's clearly something going on with Heather Novak, or the handshake wouldn't have brought you to your knees. The thing is, you clearly didn't find her dangerous, or the vibe you picked up would have been very different."

"True." Shit, she was out of toilet paper. "Can you give a girl a loan?" She waved her hand under the stall, feeling like she was back in high school again. A ball of paper was jammed in her hand. "What I felt was acute anxiety, but she might have been stressed about the event or her business or—"

"Do you really think anxiety about her bottom line would have transferred to you so brutally?" Winter's toilet flushed. When the worst of the sound faded, she went on, "I don't. I think there had to be something more…I don't know…"

"Primal?" Autumn offered and flushed too.

Back in front of the mirror, they took turns washing hands then resumed their previous positions. "Yeah, primal. Or savage or barbaric or wicked."

Autumn just stared at her friend. "Wicked." She shivered. "I think that's the right word, but not Heather. Someone close to her. And the person close to her might not actually be wicked, but that's how Heather imagines her."

"Her?"

Autumn considered the question. "Yeah. That feels right."

"So, Heather knows the unsub one, the spider? Could Heather be unsub two, the scammer?"

God, she wished she knew. She wished that her intuition offered more than just a glimpse of the person's feeling. Or... maybe she didn't. She wasn't quite sure.

"I don't know, but I guess it's possible. Or maybe Heather simply uses her businesses, both the in-person events and the online dating site, to connect the spider to the prey."

Winter nodded. "That makes sense. Maybe it's time we asked her."

Autumn thought she might have misheard. "Excuse me?"

"Well, not ask her outright, but if our covers are blown, why not get to the event a little early tonight. Wait until she's feeling the pressure of guests showing up to question her more fully. Covertly, of course."

"What are you thinking?"

"I'm thinking that I go in on behalf of my good friend Autumn who is clearly a little coo-coo." Winter circled her finger next to her ear, giving a little laugh when Autumn frowned. "I talk about how sorry I am that last night's episode happened and talk about how frustrating and sad it is to have a friend with mental health issues."

Ahhh. Autumn got it. "You hope to gain her sympathy and create a sense of openness and vulnerability with the hope that she mirrors you and shares any similar experiences."

Winter rubbed her nose. "Yeah, you took the words right out of my mouth."

"Research demonstrates that the basis of non-judgmental

chemistry is facilitated by perceived similarities within two—"

Winter's head lolled back on her shoulders, and she began to snore.

Autumn smacked her arm but got the message. "Okay... you're going to go make bestie friendsies with Heather Novak."

With an enormous smile, Winter straightened. "Exactly."

"And what exactly will I be doing during this friendship dance?"

Winter pointed a finger only an inch from Autumn's nose. "You, young lady, are going to sit in the car and stay there."

"But—"

"No buts, and if I have to handcuff you to the seat, you know I can do it."

Autumn found herself pouting and pulled her lip back into its proper place. "Okay, but can you wear those hearing aid things so that I can at least know if things are okay?"

Both of Winter's eyebrows shot straight up. "You think Heather's dangerous?"

"A cornered animal is dangerous, Winter. And humans are animals."

Winter snorted. "Well, some are vampires, apparently."

That was something else that worried Autumn. Not the fanged undead, but deranged people. She was a pro at Krav Maga, but she didn't have the training to rush in and put a bullet in someone's head. She could just see it now...she runs into the community center, yells at a bad guy to, "Put down the knife or I'll karate chop you to death."

Autumn sighed. "Just promise you'll be careful."

"Always."

Autumn rocked her head side to side, the knotted muscles

screaming at the stretch. "Can we create a code or something first?"

Winter narrowed her eyes. "What kind of code?"

"Well, for starters, we both need a code for when our intuitions are starting to freak out. I know you normally get a nosebleed, but not always, and I…" She shrugged. "I clearly start acting stupid."

Winter laughed. "Okay…so at the first sight of our nose-bleeds and stupid sessions, we hold our hands in the universal sign for timeout?" She made a T with her hands.

Autumn thought the concept through various scenarios. "If I'm shaking someone's hand, I might not be able to get away with that. How about a code word instead?"

Winter chewed her bottom lip. "How about we think on that and decide before tonight? Right now, let's go talk to Aiden and share with him, if he's alone, what happened last night and tell him what we want to do."

As Autumn opened the door, she turned back to her friend. "What was that thing in there about vanilla?"

Winter shrugged. "I have no idea, but I plan to torture Noah until he tells me."

Autumn wiggled her eyebrows. "Will you tell me when he spills the truth?"

"Of course."

They stepped back into the hallway and headed to the conference room. The room was empty except for Sun and Aiden. Autumn took a deep breath. "Aiden, can we speak to you for a moment?" She glanced at Sun. "Alone."

Sun rolled her eyes and flipped her laptop closed. "If anyone needs me, I'll be at the coffee shop down the block."

Autumn gave her a silent smile of thanks, but Sun marched her pleasant self from the room without a word. Beside her, Winter closed the door.

Looking wary, Aiden closed a folder. "What's up?"

Autumn sat across from him. She noticed that Winter stayed to the side. She was clearly making sure that it didn't appear as if she was taking sides, which was a prudent thing to do.

"Something happened last night that I need to tell you about."

Aiden's gaze flicked from her to Winter and back again. He leaned back in his chair. "All right."

Autumn shared the entire story. Well, almost. She might have left off the part about touching Heather's hand and the mental jolt she received. She wasn't ready to share that tidbit about herself just yet.

His eyes were slightly narrowed by the time she finished. "*Why exactly* did you feel the need to blurt all that out?"

The question got her back up immediately. Was he purposely pissing her off to see how she'd handle the situation or was he simply having a bad morning?

She decided to be gracious and assume the latter.

"I generally have strong intuition, which is a blessing in my field, and it simply got away from me last night."

"Do you know why?"

She didn't want to be completely truthful, but she didn't want to be dishonest either. "Most likely, it's been the strain of this case so soon after the last one, and I've felt an intense pressure since arriving in Passavant Hills to solve these murders before anyone else dies."

"That pressure won't go away."

"I agree, and I assume that, as I'm more frequently face to face with dead bodies and find myself in the pressure cooker of a case, I'll find my balance and my stride." She leaned forward, letting him see the seriousness on her face. "If you look back to your first cases, I'm sure you felt the same way."

He glanced in Winter's direction, and Autumn could have happily kicked herself. She'd completely forgotten that The

Preacher was one of Aiden Parrish's first big cases and it was a heavy weight on his shoulders for many years.

"You're right," he admitted with a long exhale, "and as seamlessly as you joined this team, I forget that you're still very new to investigations. Don't worry yourself about your slip. Believe me, you aren't the only one who found themselves in an uncomfortable position last night."

Autumn could almost see Winter's ears perk up like a cat. Hers did too. "Want to talk about it?"

He pointed a finger at each of them. "No."

As much as she wanted to poke and prod, she went back to the subject at hand. "My biggest regret about last night is that, if I could have talked to Heather Novak when I was calmer, I might have been able to get her talking, and we might have been able to learn some useful information. Instead, I effectively pushed her away."

Winter stepped up. "I have a suggestion for this situation I'd like to discuss."

Aiden nodded, looking a little wary. "Go ahead."

"Since it isn't a good idea for either Autumn or me to attend the speed-dating event tonight, I want to go back to see Heather Novak shortly before tonight's event."

Aiden frowned. "To question her?"

Winter looked offended. "Of course not. I plan to go and apologize for my mentally unstable friend. If Autumn is right and Heather is afraid for someone she is close to, I could, um, gain her sympathy and create a sense of openness and vulnerability with the hopes that she mirrors my actions and shares similar experiences."

Her gaze slid to Autumn, and Autumn gave her a discrete thumbs-up.

Aiden didn't have to think about it very long. "It's a good idea. When do you want to go? You'll need backup." He shot a look at Autumn. "You're not backup material yet."

"I was thinking an hour or so before the speed-dating event tonight."

"Take Dalton with you. Vasquez can tail me on my," his nose wrinkled, "date."

Winter grinned. "So…what happened last night?"

Aiden pointed to the door. "Out."

Autumn joined in. "Hey, I told you my story, it's only fair that you tell us yours."

His finger made little jabby points. "I said out."

Not wanting to push her luck, Autumn stood and gave him a half salute. "Well, I hope you have better luck on your date tonight."

23

Winter eased into an empty parking spot, giving the Charger another hit of gas before she put the thing in park. She could see where the Passavant Hills Community Center would have its charms—*after* the old brick building was finished being remodeled. Its history stretched backward to a time when downtown was the place where everyone gathered.

It was an hour before the speed-dating event should begin. If the fairly empty parking lot was any indication, her timing should be good.

She kept the car running, not wanting to freeze Autumn to death. "Don't leave without me."

Autumn sighed. "Don't be me and do anything stupid."

Winter squeezed her friend's hand. "I only wish I was close to being as stupid as you, Miss Einstein Psychobabble Geek."

Some of the tension seemed to drain from her friend's shoulders at the teasing. Autumn smiled. "What's our code word if you have any trouble?"

Winter shot a look into her rearview mirror, spotting

Noah in the dark SUV across the street. "Vanilla," she said, and smiled when the sound of Noah's chuckle filled her ear. She desperately wanted to know what that was all about, but right now, she had a job to do.

"See you in a few," she assured her friend, giving her hand a last squeeze.

As she walked into the building, she tried not to think too hard about how the conversation with Heather should go. *Look apologetic,* she reminded herself. *My friend, Autumn, has some, um, mental health issues, and I lied to you about the migraines. That lie has been sitting heavily on my mind, and I want to apologize. To both you and to her. Mental health isn't something to deny or explain away.*

Or something like that.

Winter searched the public areas of the building, but didn't see Heather anywhere, just the same older men playing chess, checkers, and cards at the small side tables as yesterday. She asked a couple of them, but they hadn't seen Heather either.

Terrific. All this setup for nothing.

The pass-through door to the kitchen was open, and Winter caught a movement from someone on the other side. "Hello?"

A middle-aged woman with a cheerful expression, dark hair with a hint of gray, and extra dimples appeared. "Can I help you, dear?"

"Yes, please. I'm looking for Heather. Heather Novak."

The woman's dimples disappeared. "You were here last night. You and your friend."

It sounded like an accusation.

Winter spread her hands, going for a helpless gesture. "Yes, I came to apologize to Heather for the scene we made at her lovely event. Autumn, my friend, she...well, she's been having some problems lately."

The woman's face softened a small degree. "I'm sorry to hear that, but Heather has problems of her own. You and your friend upset her very much."

Winter admired the woman's loyalty, and she decided to see how far she could push her.

"I'd like to talk to Heather, please. I promise I won't make a scene. I just want to apologize...and, well, Heather seemed so...I don't know...nervous maybe? I thought an apology and an explanation might help reduce her stress."

The woman studied Winter's face, clearly sizing her up. She took a towel off the top of a kitchen counter and wiped her hands before sticking one in Winter's direction. "Grace Henderson."

As they shook, Winter reminded herself to use her fake name. "Winter Miller."

Grace's eyes narrowed. "You have a very strong grip. What do you do for a living?"

Was she being tested?

"I worked EMS down in Savannah, but the hours and the pressure got to be a little too much. I'm currently rewriting policies and procedures right now. Working wherever my laptop goes."

"Oh, and your friend?"

Winter forced tears to come to her eyes. "Autumn has had some pretty serious struggles lately...emotionally, but she'd been doing so much better. I thought the speed-dating event would be fun, but I think it overwhelmed her."

Grace's face softened a little more. "You know, I've heard that people with emotional issues are more sensitive to others who have the same thing." She said it in a near whisper.

Winter leaned closer to her. "I've heard that too. Has Heather been having similar difficulties?"

Grace twisted the towel in her hands, but Winter could

tell she was one of those people who loved to gossip, and gossip was practically burning her tongue. "Well, Heather's mother passed recently, and she hasn't taken it well. And to top it all off, her father didn't even have the decency to wait more than a few months before dating a girl his youngest daughter's age. Can you imagine?"

Winter's heart picked up speed. "That's so terrible. I lost my mother too, and I don't think you ever really get over that loss." She held up a finger, like she just had an idea. "Autumn lost both her parents too. Do you think that's why she, I don't know, emotionally connected to Heather?"

Grace's eyes grew wide. "I bet you could be right. Emotions are powerful things."

Winter nearly smiled at the sincere and intent way the older woman spoke.

"When did Heather's mother pass away?"

Grace's eyes filled with tears. "The poor dear passed in October, and Terrance was already dating that young thing a month later." She lowered her voice. "Though I'd put money on him horning around while Amanda was on her death bed."

Winter put her hand to her chest, aghast. "That's terrible."

"Right this very minute, he and the little gold digger are on vacation."

"Gold digger? Does Terrance have a lot of money?"

The pieces were all starting to fall in place, and Winter could imagine that Autumn was on the edge of her seat listening to every detail. Noah too.

Grace made a disgusted face. "Poor as a church mouse, they were. But after Amanda passed, wouldn't you know that the slime went and won millions of dollars in the lottery."

"Wow...that's amazing. Didn't that make Heather happy? I mean, having a father have sudden riches."

Grace snorted. "Those girls didn't see a dime of that

money, and he'll probably spend every penny within the year."

Girls?

"Heather has a sister?"

"Two of them. Heather is the oldest. A real good girl. She's very sensitive, despite her smiling exterior, if you know what I mean. One of those women who works very hard to make things perfect for everyone else, because they know the pain of situations that are less than perfect."

Winter nodded sympathetically. "Autumn is like that too."

Grace looked over Winter's shoulder, then gestured toward the door to the back room of the community center. "Why don't you come to the back and have a seat? If I make you stand out here talking for too much longer, the gentlemen will get curious. Oh, they might *seem* harmless enough, but once they get to gossiping, there's no stopping them from ribbing you about every little thing."

Winter didn't hesitate, just followed Grace to an office with two chairs packed into a narrow space mostly filled with desks, filing cabinets, and computers. She settled herself in one of the chairs, tucking a leg up underneath her, and gestured Winter to the other.

As Winter sat, a phone rang from inside a small leather purse decorated with a leather patch of a beagle. Several tiny dog bones hung from the strap.

"Oh, that's me!" Grace leaned over and fished a phone from out of the purse. "Shoot. I have to take this. I'll be right back."

Winter tried to hear the conversation, but Grace's voice was too soft. Instead, she examined the cramped office. The room was sparsely decorated with a few photographs of community center events. The normal tray of paperwork sat next to an elderly looking computer. Next to a shelf of books, a huge wall calendar took up much of the space.

January featured a photograph of a small black, white, and tan bird sitting at a bird feeder. *This chickadee is especially grateful for a birdfeeder in January!* the caption read.

Grace was back a moment later. "That was Heather, letting me know that she was running late."

Winter stood, brushing her hands down her jeans. "I'm sorry I missed her. Maybe I can come back later?"

Grace chewed her bottom lip. "If you do talk to Heather, please don't tell her that I spoke so freely about her situation."

Winter mimed locking her lips. "I promise I won't say a word, and I appreciate you being so generous of your time."

Grace walked her to the door, prattling on about the community center renovation and how much she loved running the place. "You come back and see us again. And bring your friend. Tell her not to be embarrassed by anything at all."

"I will," Winter promised. "Thank you again."

She waved goodbye and strode back out to where Autumn was waiting. She smiled at Noah and gave him a little salute. "See you back at the station," he said into the device inside her ear. His lights flashed as he pulled away.

Inside the Charger, Winter held her cold hands up to the blowing heat. "Did you hear everything?"

Autumn's fingers were flying on her iPad. "Yes. I've been researching Heather Novak's family and found her mother's obituary. She has two sisters, Katherine and Courtney. Father's name is Terrance."

Winter leaned over and studied the photos on the screen. "Social media accounts?"

Autumn nodded. "Courtney, the youngest, posted frequently until a little over two years ago, then the postings were more sporadic. The second to last post was a tribute to her mother. Her very last post was a poem about not trusting men."

Winter examined Courtney's features. With skillful makeup and contouring, could she be their spider?

"Can you go back to the other sister? Katherine."

Autumn did and they both stared at the woman. Neither sister looked like the woman who'd dated the murdered men.

"What do you think?" Autumn asked.

Winter put the car into reverse. "I think we have more digging to do."

24

———————

Heather leaned back in the hotel jacuzzi and closed her eyes, trying desperately to rid her mind of the past twenty-four hours.

She hadn't slept a wink all night, and her muscles felt like plucked piano wires that wouldn't stop twanging. Her back hurt from dragging the heavy body and from digging a grave. She knew the hole should have been at least six feet deep, but they'd barely managed two in the frozen ground. Even then, the blisters on her palms and fingers were reminders of what she'd done.

When Katherine told them to simply dump the man in the river, Heather had just gaped at her. "Are you kidding? Dump a body in a river that's only about thirty feet deep in its deepest parts? A river where fishermen fish all year round?"

Katherine's eyes had grown wider with each question. She'd chewed on her bottom lip for a good thirty seconds before asking, "Is that bad?"

That's when Heather knew another truth about her sister. The missing man the news was reporting about…Edwin

Gallagher. Heather didn't know exactly where but she was sure that he was currently decomposing in a watery grave.

It had taken the three of them hours to dig this earthly tomb deep enough to ensure no predators would attempt to dig the body up. Courtney had cried the entire time while Katherine made excuse after excuse, her story changing each time she tried to explain exactly what had happened.

What happened was that her sister was crazy.

A splash had Heather jolting up, but it was only an older man who'd jumped into the nearby pool to swim laps. Still, it took her heart a while to get back to its normal rhythm. She sank into the hot water once again, not wanting to think about the time.

She really needed to get out of this hot tub, go to her room, and get dressed, but exhaustion, physical and mental, was eating a hole in her motivation.

Heather hadn't been able to stomach the thought of sleeping in their cottage while the scent of blood clung to the place and had opted to stay in a hotel. Katherine had promised to clean every surface multiple times, swearing that it would be spic-and-span by the end of the day.

But Heather knew the cottage would never be clean. Not really. And she didn't know why she continued to cling to the small home. Maybe it was because it was where her mother had lived and died, and she felt closer to her mom there than anywhere.

Now, she was ready to just burn it to the ground.

"Hungry?"

Heather opened her eyes to find that Courtney slipped in. Her baby sister was pale as a ghost, except for the half-moons of purple under each eye.

Heather shook her head. Although she was actually starving, the thought of food turned her stomach. "What time is it?"

"A few minutes after six."

Heather jolted straight up. Shit. How had that happened?

Grabbing a towel, she climbed out of the tub. "I need to get to the center."

Courtney grabbed her arm. "Seriously? You plan to go to work like nothing ever happened?"

"That's exactly what I'm going to do," Heather hissed, mindful of the man still swimming nearby. "I'm going to do exactly what I've done my entire life. I'm going to take care of everything while pretending that everything is okay."

Tears brimmed in Courtney's already bloodshot eyes. "What are we going to do?"

Heather wanted to scream. She was so very tired of hearing that question, and even more tired of having that question directed to her. "I'm not sure about you, but I'm going to work, and after I've smiled and acted normal so that we don't draw any added suspicion, I'll buy three tickets for us to get the hell out of here."

"Where will we go?"

"Maldives. I've researched it thoroughly, and I think it's our best option. We can get a thirty-day tourist visa and they have no extradition agreement with the U.S."

And they had what appeared to be an excellent mental health institute, but Heather didn't want to go down that rabbit hole just yet. She'd find a way to get Katherine admitted when they got there.

"What happens after thirty days?"

Heather pressed the towel against her face. "I don't know, but we'll have thirty days to figure it out."

"When can we go?"

Heather growled under her breath. "Stop asking me questions!"

Courtney shrank back. "I'm sorry. What can I do to help?"

Her sister would soon wish she hadn't asked. "I need you to keep a very close eye on Katherine."

As expected, Courtney seemed to diminish where she stood, but she nodded. "I will. I actually tried calling her several times, but she isn't answering her phone."

That wasn't good.

"Go to the house and see if you can find her," Heather instructed, "and the second that you do, let me know."

Courtney blew out a deep breath. "Okay. But what…" Her eyes brimmed with tears again. "But what if she's, um, hurt herself?"

It wouldn't be the worst thing in the world.

Heather nearly gasped as the thought entered her mind. How could she think such a thing about her sister? Katherine just needed help. That was all. They had enough money to live on for most of the rest of their lives. They'd amassed close to a million dollars during—

A terrible thought struck Heather, landing like a blow to her stomach. *No, no, no. She wouldn't. Surely…Katherine wouldn't.*

"What are you doing?" Courtney asked as Heather pulled up the app for the overseas bank they used to stash their misdeeds.

Two hundred thousand dollars was all that was left. At least it wasn't completely empty…but still…

Courtney grabbed her arm as Heather's knees buckled. "What's wrong?" Courtney cried.

"Do you two need help?" The question came from the swimming man, and that's when Heather knew she needed to pull her shit together.

She lifted an *I'm okay* hand to the man and gave Courtney her best big-sister smile. "Just need to eat something. Bet my blood sugar is really low."

What were they going to do? What were they going to do?

Courtney didn't look convinced. "Are you sure?"

Heather forced the smile to grow wider. "Yes. I will be. We just need to get through the night. I need to get to the office, and you need to find our sister."

"And if I can't find her?"

Then we're screwed.

Ducking her head, she made a show of wrapping the towel around her slim frame. "Then try her apartment and the other places you know she likes to visit."

Courtney seemed relieved to have something to do. "Okay, I can do that. And I promise to contact you the second I find her."

Back in her room, Heather called Grace to let her know she was running late. Grace told her that she had something to tell her, but Heather didn't have time for the older woman's gossip and disconnected the call. After a quick shower, she changed into her professional clothes, giving herself pep talks every step of the way.

They'd find Katherine. Her sister had probably just panicked. She would never rob them like she'd stolen from so many others.

Would she?

Heather tasted blood in her mouth by the time she pulled into the community center lot and realized she'd bitten her lip. "Calm down," she told herself before stepping into the building. "Keep it together. Everything is going to be okay. Do what needs to be done. Make sure these people are happy and don't suspect that anything's wrong."

As she went to open the door, she was struck by how much work she did to arrange for other people's happiness— or at least for their gratification—and how little she could imagine doing anything for herself.

She could easily be married with children by now, but the idea of being in a relationship turned her stomach. It had been a long time since she'd last been on a date. When her clients asked her who *she* was dating, she always just gave them a sly smile and changed the subject.

But the truth was that she couldn't force herself to use dating apps or social mixers for herself. She was a loner by choice. She didn't belong to a church. Friends? Hah. She had no friends.

Just family.

At first, she had given everything she had to her two younger sisters because it was obvious that none of them would make it without each other. Their mom had been a good woman, but Terrance was demanding and controlling. He was insecure, so insecure that if he thought she was spending too much time on their children instead of him, he would arrange for little things to go wrong in all their lives. No, his wife's universe was supposed to revolve around him and him alone.

And his attitude toward his daughters had been even worse. Their purpose in life, the reason that each of them existed, was to make him look good.

Heather had fallen into that trap. She had chased after good grades, a spot on the volleyball team, awards, scholarships. She even worked two part-time jobs to save for college. By the time she was a senior, she'd amassed a savings account of nearly twenty-five thousand dollars.

She'd been so pleased with herself. She was getting out of Pennsylvania on a scholarship to Columbia College in New York that covered everything but living expenses and books. She'd found a tiny apartment to share with three other girls, and if she lived on ramen and water, her savings account would last the entire four years without her needing to work even a part-time job.

She could concentrate on her studies, get her degree in computer sciences. And in four short years, she would be financially independent, and she could save her sisters from their father too.

A week before her graduation, though, her father had taken a trip with several of his friends to Atlantic City for a weekend. He'd called every day, telling her how the cards were falling for him like a miracle, and how she'd be able to afford an apartment all to herself in New York when he got home.

It wasn't until Heather tried to put gas in her car and her debit card was declined that she realized what he'd done. Somehow, her father had accessed her savings account, and in the space of a weekend, he'd gambled her future away.

Before that, she'd actually thought that she was his favorite daughter. She had actually thought that he loved her.

But when he had returned from Atlantic City, drunk, bragging about all the money he had won—two thousand dollars—and trying to pretend that the almost twenty-five thousand he'd lost didn't matter, she finally figured out the truth.

He loved only himself.

He offered to give her all his "winnings" so she could still go to college, and she'd thrown the small stack of hundreds back in his face. She'd gotten a fat lip and black eye for her efforts. "No woman talks to me that way."

Losing her respect for Terrance had made her lose respect for herself. She'd stopped caring about anything but just getting by. She'd enrolled in the local community college but dropped out the first semester.

She took care of her sisters, especially after her mother had gotten so sick. She'd waitressed, but that'd been more to get out of the house than anything. Still, she'd learned a very valuable trait while serving hungry customers.

She'd learned how to plaster a fake smile on her face to cover the turmoil inside.

She'd fallen into the dating game by accident. While she absolutely hated thoughts of dating for herself, she'd learned that she was really good at matching others.

One of the happy couples she'd matched decided to "thank" her by investing in her business. At the time, she hadn't even had a business at all, but when the opportunity had been presented to her, she grabbed hold of it with both hands and her teeth.

That's when Heart to Heart was born.

The business had grown rapidly over the years, from both online dating sites to apps and then to local social meetings like the speed-dating events that everyone seemed to love. She'd had so many other plans, looking to expand to other cities, but then, something tragic happened. The happy couple financing her ventures filed for divorce...and they'd divorced Heather as well.

It all began to fall apart after that.

Her mother's health worsened, along with her father's betrayals. Katherine was off chasing her dreams to be an actor but was also waiting tables as she waited for her big break. Courtney had headed to Pittsburgh to get the college degree that Heather never had the chance to pursue.

That left Heather taking care of her parents, even while her business prospects looked bleak. One day, Katherine simply showed up. She was wearing diamonds in her ears and Louboutins on her feet.

"Who's your sugar daddy, and does he have a brother?" Heather had quipped the moment she laid eyes on her sister.

Katherine had just shot her a very satisfied grin. "Sugar daddies...plural."

As Heather had listened in astonishment, Katherine had shared the sordid details of how dating older men was very lucrative. She lived in a very nice apartment and owned more clothes than she could wear in a year.

That had been Thanksgiving two years ago. Courtney had come home for fall break, and the three sisters had spent their time together making a plan.

Heather would stay there and take care of her business and mother. The business would be used to help the other two sisters find older men looking for love.

That's all their little crime spree was ever supposed to be. They were taking from the rich and giving to the poor. Sure, the poor was themselves, but was that so very bad? It wasn't like the men would miss the ten thousand here or there her sisters would siphon.

Katherine had even gotten one of the old geezers to pay off all the student loans for her acting classes. But that was before...Katherine changed.

Heather shivered as a gust of cold wind hit her face, but she knew it wasn't the weather that had iced her blood. Taking a deep breath, Heather walked into the building. She smiled and waved at the participants who were early and stopped to chitchat with a few of them.

She was fine.

She could do this.

Just two hours of her life to get through.

While Heather made everything seem normal, Courtney would find Katherine.

"Hello, everyone," she shouted, raising her hands over her head to gain the participants' attention. "I love how eager you are to get started, and I promise that we will be getting started soon. In the meantime, enjoy our appetizers and each other's company."

Still smiling as she walked to the little kitchen, she felt better.

She was Heather Novak, and she could do this.

25

Autumn couldn't help but grin as Aiden stepped into the conference room, once more dressed as an old man. A rock hadn't yet been placed in his shoe so, at first glance, she saw only the posture and strength of Aiden Parrish. That would change very soon.

Aiden had called the entire team in for a short briefing to go over what Winter had learned at the community center and give last-minute instructions. He had a date with what Autumn considered to be a likely spider candidate. That fact made her nervous. Nervous if Kay Nash turned out to be innocent of any crimes, thereby wasting the SSA's time, and nervous that she was guilty, and Aiden was putting his life in danger.

She ran her finger down the list of potentials. Each of their names started with a "K," which seemed to be a signature of their suspect. Powering on her iPad, she scrolled to the Rapid Start app to gain access to each of the team member's notes.

Just as Autumn had asked, Sun had taken screenshots of Courtney Novak's social media posts. Sun and her hacking abilities had been able to see inside even the private accounts and cached pages. After finding a picture of the three sisters, Autumn pulled up Kay Nash's dating profile shot.

Katherine Novak was blonde with a beautiful face and big blue eyes. She was very tanned in the picture, making her eyes appear to be even bluer.

Kay Nash was dark where Katherine was fair. Straight black hair, dark brown eyes. With skin as pale as death, her teeth were different from Katherine's too. While Katherine's were straight and brilliantly white, Kay's were a couple shades darker and sported a twisted incisor.

Temporary veneers could change teeth in such a way, though natural looking ones cost a pretty penny. Would their spider go to so much trouble? It was possible, but as different as Katherine and Kay appeared, Autumn had trouble morphing them into the same person.

Autumn turned to Sun and called her name. When the agent lifted her head, Autumn raised her iPad so the other woman could see the photo. "Can you do that overlay trick with the pictures of Katherine Novak and Kay Nash?"

Sun made a face but nodded, her fingers going to work. The projector screen lit up, and soon, the techy agent was moving one face on top of the other.

Winter, who was now watching the screen as well, let out a breath. "They match."

Sun snorted, and her fingers went flying again. "So does this one…and this one…and this one…" She was right. Three of the other spider candidates had similar facial structures. Sun stretched her arms over her head. "I compared them earlier."

Of course she had. If Sun had a personality, she could probably run the world.

Aiden grabbed a marker and moved to the front of the room. "Let's get started. I wanted us to meet before tonight's festivities begin." He nodded at Winter. "Tell the others what you learned at the community center earlier."

Autumn nodded along as Winter shared her run-in with Grace Henderson and the interesting facts she'd learned. Heather Novak checked many of their spider boxes, but especially the big one: her father began dating soon after her mother's death.

And that stressor took place not that long ago, at close to the time the killings had begun. That very well could have been their suspect's trigger.

But...Autumn couldn't help but feel that Heather wasn't their spider. Yes, she may have played a large role in the sweetheart scamming crimes, but she didn't feel like a killer. Heather had been worried about someone else, but not necessarily for herself.

Autumn pulled up a photo of Courtney Novak, and immediately shook her head. Courtney was much too young and vivacious looking to be Kay Nash.

Aiden was writing on the board, and Autumn studied him closely. Bree had done a brilliant job of aging him, so it wasn't outside the realm of possibility that Courtney could have made herself up to be the older Kay. After the meeting, she would ask Sun to overlay Courtney Novak's social media picture to that of Unsub 2, if she hadn't done that already, which was a distinct possibility.

It was so frustrating.

The urgent need to do something/anything to catch their suspect was tempered by the fact that there was very little she could do.

She was quickly learning that FBI investigations in real life were vastly different from those projected on TV. In crime shows, techs popped some miniscule piece of evidence into some machine, and a few seconds later, some case-breaking piece of forensics would appear. Or a witness would be in the exact right place at the exact right time to glimpse a face or car type, and even had the perfect memory to recall every detail. Or a camera would be at the perfect angle to get a shot of a suspect's license plate.

Real life was different.

Most investigations took a day or two to really ramp up. Until then, she had no forensics to analyze, no obscure witnesses to interview in the middle of the night, and nothing to do but sit on her hands while she waited for the ball to get rolling.

"Autumn?"

Aiden's voice jerked her back to the room. "Yes?"

"You and Winter will head to the community center and wait for the opportunity to interview Heather Novak. Dalton will be your backup."

Sun's head shot up again. "I thought they were attending the thing."

Aiden shook his head. "We've changed plans."

Sun opened her mouth to say something, but the door opened and Chief Mazur walked in, holding a thick sheaf of paper. "I've got the warrants to look into the Novak sisters' accounts."

"Excellent." Aiden took them and studied the pages for several minutes before tossing them to Sun. "You and the cyber team coordinate locating accounts and following the money trail." He wrote that on the board. "Chief, if you have someone you want to help, send him or her to Sun."

The chief seemed pleased. "I know exactly who." He clearly didn't want to waste time, because he opened the door and was gone as quickly as he had entered.

Aiden glanced around the room, his gaze stopping on Miguel, then Bree. "You two will be backup for me." His gaze slid to Autumn. "What are the chances that Kay Nash is our unsub?"

She inhaled deeply, giving herself time to think. Autumn had six possibles on her list, and they were "possible" for a reason.

"Forty percent."

Aiden nodded. He'd seen the facial structure comparison too, she knew.

"We need to know who is at the speed-dating event, and since none of us is attending," he only paused for a second when Sun threw up her hands in disgust, clearly not pleased with the change in plans, "you and Winter keep your eye on the participants the best you can."

"Why aren't they attending?" Sun demanded.

Aiden clearly knew what Autumn knew...Sun wasn't going to let it drop.

"We learned that it would look suspicious for them to go two days in a row."

Autumn hated for anyone to lie for her, but a little part of her was glad for his deceit. She wasn't up for the grilling she'd get if it got out that she'd freaked last night.

Sun appeared to be mildly satisfied, so Aiden faced the group as a whole. "Anyone have questions?"

There were a few, but they circled around the logistics of the night. Communications and the like.

"What is our code word if things start going south?" Miguel asked, his lips twisting in humor.

"South Pole," Aiden answered without missing a beat.

Even with the icy stare focused on him, Miguel just gave him a little salute before snatching up a piece of candy from the table.

Noah tapped his smartwatch, a smile playing at the very corners of his lips. "Parrish, aren't you supposed to be getting ready for your big date?"

Aiden's glare turned on the younger man just as he

reached up and scratched the side of his face, digging through a layer of makeup with his nails. "I *am* ready."

Bree groaned and pushed to her feet. "Correction. You *were* ready, but you aren't any longer."

Miguel snickered. "Yeah. Don't touch your face. You're starting to look like something from a horror movie."

Aiden's glare had transferred to his fingernails. "Shit."

As he followed Bree back to the makeup area, Sun exhaled loudly and turned on the two male agents left in the room. "What the hell is this code word stuff all about?"

Noah shrugged, his expression as innocent as a newborn lamb while Miguel busied himself with opening the candy.

Sun turned her irritation on Autumn. "And what happened to you two last night?"

Autumn stuck out her hand for a piece of Miguel's candy, and he tossed her a watermelon Jolly Rancher. Winter spoke up. "Nothing happened. Like Aiden said, we decided it was too suspicious for us to attend two nights in a row."

Sun wasn't going to be put off. "Why?"

Autumn really hated anyone lying for her. "Because I might have gotten a little too pushy with my questions last night, and now we're afraid to scare Novak off if she has anything to do with either the scamming or the murders."

That seemed to satisfy Sun. The girl seemed to have a hound dog's nose for the truth.

"You could still go," Winter said to Sun, a smirk lifting a side of her mouth.

Autumn could tell that Winter was taunting the other agent, but Sun didn't like to be teased.

Sun narrowed her eyes. "No way."

Winter crossed her arms over her chest, clearly irritated. "This is the FBI. Not a private company. If Aiden says you go, you go. We follow the authority figure, come hell or high water, unless there are ethical issues involved."

Sun narrowed her eyes. "Were you there when Autumn got a little too pushy," she air quoted the words, "with our chief suspect?"

Autumn latched on to the last word, hoping to change the subject and lead the two women away from an outright war. "You think Heather Novak is a murderer?"

Sun's mouth twisted. "I didn't say *murderer*. I said *suspect*. We have more than one crime going on here, and there is *nobody* in a better place than Heather Novak to set up con artists with their marks. I think we should be riding her hard and fast."

"Which is why we plan to also interview her again. As you may recall, my conversation with Grace Henderson happened because I'd gone back inside the community center looking for Heather, who wasn't there." She glanced at her watch. "Damn. I'd hoped to actually catch Heather again right before the next event began."

Autumn checked the time too and worried her lip with her teeth. "Maybe we should wait until afterward to talk to Heather?"

Winter didn't look happy but nodded. "Yeah. By the time we get to the community center, too many participants will be there to witness. I want to pressure her, not have her screaming for a lawyer."

"What's this about a lawyer?" Aiden asked as he strode through the door. His makeup was fixed, and he was limping now, cane in place.

Winter explained about the time dilemma, and Aiden agreed that after the event would be better. "Okay, if there are no other questions, take your stations. I won't be able to answer calls, most likely, but if you need anything, contact Miguel and Bree. They can whisper in my ear." He tapped the hearing aid.

Autumn was glad to see him smiling again, though it

wasn't close to being normal sized. She thought this entire case had been hard on him and reminded herself to make some time for him, urge him to talk it through, if he would.

Back in the Charger, Winter pulled up to a fast-food window, a reminder that neither of them had eaten since that morning. Autumn's stomach growled the second the scent of hamburgers and fries hit her nostrils.

The community center's parking lot was filled, but they found a parking space toward the back. Autumn admired Winter's ability to back into the narrow slot in one attempt. Yet another thing she needed to learn how to do in her new career, she supposed.

The first half hour went by fairly quickly as they plowed through their dinner. The second half hour seemed to drag by.

"Are stakeouts always like this?"

Winter grinned. "Wait until you have to pee in a cup."

Autumn groaned. "Maybe a desk job is a better fit for me, one with a clean ladies' room nearby."

"Nah." Winter's straw slurped as she sought to suck up the last of the drink. "Just practice your aim, and you'll be fine."

Aim.

Although she knew Winter was talking about urination, she added "target shooting" to her mental list. She wasn't even licensed to carry a gun, and although one would have come in handy a time or two since her FBI consultations began, she didn't think Aiden would sign off on giving her one anytime soon.

"They're probably eating ham right about now," Winter said, tapping her watch.

Autumn gave a baleful look at the paper sack sitting at her feet. "That was some very good ham."

"I…" Winter sat up straighter, her gaze laser focused on the front of the building. She pointed at a blonde woman who was running up the sidewalk, her face a haunted mask, tears streaming from her eyes.

Autumn had studied the Novak sisters' faces so much that she recognized the woman immediately. "That's Courtney Novak."

Winter was out of the door before Autumn could get hers open. The wind was like ice against her skin, the blast carrying Winter's voice away as she called for the girl.

"Shit," Winter muttered. "I hoped to catch her before she got inside."

"Um, what's going on?" Noah said in Autumn's ear, making her jump. She'd have to get used to those damn things.

After Winter filled him in, Autumn asked, "What should we do?" yanking her heavy bag higher on her shoulder. Why had she even grabbed it? Yet another lesson she'd have to learn not to do.

Winter checked her watch. "I say we go inside and find out what Courtney's so upset about."

"I'll move closer to the door," Noah said.

Autumn was right on Winter's heels and realized her friend had calculated the timing precisely the moment they were inside the community center. The speed-dating participants were mingling and beginning to line up for the buffet dinner.

Autumn gave the ham a longing glance, and that was when she saw her. Saw them.

Courtney Novak was still crying, and an embarrassed but equally concerned Heather had her arm around her sister and looked ready to lead her toward the back.

Time slowed.

Autumn felt as much as saw the moment Heather Novak noticed her and Winter heading her way. Normally, she needed to touch someone, but the air seemed filled with the older sister's dismay.

She said something to Courtney, and Courtney whirled around. Her bloodshot eyes searched the room, dancing over them before snapping back. The enormous blues widened even more, and her hand flew to her mouth. The sisters had clearly been talking about them.

An older lady with black curly hair came striding from the kitchen, a tray of rolls in her hands. She was oblivious to the tension building in the room and smiling as she put the bread in its proper place.

"I think that's everything," the woman Autumn recognized as Grace Henderson said. "Time to—"

Eat.

Autumn mentally finished the sentence for her because the older woman no longer could. She stood frozen to the spot, pale as the snow that threatened to fall outside.

The long blade of the knife used to cut the ham was pressed against her throat.

26

The Café Incanto was an Italian restaurant with a strange vibe. The building was painted a mixture of bright turquoise and yellow and featured a fake palm tree out front. Inside, blue neon lights behind the bar set the mood while a karaoke stage with a glittering, rotating disco ball sent dancing sparkles around the room. Fortunately, nobody was singing, although the decidedly non-Italian music would make having a normal conversation a little difficult.

If Aiden had been searching specifically for a restaurant that would make it hard to see his date's face clearly, he couldn't have found a better place. It was so dim that he could barely see Miguel and Bree sitting at the bar sharing a large plate of an appetizer so greasy looking that his nervous stomach twisted in additional knots just at the sight of it.

This case was getting to him on several levels. After a great deal of thought, he'd realized it wasn't just his ego taking a hit, but his faith in humanity was getting pushed farther and farther away.

It wasn't just the BDSM or even the vampirism Autumn

also thought was involved. It wasn't only how the men had been so thoroughly humiliated, financially and at their times of death. Or May-December relationships. Or carefully organized hookups.

It was how quickly these men had begun dating again, so soon after laying their wives to rest.

He didn't want to judge them, and he understood what Autumn said about the men needing someone to focus on them after so many years of being the head of a household. His issues went deeper than that.

Maybe it was simple faithlessness. Not just in marriage but in all relationships. Child and parent. Husband and wife. Business partners and peers. Lovers of any persuasion. Friends.

In the throw away society in which they now lived, had relationships turned into yet another disposable product?

He was shown to a seat, where he went over the six pages of the menu. The house wine was cheap and most of the items were based around red sauce—more comfort food than authentic.

A few minutes after the date was supposed to begin, the maître d' escorted a woman to Aiden's table. She had long, straight black hair, sculpted eyebrows, and lips only a few shades darker than the rest of her face. Aiden was no expert at makeup, but he appreciated the effect more than he would have a couple of weeks ago. With his increased awareness of such things, he was almost positive the woman was wearing a well-seated wig.

"Roger Applegate?" She had a lovely, lilting voice and held out a hand in one of those limp-wristed gestures that would work whether he decided to shake her hand or kiss the back of it. "I'm Kay. Kay Nash."

He stood and gave her a little bow before pressing his lips

to her soft skin. He'd noticed the older gentlemen at the speed-dating event preferred these types of gallant gestures. "Pleased to meet you."

She smiled, and Aiden noticed that her teeth were all perfectly straight except for an incisor that was slightly twisted. He held out a chair for her, inhaling her pleasant scent as he searched her face for hints of prosthetic makeup. If it was there, it was cleverly disguised by a skilled hand.

When she was settled into the seat opposite him, a fresh-faced waiter with a thin goatee appeared beside them, reaching to light the small candle in a hurricane glass at their table.

Kay's smiled practically knocked the man's socks off. "Thank you. It's lovely."

With a flourish, the waiter presented a wine list to Aiden. "We have a good bottle of—"

"Thank you." She flashed that bright grin at Aiden. "I'd like something a little stiffer." Her gaze ran down his body, and Aiden was glad that the table covered his lower half. "How about you, Roger?"

The waiter's face seemed to redden in the uncertain light. Aiden couldn't blame the kid.

"Uh…we have an extensive wine and cocktail list, but our specialties are Bellinis in a variety of flavors. Other crowd favorites are our green spritzes, and of course, our Negronis."

"I'll have a Negroni." Kay turned toward Aiden. "What about you?"

Aiden spread his hands, remembering their spider's penchant for submissive men. "What can I say? I like a deci-sive woman. Decide for me."

Something flickered in her eyes before the smile grew even wider. "Negronis for two, then."

After the waiter retreated, Aiden leaned back in his seat, tilting his head and giving Kay what he hoped was an admiring smile. He was wearing a long-sleeved shirt that was unbuttoned at the neck a little. Suddenly, he was glad that his arms were covered. His skin was covered with goose bumps.

She leaned toward him, and the low-cut burgundy wrap dress teased at a hint of cleavage. She had brushed the mounds with a light dusting of silver glitter that caught the light. "So, Roger, how are you?"

"Delighted."

She leaned back in her seat a little, lowering her eyelashes to give him a sultry look. "Delighted?"

"It's not every day that I meet a woman so refreshingly direct in ordering drinks. Are you always this direct...when giving orders?"

The woman's aggressive attitude definitely brought thoughts of bondage to mind.

She gave him a smile that could only be described as smug. "I'm always very direct when giving orders."

"I admire that in a woman." Aiden wondered whether Kay intended to proposition him that night or not. It seemed like the spider's cycle of killing was intensifying and escalating. He'd have to be on his guard, and not let her drive him anywhere or otherwise gain control.

Their waiter appeared, delivering their drinks and two glasses of iced water. "Are you ready to order?"

Kay hadn't even looked at the menu. "Penne arrabbiata with the insalata fennel."

She clearly was a frequent visitor of the place.

Aiden decided to be equally decisive. "Pollo alla cacciatora with the polenta. And a small antipasto platter as well as," he raised his eyebrows toward Kay, lobbing the decision-making back to her, "a bottle of the pinot noir?"

She smiled. "The Meiomi."

The waiter took their menus, and once again retreated.

Kay winked at him. "You're not bad at giving orders yourself."

Aiden lifted his drink and held it between them. "To orders well given and received."

She laughed, and he thought it might have actually been genuine. "I like that." Their glasses clinked, and they both sipped deeply.

He gave an appreciative sigh. "Negronis aren't my usual drink, but this isn't bad."

He noticed that her lips barely left a smear on the rim of the glass and realized she was only wearing gloss, not lipstick at all. She really did have pretty, bow-shaped lips.

"What's your usual drink?" she asked, running her finger around the rim of her glass.

He was normally a gin-and-tonic guy, or maybe a bourbon, but it seemed disturbingly over-intimate to confess his real tastes in front of this woman. "Scotch."

"Do you have a favorite brand?"

Unfortunately, he didn't have much taste for Scotch and couldn't rattle off any specific ones off the top of his head. "I'm not picky. As long as it's not too smoky, I'm game. I save those for going camping with the boys."

Aiden found himself thinking of the undercover CIA officers he knew. His appreciation of their acting skills had just increased tenfold. Being undercover also took a great deal of preparation, and he realized he'd enormously underestimated the amount of backstory he'd needed to come up with to pull off Roger Applegate successfully.

Like favorite drinks, for one.

But Kay just laughed. "I know what you mean. Some people get married to one brand and act devastated when they can't order that brand at every bar in the state." She sipped her drink, barely touching it to her lips before once again stirring the liquid with her straw. Her face grew sad.

He reached over and touched her hand. "Is everything okay?"

She sighed and turned her hand until their fingers linked. "I'm sorry. I'm not at my best this evening. If your profile hadn't seemed so interesting, I would have canceled."

"You found my profile interesting?" Aiden prompted her toward the subject he knew "Roger Applegate" would have been most interested in...himself.

Kay's face darkened, but only for a second before she chuckled, her hand slipping from his to pick up her glass again. "Yes. I've always been into older men. Silver foxes and all that. I love their intellect and wisdom, though I've found that most talk a big game about staying in shape and taking care of their bodies. Most don't actually follow through, though. I think I could out-lift most of them."

"You lift?" He forced his eyes to graze down her body and was disgusted by how lecherous he felt. "You're such a tiny thing. How much do you weigh?"

She fluttered her eyelashes at him. "Isn't that an intimate question to be asking a woman on the first date? I'm actually trying to put on a little weight, and if I eat everything I ordered, I'll probably do just that." She leaned forward, her voice dropping. "Unless you work the calories off me later."

Aiden decided to play dumb. "Are you a member of a local gym?"

Her disappointment was palpable, but she covered it quickly. "No. I like my workouts to be more..." her gazed dipped to his lips, "natural."

In his "hearing aid," muted laughter filled his ear.

God, not again.

Aiden nodded and took another sip of his drink. "The gym saved my life. Had a health scare a year or so ago, and it brought me to my senses. Started taking care of myself after that."

"You look very fit."

Aiden smiled, deciding he needed to flirt a little more. "So do you. You're very beautiful, and I feel very privileged to be with you right now."

Her expression softened, and her gaze fell to the drink she continued to stir with her straw. "That's very kind. I'm very surprised that a man like you," her eyes came up and met his, "isn't married."

His balls tightened, and the goose bumps rose on his arms once again. Earlier that day, he and Autumn had spoken about this very topic at length. Autumn had shared her "stab in the back" theory and how she felt sure that the knives left near the victims' spines were a message that they were being punished for stabbing someone else—namely their dead wives—in the same way.

He waved a dismissive hand. "Not anymore. Guess I'm looking for the right woman."

Kay's face stayed neutral, and if she was irritated with his answer, it didn't show. "Finding the right person is very difficult, I've found."

"I agree. And I'm not the type to go out to bars or places like that, so I decided to toss my hat into the online ring and see what might happen." He smiled, making his voice go deeper as he held eye contact with her. "I'm so very, very glad I did."

She blushed, which was interesting. People could fake embarrassment but actually having color rush to the cheeks was an involuntary response. Sure, a person could some-times fake it by thinking of a past event they found embar-rassing, but Kay wouldn't have time to have done such a thing.

Maybe she wasn't their spider after all.

Reaching out, she covered his hand with hers again. "I'm glad you did too."

Their food came, giving Aiden time to recollect himself. Kay Nash was very attractive, much prettier than the online profile pictures of the woman who dated the murdered men.

Was this Unsub 2? The scammer? It was a possibility of course, but Unsub 2's cheeks had been a bit broader than Kay's. Could that be a makeup trick too?

"What are you thinking about?" his date asked, her fork in the process of twirling a bite. "You seem very far away."

He had been.

He smiled and picked up his own fork. "It's nothing, just woolgathering I suppose."

She laughed. "I've not heard that term in a very long time."

"Well, I learned the phrase from my grandfather..."

Aiden launched into a yarn spinning tale that took several minutes to finish.

Woolgathering? Spinning yarns?

Geez, he was getting old.

Moving away from the idioms, he took a sip of the wine. "Do you have family here?"

Her face went sad. "No. My entire family is gone."

"What hap—"

"There's a problem at the community center."

"—pened to your family?" Aiden managed to finish the question through Bree's soft interruption.

A glance toward the bar showed Miguel on the phone, his finger in his ear as he spoke animatedly.

He tried to focus on Kay, who was talking about a terrible accident that killed both her parents and siblings. How she should have also been with them but had been a typical bratty teenager and refused to go.

"The guilt has eaten away at me all these years," she said,

lifting a napkin to her eye. Real tears were involved, he noted.

"Heather Novak is holding a knife to a woman's throat."

Shit!

Aiden reached for her hand. "I'm so very sorry that happened to you. Losing people we love is such a terrible thing." Aiden forced his voice to break on the last word. Clearing his throat, he pushed his chair back. "I'm so sorry. I need the restroom."

Better Kay Nash think him an emotional asshole than he spend another moment not knowing what was happening with his team.

Kay dabbed at another tear as he walked away. Miguel handed the phone to Bree and followed him down the hall.

"What the hell happened?" Aiden demanded, whirling on the agent the moment they were out of sight.

"From what I understand, the youngest sister, Courtney, came to the center when the speed-dating event was breaking for dinner. She was crying, so Winter and Autumn decided to follow her in. When Heather Novak saw them, she grabbed a knife from a table and put it to her employee's throat."

"Dammit." Aiden gave himself a moment to think it all through. He'd been in the building just last night and had paid attention to each exit. "You and Bree head over there. Dalton can cover the front while you and Bree cover the back and side. Call Mazur for additional backup. When they get there, work on getting the dating participants out as quickly as you can."

Miguel glanced back toward the eating area. "We can't leave you. One of us, at least, needs to stay."

Aiden was already shaking his head. "That's the priority and a direct order." Miguel's jaw popped but he didn't argue. "Besides, I'm perfectly safe in a crowded restaurant."

Miguel didn't look convinced, but finally nodded. "Stay put. Don't go anywhere."

Aiden nodded agreement and strode to the restroom to give himself a moment to calm as Miguel marched off. After washing his hands, he found Kay typing on her phone, her facial features a tight mask.

She jumped when he pulled out his chair. He glanced at the device. "Everything okay?"

Her lips didn't seem to know what to do as they first attempted a smile, then collapsed into a frown. She tossed the phone into her bag and lifted her napkin to her eye.

There were no tears this time. Instead, he could almost feel anger coming off her in waves.

She sniffed. "I'm sorry. I just got some very upsetting news."

So did he.

He reached for her hand and squeezed. "I'm so sorry. Is there anything I can do?"

She sniffed again, though her eyes were still dry as bone. "No, but thank you. You're such a kind man." She rubbed her thumb across his fingers. "Would you be very upset if I shortened our time together?"

Hallelujah.

"No, not at all, but I do hope to see you again."

Kay linked her fingers in his. "Absolutely. I'd like that very much."

He stood as she did and kissed her cheek when she offered the powdery skin. She grabbed her bag. "Oh, the check." She began rummaging inside. "Let me give you my share."

Aiden waved her off. "No need. I'm happy to buy a lovely lady a lovely dinner." He gestured to her uneaten food. "Would you like to take this for later?"

She shook her head. "No, thank you. After this news, I'm afraid I won't be able to eat another bite."

Then she was gone. He watched her rush to the door, then her car. A moment later, her headlights flashed on, and with very little hesitation, she pulled out of the space and was soon out of sight.

The waiter reappeared. "Anything wrong?"

"No…not at all. May I have the check?" He offered his card to speed the process up.

The kid gave him a sad look. He clearly thought that Aiden'd been dumped. Which he very well might have.

"Of course, I'll be right back."

If Kay Nash gave him three stars…

"Here you go."

He thanked the kid, took back his card, and signed the slip, leaving a twenty-percent tip. He was tempted to have the food boxed up for him, but he had no idea how long the community center fiasco would last.

Specks of snow and ice hit his face the moment he stepped outside. Poking his hands in his pockets, he was glad for the keyless entrance feature so he didn't have to fumble with the buttons to figure out which one unlocked the doors in the inadequate parking lot light.

He wished cars also had an automatic opener so he wouldn't have to touch the cold metal. He pulled out his phone, intent on calling for an update the very second the motor began to run.

Opening the door, he bent to get behind the wheel. A powerful force gave him a mighty push, and Aiden found himself projected nearly in the passenger seat.

What the—

A surge of electricity locked his muscles and brain before he could get through the rest of the thought. His entire body continued to cramp as hands pushed him all the way over the console. He was splayed awkwardly against the passenger side door, his legs higher than his head, but he could do absolutely nothing about it.

He couldn't move. He could barely think.

But he had no trouble watching Kay Nash slide behind the wheel, a stun gun in her hand. And he had no trouble watching her smile or hearing her say, "Told you I workout."

27

Heather's heart beat wildly in her chest as she stared at the black-haired woman and the redhead. They looked so different today in their well-fitted pant suits. Their hair was pulled back tightly from their faces.

Cops.

Her instincts had been right.

Very slowly, the black-haired one pulled something from her jacket pocket. A badge. "I'm Special Agent Winter Black with the FBI, and this is my associate, Dr. Autumn Trent. Put down your weapon and step away from your friend."

Friend?

Friendships are like apples, clinging to a tree.

They either ripen and grow, or they rot and fall free.

Heather and her sisters used to love to make up rhymes. They'd write songs and poetry, then very seriously present them to each other. In their little cottage, she had a trunk that still possessed every word they'd ever written.

Around the room, her speed-dating participants stared on in shock as they backed away from the table. To her side, Courtney was on the floor, her face pressed into her hands as she sobbed uncontrollably. Of course, that was nothing new. She'd been sobbing when she rushed inside only a few minutes ago. Sobbing and speaking in a voice so threadbare, Heather wasn't sure how it hadn't completely unraveled with every word she'd attempted to say.

Heather'd only caught a few of them. Something about father...asshole...honeymoon...t-shirts. Then it clicked. Their father, the asshole, had returned from his honeymoon, and all he brought them was a t-shirt.

Heather laughed, the sound more hysterical than she remembered it ever sounding.

"What...are you...doing?" Grace's entire body trembled as she asked Heather the question.

Heather didn't answer. She wanted to because Grace had been a wonderful employee, but she didn't know how.

Instead, she lightened the pressure on the woman's skin. Grace pulled in a deep breath, a sob escaping on the exhale. Only then did Heather feel the warm trickle of blood on her fingers.

Sorrow rose inside her. She'd never meant to hurt anyone, not really. She wasn't like her sister.

"Where's Katherine?"

The thought had been in her head but somehow found itself coming from her mouth. It was Courtney who answered, "I can't find her." Her eyes were swollen as she silently pleaded for Heather to fix this. "He, our bastard sperm donor, sent us a group text...about the t-shirts. I tried calling her so many times." Her voice finally unraveled, and she began crying again.

Heather looked away.

She was tired, so very tired.

"Katherine is sick, isn't she?" It was Autumn Johnson...no, Autumn Trent. *Excuse me*, Doctor *Autumn Trent*. "She's the one you're so afraid for?"

"Afraid for? Afraid of?" Heather made a very unladylike sound. "Does it matter?"

"Yes." Autumn took a step forward, her hands out, beseeching. "It does matter, Heather. It matters to both you and to Courtney."

Tears burned in Heather's already scalded eyes. "You don't know us. Any of us."

"I know you're scared, and you don't know how to help your baby sister."

Pink is for girls with pretty soft curls.

Wearing their pretty silk dresses and pearls.

Laughing and singing all day while they danced and twirled.

Heather forced the corny little childhood song away. She used to sing it over and over while rocking Katherine on the front porch.

Katherine had been so sweet as she gazed up at her big sister, her big eyes glowing with love as she said, "Sing it again."

"Sh-sh-she's ch-ch-changed." Heather's voice didn't even sound like her own.

Another step closer. Autumn's green eyes were very pretty. Why hadn't she noticed that before?

Heather realized that the knife had dropped several inches from Grace's throat. The speed-dating participants gasped when she gave herself a mental shake and jerked it back in place. Grace gasped too and began to cry again.

Heather noticed the FBI agent mouthing instructions to her hostage. She also noticed that Autumn was even closer now. And more people dressed in black were in the room.

"Don't come any closer," Heather screamed, her heart slamming again. What was she doing? Why was she doing it? She couldn't think with so many people staring at her. "Get out! Leave me alone."

No one moved, and Heather's vision blurred as she realized just how alone she really was.

"It started out as a way to support your family, didn't it, Heather?" Autumn smiled, and Heather didn't see a hint of malice in the expression. Not even pity. Just understanding and a deep desire to help. "Did the three of you joke about robbing from the rich and giving to the poor?"

Courtney's head jerked up, and the sisters' gazes met. It was Courtney who spoke. "Yes. We called ourselves The Three Robins." Her laugh was mostly a sob.

"Hush!" The demand came out louder than Heather had intended, making Grace and Courtney both jump. "Don't say anything, Court. We'll get out of here, you'll see."

Sirens blared outside, and she knew she'd just lied to her sister. From the look in Courtney's eyes, she knew it too.

It was over. For all of them.

Except Katherine, the bitch. The betrayer. The stabber in the back.

Fury began to burn through the pain. Her sister was probably on a plane right now, sipping champagne in a spacious first-class cabin. She'd probably already erased her family from her mind and was dreaming of who she'd screw over next.

Just like their father.

Yes. Just like him, Katherine had robbed her of her future. No more.

No one was ever, ever going to hurt her like that again.

"Katherine took almost all the money," she told her sister, and Courtney's mouth dropped open in surprise. "There's a little left...enough for you to get a good attorney." Heather turned her attention on Autumn. "The username and password are in a purple and pink notebook. Page sixty-three. Bottom drawer of my bedroom desk. Make sure she uses the money for a good attorney. And make sure the judge knows that Courtney was the only innocent one of us."

Feeling much calmer now, she gazed down at her sister. "I love you, Court. Sell the house and move away, okay. Go to California where it's sunny all the time." Emotion deepened her voice. "You need sun."

It was like her words had triggered fear inside her sister. Pain was replaced by terror as Courtney pushed back on her heels, ending in a kneeling position. Gazing up at Heather with those big blue eyes she knew so well, her baby sister held out a trembling hand. "Give me the knife. Please."

Heather took a step back, taking a trembling Grace with her. Her speed-dating participants cowered away. They were huddled in groups, holding on to each other.

See? I really am good at bringing people closer together.

Courtney moved again, getting to her feet this time. Her hand was still outstretched…reaching, wanting. "Heather, I love you. You're all I have left. Please give me the knife."

All the regrets in the world spun through Heather's mind.

How Heather wished it could all be different. How she wished she hadn't failed so badly. How she wished Courtney wouldn't have to witness this part.

"I'm tired," Heather admitted and dropped the knife from Grace's throat, pushing her employee away.

"Don't." Courtney's words were whispered, but they rang in Heather's head.

As her hand moved, the agent and the doctor began to shout. Heather didn't understand what they said, her focus was solely on her sister.

"I love you."

She hadn't expected it to be so easy, and it didn't really even hurt as much as she'd expected. Her blood was surprisingly warm as it flowed down the front of her shirt.

"No!" Courtney lunged for her just as Heather's knees began to buckle.

Three little sisters jumping on the bed, one fell off and bumped her head.

Mama called the doctor and the doctor said, "No more sisters jumping on the bed."

"Heather…don't go. Don't leave me…please."

Two little sisters jumping on the bed, one fell off and bumped her head.

Mama called the doctor and the doctor said, "No more sisters jumping on the bed."

"We need medics…now!" So many faces. So much pressure. So many touching her.

One little sister jumping on the bed, she fell off and bumped her head.

Mama called the doctor and the doctor said, "No more sisters jumping on the bed."

Courtney's lips on her forehead, her tears on her cheeks.

Heather wanted to tell her that she loved her again, but her voice didn't seem to work.

Darker. Dimmer. Courtney's bright hair fading away.

No little sister jumping on the…

AUTUMN SAT IN SHOCK.

She still couldn't believe what just happened, even though it'd happened before her eyes.

Courtney Novak was sobbing uncontrollably, holding on to her sister, refusing to let go even when two burly paramedics tried to pull her away. When it was clear that there was no hope of saving Heather, Winter had told the men to just leave the youngest Novak alone.

Grace Henderson was crying too, a silent trail of tears dripping off her chin as a third paramedic began treating the small wounds on her throat. "I don't understand what just happened," she kept repeating.

By the looks on everyone's faces, no one did.

The speed-dating participants were herded to another section of the community center. There, Autumn knew their contact information would be gathered for later questioning.

Noah dropped to his haunches in front of her, his big hand coming down on her shoulder for a squeeze. "You okay?"

She blinked and tried to focus. "Yeah."

She wasn't, but she would be because she had to be. There was no other choice.

From the corner of her eye, she spotted Bree and Miguel. "When did they get here?" she asked Noah.

He turned to see who she was speaking of. "Hell, I'm not sure exactly, but I'm thinkin' they broke every land speed record on the books."

She glanced around the room, studying every face. "Where's Aiden?"

Noah frowned, but instead of answering, he stood up. In just a few steps he was in front of the two agents. Pushing to her feet, Autumn gladly took the small package of wet wipes one of the medics handed her.

She couldn't watch as the white sheets turned pink from the stains on her hands. Autumn had tried to hold pressure on Heather's neck, but the wound was just too big. She could still remember Courtney's screams and her tears that fell onto her sister's face.

Sister.

This entire case, she hadn't allowed herself to think of her own sister, but Sarah's name had been nagging her mind. Just not here in Pennsylvania. For the past few months if not years, Autumn's desire to find Sarah had increased.

And now that she'd witnessed the bond between sisters so intimately, that desire had spread.

Later. She would think about that later, but now, she

didn't like the expression that was on Noah's face.

Still wiping the blood from her hands, she moved closer to their discussion. Miguel had a phone pressed to his ear while Bree spoke into a little mic.

"What's happening?" she asked.

Noah's expression was grim. "Aiden sent them here to help us."

Goose bumps raised on Autumn's arms, and she turned on her heel, heading back to the crying blonde still on the floor. She had a terrible feeling.

"Courtney!"

The girl jumped but didn't stopped rocking her sister.

"I need you to listen to me," Autumn demanded, using a firm voice to gain the girl's attention.

Very slowly, Courtney's eyes moved to meet hers. Good enough.

Legs appeared in her periphery, but she ignored them all. "Courtney, do you know where Katherine is?"

Courtney didn't answer, just continued to rock.

After what felt like a lifetime, Courtney shook her head, still rocking her sister, blood everywhere. "I don't know. I've looked everywhere for her. She wasn't at the cottage or at her apartment."

"What did Heather mean when she said that Katherine had taken all the money?"

Courtney looked at her in abject misery. Her eyes were filled with so much pain that Autumn ached for the young woman. "We...we did bad things to get money. We were trying to get enough to leave this place." Her face crumbled. "I'm so sorry." She began to cry hard again.

Winter placed a comforting hand on the young woman's shoulder, and Autumn exhaled a soft breath, grateful to not be the one to touch her. She didn't think she'd survive the onslaught of pain.

"Don't worry about any of that right now," Winter said. "Was Katherine supposed to have a date tonight?"

Autumn's gut began to twist as the seconds turned into minutes. Finally, Courtney's keening grew softer and Winter repeated the question.

Courtney wiped her nose on her shoulder, her hands busy stroking her sister's face and hair. "Sh-she was supposed to have a date, but she said she was going to cancel it. After last night…" The girl closed her eyes and turned so pale that Autumn worried that some of the blood on the floor might be hers.

Autumn leaned forward, catching Courtney's gaze. "What happened after last night?"

They'd get to their other questions about last night later, but right now, they needed to focus on one thing…finding Aiden.

The girl's eyes looked angry and raw as she met Autumn's gaze. "She promised me that she would stop, that she wouldn't go on anymore dates."

Autumn swallowed the bile that wanted to rise. "Did she have one scheduled?"

Courtney nodded. "But she said she would cancel."

Autumn's guts churned and twisted even tighter. "Courtney, honey, do you know the name she was going to use for the date?" When Courtney shook her head, Autumn tried another question. "Do you know the name of her date?"

Courtney stroked her sister's hair, her bloody hands leaving bloody streaks. After a while, Autumn didn't think she would answer, then she frowned. "Richard maybe? Robert? No…" Her frowned deepened.

"Roger?" Autumn offered slowly.

Courtney's head snapped up. "Yes. Applegate. She was going out with Roger Applegate."

28

That was exciting.

Well, not at first.

Roger Applegate had been about to blow me off. I had a nose for things like that. He'd been distracted on our date, glancing at his phone when he thought I didn't notice. Looking around the restaurant. Paying attention to every-thing but me.

Had he been searching for the door?

Or searching for someone better?

I didn't like that. Not at all.

Being ignored did nothing but piss me off.

After training to become a professional actor for several years, I'd been ready for the spotlight to fall on me the moment I moved to New York. It hadn't.

What fell on me instead, was the slobbering lips of much older men. They made promises and gave me gifts to buy both my body and my silence.

For a while, it had been a good exchange. I'd enjoyed the clothes and shoes and jewelry. My sweet little apartment was beautifully furnished. But as I began to hit my mid-twenties, the offers of support withdrew, and I knew I needed a more sustainable plan.

Convincing Heather and Courtney to team up with me had been easy. They too had grown tired of living on the very fringes of attaining a happy life.

They both tried. Heather worked hard, not only in her growing business but in keeping our pitiful little family together. Courtney, the baby, just wanted everyone to fix things for her.

I'd fixed it, all right. Showed them the way out of Pennsylvania. Gave them a very specific plan toward having our own independence. It had worked beautifully for over two years, beginning the moment Courtney and I went back to my place in New York and began working the city's lonely even older men.

A few hundred thousand dollars later, both Courtney and Heather had been hooked. We moved from city to city, dating the men Heather connected us with after she broadened the reach from local to national. A few thousand here and a few thousand there turned into six figure hauls.

Then Mom got sicker in the body while Dad got sicker in the head.

He'd always been a horrible person. He'd even stooped so low as to steal Heather's "get the hell out of here" fund.

But as Mom lay dying, I learned that he had met someone. I followed him once, stood at the window of Deena's home and watched as she gave him head.

My world shifted in that moment. I felt it give under my feet, just like an earthquake tremored under the earth.

Mom died, and my world shifted again.

Weeks later, Terrance called with "great news." He'd won the lottery, eleven million dollars.

"And don't you worry," he'd gushed, his voice booming over the phone. "I'm going to take good care of my girls."

I'd been so gullible, so desperate for my father's love, that my heart had filled with so much hope. At twenty-six years old, my daddy was finally going to take care of me.

"I'm transferring the title to the house to you and your sisters. Paid off, free and clear."

I'd waited. Waited for more? Waited for something that didn't feel like a knife in my back.

"The cottage?" I'd finally managed to ask. "You're giving the three of us a broken-down cottage?"

He'd laughed. *Laughed.* "I'm sure you girls will fix it right up."

My world shifted with that laugh.

It shifted again when he brought Deena to Thanksgiving dinner.

It shifted one more time when that envelope arrived in the mail. A thick stock, cream with gold letters could only mean one thing. Opening it revealed the truth.

Dad and Deena had gotten married. Three months after Mama's death.

That had been the shift that spun me into a vortex of self-destruction.

I'd spit on the announcement. I'd ripped it to shreds. I'd cursed and cried and raged. I did everything but...I didn't tell my sisters.

The game changed after that day.

Men were no longer my targets. Men became my prey.

"Ah...ah...ah..."

Roger's face had transformed into a brutal sort of red, and saliva dripped from his mouth and onto the floor of this very nice Lexus. I sighed. Time to pull over and make a few decisions.

It was very dark behind an abandoned strip mall, which was exactly what I needed. Looking around, I searched for hidden cameras, but didn't find a single one.

Getting out of the car, I kept the stun gun in my hand. Roger nearly fell out onto the cold concrete when I opened the passenger side door, but I managed to muscle him back in. Once he was in a more upright position, I gave him another little dose of electricity before opening my Mary Poppins bag and pulling out a set of handcuffs.

Leaning his stiff body forward, I cuffed his wrists together then kissed his cheek as I buckled his seat belt in place. "Safety first."

That was when I saw it…the makeup on his face. Licking my thumb, I wiped more of it away. Smooth skin appeared.

Heart pounding, I searched through his pockets. A wallet. A badge. This man wasn't Roger Applegate. He was Aiden Parrish, Special Supervisory Agent of the fucking FBI.

Stumbling back, I nearly fell on my ass.

The FBI. This man had been setting me up.

I was in so much trouble.

"Calm down," I told myself as I began to pace. "You've planned for this moment. You knew you could get caught."

I had planned. Planned enough ahead to get a set of documents in a new name.

Once it had become clear that my sisters were beginning to turn on me, I'd siphoned off my share of the money—it had been my idea, after all, so the larger share should go to me. Now, all I had to do was get on a plane and leave the country.

Grabbing my phone, I opened a travel app and tapped on flights to Cuba. Nothing available until the morning, so with no other choice, I booked a one-way ticket using my new identity for butt crack in the morning. First class, of course.

"Ah…ah…ah…"

Picking the stun gun back up, I walked over to the passenger side of the Lexus, studying the man inside with new eyes.

"So, Mr. Aiden Parrish of the FBI," I grabbed his face, turning it until he was looking directly at me, "it seems we have a little problem."

That was an understatement.

Getting Roger/Aiden into this car had been so easy. Toward the middle of our date, I'd sensed his distraction grow. By the time he'd excused himself to go to the restroom, I'd made a decision.

Instead of him rejecting me, I'd reject him first.

Roger had been perfectly nice as I made my excuses, going so far as saying that he wanted to see me again. But as I got into my car, my false tears still drying on my cheeks, rage began to consume me. How dare he! How dare he reject me!

Then the worst thought of them all...*what was wrong with me?*

That question had been the turning point, and instead of driving away, I'd turned around and waited.

I hadn't used a stun gun before. I'd never been forced to do so. The website promised that the one I'd purchased was powerful enough to take down a man, even through several layers of clothing.

The website had been right. Roger had locked up like the Tinman on the *Wizard of Oz*. It had been a simple thing, really, to give a hard push. The way he landed, head down and feet up, still made me smile.

"Ah...ah...ah..."

I held the stun gun in front of his face. "Hush, I'm thinking."

I didn't dare go back to the little cottage or my apartment.

Where? And what was I going to do with this man?

My phone pinged, and I closed my eyes in frustration.

Was it Heather, or Courtney, or dear old Daddy this time?

The thought of Terrance paused my pacing...and gave me an idea.

He and his little wifey got home from their honeymoon, I remembered. And he said he had a present for each of us too.

I smiled.

It was perfect. Absolutely perfect.

Leaning close enough to the agent to smell his aftershave, I pressed my lips to his ear.

"Ready to meet my daddy?"

29

"She's always been selfish, but she'd never been bad."

Courtney Novak blew her nose into one of the tissues gripped in her hands. They'd finally been able to pry her from her sister and lead her to another room in the community center.

Normally, this was the point where they would take her to jail for booking, but with Aiden in the clutches of her sister, they had no time.

"Courtney," Autumn said softly, Winter by her side. "I'm so very sorry all this has happened to you and your family."

The girl had been speaking in great gushes of words, explaining everything that had happened over the past two years. Their scheme to be financially independent. Their mother's death. Their father's betrayal. Katherine's change.

Autumn took the young woman's hand when she began to cry again and closed her eyes against the rush of sadness and guilt.

"Courtney." Her voice was firmer now. "Katherine may have taken our colleague, an FBI agent, hostage, and I need you to tell me where they may be going."

When they'd first realized that Aiden was missing, Miguel and Bree had rushed back to the restaurant, finding nothing but Aiden's phone in the parking lot. They were working on getting a warrant to have the Lexus's rental company help them locate the car.

Nothing was happening fast enough to suit Autumn, though, and she knew questioning this poor girl was one of their last options. And she needed to do it before Courtney was formerly arrested. If Autumn avoided talking about her involvement in the spree of crimes, it would be fine...if Courtney would stop talking about the spree of crimes and focus.

"Did you try our house?" Courtney asked.

Autumn nodded. A patrol car had been sent there right away. "We've also tried her apartment. Please think. Earlier, you said something about your father."

Courtney blew her nose again. "Terrance." She practically spit out the name. "He got back from his honeymoon today. Married that bimbo three months after Mama died."

Stabbed in the back. It made so much sense.

Autumn glanced over at Winter but directed the question to the young woman. "Terrance Novak got home today?"

Courtney's head bobbed. "Yeah...and he brought us all a t-shirt." Betrayal and disgust and hurt mingled in the words.

"Does Katherine know that Terrance arrived home with his new wife?"

The young woman shrugged. "I guess. He sent a group message. Couldn't even be bothered to send us anything personal."

Autumn's heart was picking up speed. "What's his address?"

She shrugged again. "I don't know. He just bought it after winning the lottery and I've only been invited there once." She laughed, the sound filled with bitterness. "He gave us a run-down house that leaks each time it rains and buys himself a mansion. Typical."

"Courtney, we've searched for properties in your father's name and haven't found anything."

"That's because he put everything in *her* name. Even changed his will so *she* gets everything."

Autumn glanced at Winter again, who was now on her feet. This admission was new.

She squeezed Courtney's hand. "What's Deena's last name? Her maiden name?"

Courtney's nostrils flared. "Watkins."

Winter was out the door before Autumn could get to her feet. "Thank you," she said and glanced at the man standing in the corner. "She's all yours."

Chief Mazur had cuffs in hand, but Autumn didn't stay to listen to the charges or Miranda rights. She found Winter hovering over Sun's shoulder as she typed.

"Passavant Hills Estates," Sun said and rattled off the address.

Seconds later, they were all piling into their vehicles. The Charger started with a mighty roar, and the tires squealed as Winter pulled from the parking lot and onto the road.

"Hang on, Aiden," Autumn murmured as the car hit one hundred miles per hour. "We're coming."

_____

30

Aiden Parrish stumbled on legs that felt like wood. The damn woman had stun-gunned him again before hauling him from the vehicle. If she wasn't surprisingly strong for her size, he would have fallen on his face.

"Ah…" Dammit, his mouth wouldn't work.

"Hush," she demanded. "Don't want to wake the neighborhood."

And some neighborhood it was. On the drive there, Katherine Novak had ranted and raved about her father and his new home…his new bride…his new everything. And she hadn't lied. The house was massive.

She led him straight to the front door, and without hesitating, pressed her thumb on the ringer. Then again and again. Finally, she left her thumb in place.

Instead of the typical "ding dong" coming through the door, some mysterious music took its place. If he'd been able to think right, he would have been able to name the tune. But everything was blurred and spinning, and when he tried to speak, the words got lost somewhere between his tongue and his lips.

The sensation would go away in a short time, he knew. In the meantime, he tried to focus on what he would do the moment it did.

"I'm coming, I'm coming," came an angry voice on the other side of the door.

Did Katherine seriously think she could handle this situation? Her against two grown men.

The porch light flipped on. "Who is it?"

"Daddy," Katherine cried, a sob making the word hitch.

If Aiden'd had better control of his head, he would have turned it to see if someone different had taken his captor's place. The raging woman had morphed into a little girl.

"Daddy. It's me. I need help. Please."

The door opened, and a sleepy looking man appeared in boxers and a t-shirt. "Katherine? What's—"

She launched, the stun gun pressing directly on the man's stomach. Like a tree felled by an ax, Terrance Novak collapsed to the floor.

Katherine laughed and pulled Aiden inside. "Aiden, meet Daddy. Daddy, meet Aiden."

"Who is it, Ter?" a woman's voice called from down the hallway.

Aiden opened his mouth to warn her. "Ah—"

His body seized as the gun once again fulfilled its purpose, but this time, stars exploded into his vision as his temple connected with a marble table he had no reflexes to avoid.

His world went dark before he hit the floor.

SOME TIME LATER, he didn't know how much, the world brightened then focused. He tried to move, but his body still wasn't under his full control.

"Oh, look who's awake?"

Katherine Novak's voice was high-pitched and overly sweet, her smile much too big for her face.

She was different now. The black wig was gone, and in its place was her natural hair, a short blonde pixie cut that suited her much better.

Her eyes were blue now, and her nose was…different. So was the shape of her eyes.

"Nice disguise," he managed, though it took several long moments to get the words out.

She practically beamed at him. "Thanks. I'm an actor, you know. It's my job to become whoever I need to be."

He swallowed hard, which was when he felt the rope around his neck.

Panic hit him like a train, and he tried to get away, jerking his hands so hard the skin began to break from the bite of the metal trappings.

Smile still in place, Katherine reached over her head. Aiden looked up, watched her hand wrap around the end of the rope that was tied to a stairway rail…and pull.

The noose tightened until he was forced to sit up. It tightened even more, and he scrambled until he was on his knees on the floor.

She stopped there, tying the rope back to the rail. "Perfect."

Aiden looked up, following the line of the rope. She'd flung it over one of the many exposed beams. No, not only his rope. Two additional ones were strung beside it.

Turning his head, he found the man in the boxers kneeling too. Beside him, a young woman was equally bound.

They both disappeared as Katherine stepped in between Aiden and the couple. Aiden tried to cringe away from her touch as she stroked his hair, but the rope tightened a frightening degree.

Aiden cleared his throat. "What...want?" It wasn't a full sentence, but it was better than the mumbling idiot he'd been before.

She dropped to her knees in front of him, her blue eyes focused on his forehead. When her thumb brushed over an open wound, he groaned but didn't cry out. She brushed it again, harder this time, not stopping until fresh blood, warm and thick, dripped into his eye.

She smiled. "I'm going to combine our DNA, take you inside of me in a way much more powerful than sex."

Her tongue was warm as she licked the blood from his cheek. He shuddered in revulsion as she began to suck the gaping wound. He wanted to pull away, wanted to fight, but bound as he was, he could do nothing except wait until she drank her fill.

Lips a brighter red now, her expression was much more serious as she pulled away. "I regret that we don't have more time to play, but as I'm sure you know, I'm rushed for time." She ran her hand down his cheek. "A pity."

"What...you...want?" His voice was better now, though each syllable caused his head to throb even more.

In one graceful movement, Katherine Novak pushed to her feet. "How about a little game of show instead of tell?"

From her giant-sized purse, she pulled out a knife that was the exact replica of the ones found in her victims' backs.

Beside him, Deena Novak began to cry, which seemed to bring Terrance out of his stupor.

"Katherine...what are you doing?"

She licked her lips. "It's called poetic justice, Daddy."

With her attention off him, Aiden began to work to free himself of the cuffs. The steel was strong, and the links close together. Without another option, he began to work his thumb, hoping to dislocate it so he could slip his hand through.

He couldn't die like this. Not on his knees, the victim to a homicidal woman with daddy issues. He thought back to Brice Sutter and Allen Newhouse, and although he knew his situation could be worse, he took no comfort in the thought.

He'd been so stupid to leave the restaurant without a member of his team. So ego driven that he didn't think that anything like this could ever happen to him.

He'd been wrong. So very wrong.

His ego might have very well cost him his life.

"Do you know the man you married?" Katherine asked Deena. "I mean, other than the number in his bank account."

The woman was sobbing, but she raised her head and hissed, "Go to hell."

Katherine's laugh was more like a hysterical giggle as she walked over to the woman, pressing the knife to her throat. "I'll meet you there."

"No!" Terrance screamed, and instead of cutting the woman's throat, Katherine's head turned, her face as blank as a doll's as she looked down on her father.

"No?" She began to pace in front of them. "You know, you're actually right. I can't let her meet the devil downstairs without knowing more about the devil in her bed."

"Shut up!"

Aiden would have kicked the man had he been able. Instead, his daughter did it for him. A good one straight in the gut. The man would have collapsed if not for the rope holding him up.

"I like your house, Daddy." She looked up at the beams. "Nice architecture and all, unlike the piece of shit wreck you left to us. But I digress…"

She began pacing again, stopping in front of Deena.

"My previous question stands…do you know the man

you married? Do you know how many women, and children, have been in his bed?"

Deena blanched while Terrance began to sputter. Very calmly, Katherine pressed the blade against his mouth.

"How I love my baby in our special way..."

Aiden blinked at Katherine's surprisingly pleasant voice. Katherine stopped and smiled at her father. "Remember that song, Daddy?"

Tears ran down the man's cheeks.

"Crawl into my bed and we'll begin to play..."

"No!"

The anguished cry came from Deena, and Katherine turned her attention to her stepmother. "Oh, yes. Were you under the illusion that you were his youngest plaything?" She laughed. "Not by a long shot."

Katherine pulled the knife away from her father's lips. He immediately took advantage. "Katherine, I—"

"Shhh, Daddy." She sank to her knees. "Sing our special song for me again."

When Terrance did nothing, Katherine lifted the blade, not stopping until the very point was pressed into his throat.

Terrance swallowed and licked his lips. When a dot of blood appeared on his skin, he began to sing.

"How I love my baby in our special way.
Crawl into my bed and we'll begin to play."

Katherine began to sway side to side. Aiden swore under his breath as his thumb finally popped from its socket.

"Let me touch you places that makes all worries fade away."

Bile rose into Aiden's mouth, brought on not only by pain but the man beside him.

Headlights flicked through the windows as Aiden's hand slipped through one cuff.

"Aiden...?"

The voice coming through his fake hearing aids was

Autumn's, and it was the most beautiful sound he'd ever heard. He very softly cleared his throat. Just once. *Yes.*

"Kissing and touching gives Daddy so much pleasure."

"We've covered all the entrances, and we can hear everything that is happening inside. Do you understand?"

One small cough. *Yes.*

"Especially from the one I most treasure."

"Does she have a gun?"

Two tiny coughs. *No.*

"We've rallied local SWAT, and we have eyes on you."

Aiden glanced at the blinds across from him. His eyes might have been playing tricks, but he thought he saw the reflection of a sniper's lens.

Katherine began clapping. "Bravo, Daddy. Just the way I remember it."

Deena glared at her husband, her mouth trembling. "How could you?"

"It's not what you think!" Terrance cried. "I would never do—"

The blade didn't stop this time when its point met Terrance's skin. Katherine thrust, then swiped, and a geyser of blood erupted from her father's throat.

Deena's screams pierced Aiden's ears as Katherine swung the blade toward her.

Glass shattered, and it was like a gust of wind blew Katherine Novak backward. She hit a wall before slowly sinking to the floor.

Hands free, Aiden pulled on the noose as the doors and windows slammed open all around. His legs were unsteady as he forced himself forward, not stopping until he'd kicked the knife from Katherine's hand.

Voices were everywhere, then an arm came around his shoulders. Autumn. As cold as it was outside, sweat dripped from her forehead. "You're all right."

His throbbing head wanted to disagree, especially when he nodded. "I will be."

Paramedics tried to urge him away, but Katherine was reaching for him, and he didn't have the heart not to reach back. Her lips began to move as he took her hand.

"Step into my parlor, I said to the fly."

She really did have a beautiful voice.

"Dance into my heart and let me taste your soul."

Someone pressed something onto his forehead, and he missed a couple lines.

She began humming as an IV was started in her arm. Though the paramedic worked frantically to save her, she was fading before his eyes.

"Confirm...nothing to forgive."

She was dying. The spreading blood was proof of that certainty.

"And in return...gratitude...you."

With a shaky breath, Katherine's eyes lifted to meet his.

"In return, I'll...let you..."

Her eyes glazed over as her mouth struggled to continue, than all movement stopped and the hand he was holding fell into her lap.

Katherine Novak—their spider and vampire—was gone.

31

Autumn smiled at Winter and took the cup her friend offered. She sipped the warm vanilla latte and closed her gritty eyes. "I may live yet."

"Take a break," Winter murmured, keeping her voice low, although nurses bustled by them a mile a minute. Aiden had just been taken for a follow-up x-ray and they were standing in the hallway while a custodian mopped the floor.

"I will soon, I promise."

Instead of going back to the hotel after their headlong rush to Terrance Novak's house last night, Autumn had followed the ambulance containing Aiden to the hospital. Since her clothes were still covered in Katherine Novak's blood, the ER staff had graciously given her a pair of old scrubs to change into.

Winter, Noah, and the others had left the hospital in the early morning hours, after it was clear that their SSA would be fine. His concussion had been just bad enough that the doctor wanted to keep him overnight for observation. Autumn had volunteered to stay with him.

"Have you eaten?"

Autumn smiled at her friend. "I had a PayDay and some nuts in my bag, so I'm fine. You?"

Winter rolled her eyes. "I was with Noah, so of course I ate. Guess what?"

Autumn raised an eyebrow. "What?"

"Courtney Novak got released on bail this morning, and guess who paid it?"

Autumn frowned, trying to think who in the young woman's life would do such a thing.

The team had gotten to Terrance Novak's house in time for Autumn to hear Katherine Novak's accusations against her father through Aiden's earpiece.

They had desperately hoped to bring the disturbed woman out alive, but after she slit her father's throat and was turning the knife on Deena Novak, the sniper had no choice but to take the shot.

"Her stepmother paid it?"

Winter snorted. "Nope."

Autumn gave up. Every person Courtney was close to, that she knew of, was dead. "Just tell me."

"Woody Waller."

Autumn's mouth dropped open and her coffee almost slipped from her hand. "Woody from the speed-dating event?"

"That's the one."

Autumn was still stunned as Winter shared everything that had happened while she stayed here playing nurse to her future boss.

"Woody showed up at the courtroom, and we recognized each other. He told me about how Courtney, well Connie #16 as he knew her, had gone home with him after the event." Winter rolled her eyes. "He said it was love at first sight."

Autumn could do nothing but gape. "And he knows what she was charged with?"

"Yep."

"And he still posted her bail?"

"He sure did. He told me about how she began to cry when he was showing her his old car collection and how touched she had been that he didn't toss away older models and buy new." Winter sipped her own coffee. "He said that he could tell she was a good person who'd simply gotten dragged into a bad situation."

Autumn blinked. "She helped her sisters bury a dead body."

"That's true, but Woody insisted that he was intent on getting her help." Winter shrugged. "And I guess he can afford it, so who am I to argue?"

Autumn mentally scrolled through the laundry list of charges against Courtney. "He does realize that she most likely won't be able to avoid jail time, right?"

Winter rubbed her fingers together. "Money talks, so I wouldn't be so sure of that. Woody is loaded, and I'd bet all the coffee in the world he gets her an attorney that pleads her down to misdemeanors and house arrest."

Autumn considered it. "Well, she has been very open about everything. The sisters didn't spend any of the money they took. Her willingness to help us locate the funds and return it to the rightful owners would sway any judge."

"And she told us exactly where George Marsh's body was buried, and she said that she believed her sister killed Edwin Gallagher and tossed him in a river somewhere. They started dragging for a body this morning."

"At least those families will have some closure." Autumn thought of Peter Kelley and his daughter. She bet Tina was tap dancing to learn that her father was getting his money back.

"Yes, and sometimes that's the best we can all ask for."

Autumn lifted a shoulder. "I guess. It's so fascinating to me that three siblings from the same parents can turn out so different."

Winter's face fell, and Autumn could have kicked herself. "Nature versus nurture and all that, huh?"

Autumn squeezed her friend's hand. "I'm sorry. I know how close to home that hits."

Winter squeezed back. "You have a sister too, so it's not exactly outside your family tree."

Autumn sighed. "I've actually been thinking of my sister a great deal lately. So much so, that last night while I was sitting with Aiden, I entered her name in several missing persons databases."

Instead of smiling like Autumn had expected, Winter looked down at her feet. "That's good."

According to her friend's expression, it wasn't good at all.

Autumn's heart thumped. "What?"

Winter blew out a breath and looked her in the eye again. "Just be careful what you wish for, is all."

A clamp pressed on Autumn's heart. She knew exactly what Winter was and wasn't saying. What if she found Sarah and regretted it?

Which was worse?

"Most criminals don't start out as bad people," Autumn said softly. "The cards were just stacked against them. One thing went wrong...then another. Often, the thing that went wrong can be traced to childhood."

"Like Justin."

It wasn't a question, and Autumn just offered her friend a small nod. "Once the competency assessment is over, I'm going to attempt to attain approval to scan Justin's brain."

Winter frowned. "Why?"

"You know that I very much want to help Justin get

better," Autumn bit her lip, trying to be careful with her words, "but I also very much want to study him. I've shared that interest with you before."

Winter smiled, her blue eyes brimming with tears. "I know, and I think you doing both of those things is wonderful. Helping him, and then better understanding how his mind works so we can hopefully catch more people like him in the future."

"Exactly. I want to better understand how killers are made."

"Nature versus nurture," Winter offered again.

"Yes, but even deeper than that. Let's look at the Novak sisters. All three from the same family, but only one of them ended up murdering men, even though Courtney told us that they, all three, had been molested by their father. So these girls, same house, same experiences…two go on and attempt to build a life while one…" She held out a hand, not needing to finish the statement.

"What do you hope to find?"

"I hope to find out if a certain part of the brain is different in the one sibling who ends up taking a gun to school and opening fire." Autumn felt her excitement grow each time she thought of the brain. "I'm specifically interested in learning the size of Justin's amygdala."

Winter squinted. "Sorry, I'm going to need a neuroscience crash course."

Autumn grinned. "The amygdala consists of two tiny clusters of nuclei located deep in the temporal lobes and is directly linked to empathy." Autumn set down her cup on a nearby chair so she could use her hands better. "Essentially, those with a large amygdala have strong social connections and are people like caregivers and volunteers. Those with a very small amygdala are most likely psychopaths."

"What if Justin's amygdala is normal?"

"Actually, that's exactly what I'm expecting to see." When Winter frowned, she went on, "If Justin's amygdala is within the normal size range, then we can better understand that it was his environment, nurture, that played the larger role in decision-making."

Winter's face went cold. "Douglas Kilroy."

Autumn didn't want to go down that rabbit hole. "I'll also want to see if Justin has what is commonly called the 'warrior gene.' That, along with the brain scan will better help me not only help him but have more insight when developing profiles in the future."

Winter straightened, a smile coming to her face as she looked past Autumn's shoulder. "Speaking of brain scans..."

Autumn turned to find a hospital-gown-wearing Aiden being wheeled down the hall. White gauze created an almost crown appearance on his head. "He looks grumpy," she murmured.

Winter laughed softly. "When doesn't he?" She focused on Aiden. "How are you feeling?"

"Left out of the loop." He waved for them to follow him inside the room.

They ended up talking to the nurse while the grumpy patient was safely tucked under the covers by an orderly. "He'll be under concussion protocol for the next week, but he should be fine with time. Upon discharge, we'll make sure that you know of any warning signs to look for."

Once all the caregivers had left, Aiden barked, "Tell me what's been going on."

Autumn left the telling up to Winter and let her mind wander during the synopsis of the past twelve hours and then through the barrage of questions Aiden tossed at her afterward.

"Autumn!"

She snapped her mind back to the room. "Sorry." She rubbed her eyes. "Zoned out on you a little."

Aiden's gaze softened a fraction, and he scratched his jaw. "You didn't need to babysit me all night."

Winter snorted, making Autumn laugh. The women shared a look before Autumn raised an eyebrow. "Someone had to make sure you didn't leave against medical advice."

The SSA attempted to look offended. "I'm perfectly capable of following orders."

Autumn waved a finger. "Being perfectly capable is very different than actually following them."

He didn't argue. "My question was about when you two were heading home. Docs don't want me to fly for at least a week so I'm going to get a rental and drive home."

Beside her, Winter stiffened. "Not by yourself, you're not."

Autumn agreed. "One of us will drive you."

"Two of us," Winter said, tapping her thumb on her chest.

"I'm guessin' that makes three of us."

Autumn turned to find Noah in the doorway. Bree, Miguel, and Sun came in behind him.

Miguel popped candy into his mouth. "Four."

Bree grinned. "Five."

Sun just stared at everyone like they were crazy. "Count me out. I'm on the next plane out of here."

AUTUMN LEANED against the inside of her apartment door, leaving her rolling suitcase and other belongings at her feet. She kicked off her loafers and peeled off her sweaty socks.

She inhaled deeply. Experience in moving from place to place had taught her that the worst thing to come home to was a bad smell: smoke, backed up sewers or flooding from the apartments overhead, dead mice in the heating vents, animal poo from her pets, or garbage she'd forgotten to take out.

But nothing in the apartment smelled. Once again, she had made it home without having to deal with an emergency.

Toad, her adorably cute Pomeranian, was just about wagging himself into a coma by the time she opened the door to his kennel. She smiled at the little sweater he wore... frogs on red fabric.

"Did Ms. Leslie make you that?" she asked as she scooped him up and accepted a face full of licks.

Ms. Leslie was an absolute doll of an older woman in her building who watched her pets when she was out of town. She was the entire building's grandma, pet-sitter, and cookie baker, and they were all prepared to pay her rent if she ever needed it.

She'd bet her entire future income that Ms. Leslie had an amygdala the size of a house.

Autumn made a kissing noise as she walked from room to room. "Where's Peach?" she asked the little dog.

After she'd given up looking, her ginger tabby oozed out from behind the couch. Her tail was straight up, and her face showed great malice. Peach was not pleased with her at all, but after a handful of treats, she finally began to purr.

Although playing with her pets helped, she was tense from head to toe. She was also dirty and hungry. Maybe takeout from her favorite Italian restaurant and a hot bath might soothe her, mentally and physically.

Digging her phone from her bag, she practically melted onto the couch. Toad jumped up beside her while Peach headbutted her leg, wanting some additional ear scratches.

While Autumn scrolled for the restaurant's number, her phone vibrated in her hand. She'd put it on vibrate during the trip, which had been more fun than any six-hour ride with six people should have been.

They'd had to keep their voices low for the sake of Aiden's head, but they'd talked the entire way...about everything but murders.

Staring at the screen, she debated on ignoring any messages until later. Knowing she would only worry and wonder if she did that, she tapped the messaging app with an irritated grunt, and stared as her heart picked up speed.

Just last night, she'd entered her sister's name into several websites, including the National Name Check Program. She'd set the notifications up so that she'd be texted with any news about her sister.

There was a possible match in Florida.

Was this a good thing or bad, and was this particular Sarah even her sister? After all, Autumn had tried looking for her a couple years ago with no luck. Back then, she'd gotten a number of false leads. What made her think this time would be any different?

Toad whined, feeling her raised anxiety, and she put her phone down to snuggle him closer.

Maybe it'd been a bad idea to look for Sarah, or at the very least, bad timing. What if Sarah wasn't interested in being found? After all, Autumn had never once heard from her sister either.

Her phone vibrated again, and she almost didn't look.

Food. Bath. Bed.

Shit.

She snatched the phone up. A message from Sun.

Heads-up. We may have another case coming up in the next couple days. Several pregnant women have gone missing in Florida. I don't have all the gruesome details yet but wanted to make you aware in case Aiden calls you in to assist. Which he probably will!

Florida?

She blinked several times to make sure she was reading the message correctly.

Was this a sign?

Autumn's throat tightened and tears burned her eyes.

Within the past couple minutes, she'd learned that her sister might be in Florida, and that a case involving pregnant women was in that same state. Maybe even close together?

Was this Autumn's break into finding some sort of closure to her past?

A feeling she didn't like bloomed in her chest. Hope.

She kissed Toad's head. "Well, buddy, looks like Mama might be heading south."

For the new case…and for herself.

She typed in three little words: *I'll be there.*

The End
To be continued…

Thank you for reading.
All of the Autumn Trent Series books can be found on Amazon.

ACKNOWLEDGMENTS

How does one properly thank everyone involved in taking a dream and making it a reality? Let me try.

In addition to my family, whose unending support provided the foundation for me to find the time and energy to put these thoughts on paper, I want to thank the editors who polished my words and made them shine.

Many thanks to my publisher for risking taking on a newbie and giving me the confidence to become a bona fide author.

More than anyone, I want to thank you, my reader, for clicking on a nobody and sharing your most important asset, your time, with this book. I hope with all my heart I made it worthwhile.

Much love,
Mary

ABOUT THE AUTHOR

Mary Stone lives among the majestic Blue Ridge Mountains of East Tennessee with her two dogs, four cats, a couple of energetic boys, and a very patient husband.

As a young girl, she would go to bed every night, wondering what type of creature might be lurking underneath. It wasn't until she was older that she learned that the creatures she needed to most fear were human.

Today, she creates vivid stories with courageous, strong heroines and dastardly villains. She invites you to enter her world of serial killers, FBI agents but never damsels in distress. Her female characters can handle themselves, going toe-to-toe with any male character, protagonist or antagonist.

Discover more about Mary Stone on her website.
www.authormarystone.com

Connect with Mary Online

facebook.com/authormarystone
goodreads.com/AuthorMaryStone
bookbub.com/profile/3378576590
pinterest.com/MaryStoneAuthor
instagram.com/marystone_author

Made in United States
North Haven, CT
21 April 2022

18455985R00183